Ignatius

Ignatius

Published by The Conrad Press in the United Kingdom 2020

Tel: +44(0)1227 472 874
www.theconradpress.com
info@theconradpress.com

ISBN 978-1-913567-35-4

Typesetting and Cover Design by:
Charlotte Mouncey, www.bookstyle.co.uk

The Conrad Press logo was designed by Maria Priestley.

Printed and bound in Great Britain by Clays Ltd, Elcograf S.p.A.

Ignatius

Dan Wood

Prologue

July 2008

The four soldiers were cautiously approaching an old rice storage warehouse just outside Jinan, in the Shandong region of China.

The assault team leader, Ignatius Winter, spoke to the team through his field radio microphone. 'Stay alert.' It was a sentiment spoken out of habit, rather than necessity. All four of these men were the best of the best. They were always alert.

Each one of them was carrying a C8 Carbine as their primary assault rifle with a Sig Sauer P226 handgun as a backup. The air felt unnaturally heavy and Winter wasn't feeling good about this operation.

The street running centrally through this small village was almost deserted, but they were expecting that. It was an almost derelict village with only a few stubborn locals still choosing to live here.

The properties that weren't in an unliveable state of disrepair had their window blinds shut. Was this usual here, and just a consequence of trying to keep the heat from the sun out, or was it due to another reason? Winter and his team didn't know. He wished they'd had more time to prepare, but they didn't, so they had to carry out the operation using the Immediate Action Plan they had formulated.

Spread out across the street as this was the only viable

approach to the warehouse, they were now within sixty metres. Winter caught a movement of shadow out of his left eye's peripheral vision and instinctively sidestepped to his right. A fraction of a second later a bullet hit the ground three feet behind the space he had just been occupying.

The battlefield opened up. Gun nozzles flashed like cameras at a sporting event, the explosions were deafening and the air was displaced with rifle rounds pouring down at almost 3000 feet per second. It was hell, but these men operated in hell and training kicked in. They moved like ghosts and to the aggressors it seemed that every time they fired a shot, the bullet hit where the Soldiers had just moved from.

The assault team were expecting an enemy of between six to nine, but they were facing a force of thirty-three combatants, who had every tactical advantage. Had they been outnumbered four to one, no problem, but at over eight to one, it was an issue. Despite this, every time one of these four men pulled the trigger a hostile fell down.

As good as they were, the sheer volume of enemy fire meant it was similar to trying to dodge rain, and eventually the bullets started connecting with their bodies. Some were stopped by kevlar body armour, but others hit vital organs and three of the four soldiers had been hit with what would become fatal wounds. Even with the last breaths in their bodies, these three warriors kept putting down firepower.

The enemy combatants had only seen four men approaching, but with the level and accuracy of firepower that had come their way, they assumed that there were at least four times that amount of men. Twenty-five of their own were already dead and they only had eight left, two of whom were badly injured.

They had no doubt that more soldiers were on their way, and out of fear they fled via a narrow side alley.

Ignatius Winter lay wounded on the street behind a pillar. He hadn't heard any gunfire for a few seconds, so he persuaded his body to move over to his brothers in arms and check on them. Two were already dead and one was taking his last few breaths. He sat with him, holding him in his arms whilst he died on a street over five thousand miles from home.

On the sun baked street, Ignatius Winter made a promise to himself and his dead brothers: he would one day find out who had betrayed his team and he would take vengeance.

1

Present Day

May 11th, 1pm

Bambi lay down on the grey, sheet metal, industrial grip pattern plate and found his nest amongst the snaking of cables required to operate a sightseeing boat on the River Thames. He had been on this very boat several times before, in preparation for today.

The boat did multiple daily tours between Greenwich and Westminster and took in historic London landmarks, such as *The Cutty Sark*, St Paul's Cathedral, Tower Bridge and most importantly, The Houses of Parliament.

It was a two-tier metal shelled vessel. The first floor had extensive porthole windowing along the sides. The second tier was open-air, and even on a cold London winter day it was still the most popular deck. It had flooring on both decks made of a cheap wooden panelling. This was for aesthetic purposes, but that covered two other layers of flooring on each level; one of which was sound proofing, so that the paying customers were spared the hum of the engines and mechanical workings.

As Bambi lay within the engine room below the first deck, he set to work removing the circular metal hole that he had cut along the side of the boat on one of his previous visits. He had replaced the circular metal sheeting that had initially been removed, using a waterproof industrial glue. He also painted the edging to hide any evidence in the unlikely event that anyone was inspecting the structure.

The boat had recently undergone its mandatory safety inspection, so he was as confident as could be that any inspection of credibility wouldn't be undertaken. He fired up his hand-held plasma torch and traced the edges of the cut. The heat from the torch would weaken the glue strength enough, without compromising the metal shell. Then using an aluminium suction pad bought from a hardware store for £14.99, he freed the previous cut sheeting while simultaneously sliding a piece of cardboard painted with a metal effect finish to replicate the exterior of the boat. This was a necessity in case someone walking alongside the river suddenly saw a hole appear in the boat.

This way, in case an eagle-eyed stroller thought they saw a hole, by the time they did a double take, the painted cardboard from that distance would be indistinguishable from the rest of the frame; and it would be dismissed as a viewing anomaly.

Setting to work on his final preparations before the big show, and more importantly, big pay day, he used an electric screwdriver to remove the screws for a section of the flooring and replaced them by sticking on previously decapitated screw heads that he had brought with him. He slid it aside to check the rest of his equipment was in place. It was.

Putting on a wetsuit in ample space is a pain, putting one on in very limited space, whilst having to be certain not to knock into anything, was just reason enough to hurt someone.

He stripped off all his clothes and put them in his backpack, after removing what was currently in there. The bag had a waterproof compartment to ensure they remained dry. Fully naked, barring the plastic surgical gloves he wore, he put two plastic shopping bags over his feet and used them to slide easily into his wetsuit.

From below the flooring panel, where he had removed the screws, he retrieved his L129A1 Sharpshooter gun. The L129A1 Sharpshooter is a marksman's rifle that has been fielded, predominantly by UK elite forces since late 2010.

The weapon was procured in order to fill a capability gap identified by experience in Afghanistan, where British infantry units were often engaged by small arms fire from outside the range of their own assault rifles and light machine guns, at ranges between 500m and 800m.

The width of the river at that point is 252m , so the rifle was arguably overkill. But after endless hours on the range, exhausting the weapon, this was what Bambi was most comfortable using for the operation. It was also the best barrel to fit his custom made silencer without compromising the trajectory of 7.62x51 NATO ammunition. He set to work stripping and cleaning the weapon and checking the ammunition as he'd never used this exact rifle before. No one had.

Three weeks previously it had been stolen from a deniable British Military store in Istanbul, which was on hand for Special forces and Security Services use as required.

The building fronted as an industrial cleaning unit and had staff turn up each day to live this ruse. The business, whilst heavily protected by infrastructure had a human presence which was minimal, and stock checking was loose at best. It would take an amount of time, if at all, to realise the weapon was missing. Managing the procurement of these types of sites worldwide was not a priority. Being deniable, even to most senior figures within the UK Government, there was no reporting required.

Timings wise, the boat was four minutes behind schedule, but that wasn't a major issue. Allowances had been built into the operational planning. He had plenty of time.

The boat slowed to an almost standstill as it was preparing to dock and allow the current passengers off and refill with new customers for another river tour of London. Now, Bambi removed the piece of cardboard from the hole. He was unlikely to be seen from across the river at over 200m, and walk by traffic was non-existent. This was due to the fact he was directly opposite the Houses of Parliament Terrace Pavilion.

The Terrace Pavilion, Bambi knew, was an event venue for larger receptions at the House of Commons with access out onto the Commons' Terrace. The east front of the Pavilion measures 265m, and is the longest façade of any building in London.

A purpose-built heated marquee provides an ideal venue for all weather conditions. The panoramic glass doors offer uninterrupted views of the river Thames, and open out onto the terrace.

The pavilion had traditionally been used for Members to entertain their guests but was also now available for private hire, assuming you had a healthy bank balance or healthy influence, of course.

Today, it was very much being used by a Member. The British Prime Minister, Mary Henshaw, along with leading front benchers within her cabinet and the shadow cabinet were entertaining guests, and eating a bizarre fusion banquet of Chinese and English dishes.

The reason for what most chefs would consider a culinary insult, was that the Prime Minister was hosting a small but distinguished contingent from China, including Li Jintao the President of the People's Republic of China, Zhang Jinping, the Premier of the State Council of the People's Republic of China and the Minister of National Defence, Xu Hua.

Bambi had already entered his trance-like state as he prepared his body once again for the shot. He had removed his surgical gloves as he always did for this part. He didn't need to worry about any fingerprints as he had covered them and his palm in superglue beforehand.

The surgical gloves were an extra level of protection for DNA leakage. He knew the gloves themselves would have been little use against fingerprint prevention, anyway. Many burglars had been caught out before, not realising that fingerprints can often be transferred onto surfaces whilst using surgical gloves; a thicker weave was needed to hide prints. He had pressed the button to begin the timer eighty-eight seconds ago. There was no need for him to use any device to measure this period of time. His body knew exactly how long each part of this ritual took.

The glass doors on the Terrace Pavilion were built using P4A armoured glass sourced from a company in Germany. Although it wouldn't have been difficult to find and use ammunition to pierce the glass, it might cause the flight of the bullet to deviate. This wasn't an issue for Bambi, because as promised, the doors on the Terrace had been slid fully open, which wasn't unusual on a warm day of May.

The target was clearly in his sights for a full two seconds

before he pulled the trigger on his L129A1. Almost instantaneously he saw the pink mist that confirmed he had hit his target's centre forehead whilst the target looked out onto the river from the Terrace balcony. Additional confirmation came in the form of the target collapsing to the ground like a discarded jacket. Within a second of the bullet impacting bone, the button that he had pressed ninety-seven seconds previously, set of a low-level flash bang on the third floor of the building, south side of the river opposite the Houses of Parliament.

Bambi didn't hang about admiring his work. He glued back in place the removed pane of metal, stripped down the weapon and put everything, that wasn't previously part of the boat, in his rucksack. He moved the loosened panel so that half the width was open and slid under it into the bilge of the boat, then reached above his head to slide it back in its place.

He was now in a cramped metal triangle where he had spent most of the time on his previous visits. Awkwardly, he put on his flippers and goggles and slid the mouthpiece of his breathing apparatus into his mouth. This was attached to a small tank of oxygen, giving him approximately thirty minutes breathing time, which on top of the comfortable eight minutes he was able to hold his breath, gave him enough time for what he needed.

Collecting the last parts of his equipment, he put a door handle on the centre part of a piece of the metal frame, pressed a button to engage the magnet and pulled. What seemed to be a single sheet of metal folded inwards opening a gap on the bottom of the boat, so he could shimmy into the water after he pressed another button on the handle to disengage the magnet, freeing it and taking it into the water with him. He then engaged the magnet on the outer shell and pulled again to close the hole into the boat. This had taken a matter of seconds, but inevitably had let water into the boat. However, this would spread along the whole length of the boat and would be unnoticeable on performance or use of the boat for the immediate future.

Bambi positioned himself so that his head was pointing towards the bed of the river and used his flippers to kick down and towards the centre of the river. At this tide the Thames was between twenty to twenty-one metres deep. Bambi just needed to be below seven metres to ensure that his silhouette or heat signature wasn't visible from any passing boats, nosy drone or other aircraft that might be flying overhead.

Bambi used an Oceanic OCI personal wrist dive computer to measure his depth and maintained it once his dive computer showed him at ten metres. It was when he was at this depth that he activated his last bit of equipment for this part of the operation. The TUSA SAV-7 EVO3 Scooter Diver Propulsion Vehicle. The underwater propeller once brought to life, towed Bambi along at six knots.

Just after twenty minutes later, Bambi pulled up alongside a wall on the south side of the Thames at approximately three metres deep. During the journey, which was the equivalent of two and a half land miles, he had discarded the equipment that he no longer required, including the weapon which had been stripped to parts; and he'd discarded each part sporadically along the journey.

It would take nothing short of a miracle for anyone to recover every bit of the gun and link them together as one weapon. Even if they did, it didn't matter. It couldn't be traced back to him, or anyone for that matter, but there was no point making things easier for people.

He took out his pliers and cut the zip ties that were holding a metal grate in place. The grate covered a wide pipe leading into a larger structure. A week previously, Bambi had used an underwater torch to cut free the metal grate and had secured it in place with the zip ties that he was now cutting.

Once he'd released the grate, he sunk the rest of the equipment he'd no longer need, including his propeller, dive computer and weighted wetsuit.

Naked bar his rucksack, he used a mixture of swimming and crawling along the pipe until he reached an exit part of the piping that led into an underground and unused store room. In the room he shook excess water off himself and opened his rucksack to reveal completely dry equipment inside the waterproof compartment.

Using a towel, he was sure to dry himself thoroughly, before putting on his clothes: some cycle pants and a cycle jersey, as undergarments. Then, over that, some black trainers that looked like smart shoes at a glance when covered with trousers. They were also practical for high levels of activity. Next, some black non-descript trousers, a black shirt and finally a thin, black waterproof jacket that had the insignia of a local catering company.

He made his way up some tight spiral stairs used for trade and slid unnoticed into a large room with a hive of frantic activity going on. He was in the industrial kitchen of Battersea Power station, which was currently hosting a high-end lunch for over sixteen hundred guests with over a hundred and fifty staff on site, working in a variety of capacities. Since the power station had been decommissioned it had been used success-fully as an event venue, whilst its long term future was being argued over.

He was by the indoor dustbins and went about emptying two of them, one which was almost empty and one which was half-full. He took them outside and headed towards the vast trade bins. No one even gave him a second glance. As soon as he'd entered the room, he'd put his backpack in the almost empty bin bag, before tying it up. Now outside and confident he was out of sight of anyone, he opened both bins bags and emptied the half-full one into the other bag to cover the ruck-sack and then put the now empty bin bag on top of that before tying it up to look like one full bag. He disposed of the full bag into the industrial hired event bins outside, which he knew were being collected at 6am tomorrow morning.

He walked around the side of the bins, which rested against the back of some old and vast store rooms that had once been used to store fuel for the power station and were now used to store a multitude of equipment. They were secured with a padlock which took Bambi less than a minute to pick. Inside, he moved aside some spare plasterboard and pulled off a dust sheet to reveal a bike with a logo heat bag attached to the back, inside of which was some Sushi that had been sitting there for over twenty-four hours now. It wasn't a snack that he had any intention of tasting.

He removed his jacket and reversed it, before he put it back on. His black jacket was now a green and grey jacket and he had a grey cycle helmet. To anyone who saw him, he was a Deliveroo cyclist courier for fast food. The success of the company, meant that they were a regular sight around London, which helped make them effectively invisible, in the same way a road worker is.

From Battersea Power Station, it was an 8.8 mile ride to West Croydon Rail Station. On average the cycle time would be close to fifty minutes. As he was cycling out of the power station, he very nearly crashed into a site security guard, who yelled some form of abuse at him as he carried on, but he was too far away by this point to hear or care what was said. He had a pretty good idea though what was the gist of the message.

Bambi pulled into West Croydon Rail Station within thirty-five minutes, without any further incident. He walked into the toilets with his bag and took of his outer clothes and put them in the bag, so he was now wearing his cycle pants and jersey.

He peeled of the logo he'd added to the bag, so it was a non-descript black bag. One of the reasons he'd chosen West Croydon Rail Station was due to the fact that it was currently undergoing extensive maintenance and building work as well as the issue that Deliveroo cyclists would only deliver to a restricted radius. A Deliveroo cyclist too much further south of Croydon, would turn from being invisible to being suspect, hence why he had now taken on the persona of amateur but keen cyclist. He casually waited until one of the many skips was free and discarded his bag in one, which he buried under heavy rubble from the ongoing works.

The final part of his journey was certainly for him the most relaxing, although for most it would be physically taxing. He had a thirty-one-mile cycle ride to Mannings Heath, a village on the outskirts of Horsham in West Sussex. The journey took two hours and fifteen minutes, which was a quite leisurely pace for him.

He pulled up to the farmhouse in Mannings Heath at 4.43pm and entered his humble room in a converted barn where he had been living in for the past six months.

2

It had been eight months since Bambi had first been contacted about this job via his agent.

Bambi didn't know what path in life you had to follow to become a broker for mercenaries but he wasn't exactly one to talk, and wasn't here to judge. His agent wasn't typical of agents in other industries. He was simply used as a means for potential contacts to get in touch with Bambi with a job request. The requests weren't overly varied. He only offered one service: death.

The service was categorised from A – D. Category A was a high-level public figure with influence and resource, which meant the fallout from the job would be significant. Category D was cheating-spouse-type level with limited fallout. The agent would contact Bambi with the request, timeframe and money offered. From there Bambi would decide if he would speak with the client. Even just to speak to Bambi, he charged five thousand US dollars with no guarantee he would take the job. At this stage, he usually only accepted around twenty per cent of the jobs offered.

The job offers were few and far between, but that was no reflection on the service offered. Even amongst the world of people who would hire an assassin, the vast majority had never heard of Bambi and for those that had, most didn't believe he was actually real.

The security services with any credibility throughout the

world were convinced of his existence, but there was debate between them, whether it was a 'he', a 'she' or a 'them'. The only information that had repeated itself about him, to the few people who believed they might have had contact, was the rumour that when he was a child his mother had been shot.

The intel suggested that this was a serious cause of anguish for him. It was using this titbit of information, that some wise-cracking MI6 officer had given him the nickname Bambi.

The name had stuck, not just within British Intelligence but globally.

This job wasn't the type of publicity that he was seeking and he wouldn't normally be interested. But the fifteen million dollars plus expenses price tag had got his attention and meant that, should he accept it, this would be his last job before he retired to a small ranch somewhere, to live out his days in peace.

He took the call from his client who introduced himself as Jerry and was using a sophisticated scrambling network and voice contortion system to ensure his location and identity couldn't be traced. Bambi knew this because he had tried to do exactly that.

Jerry outlined who the target was, which immediately put Bambi off, but the help that Bambi would be receiving on this mission, would make his life a lot easier. He would be getting unprecedented access to equipment and the target's schedule. They agreed the price tag, with Jerry also agreeing to pay twenty-five per cent upfront and a hundred and fifty thousand dollars to cover expenses.

Bambi set about the job immediately and within two months of accepting the assignment, had moved from his temporary residence in India to the UK. He had taken the job as a farmhand in West Sussex, under the guise of a Spanish seasonal worker, who was looking for a job until the tourist season in the Spanish summer was back in full flow, and he could go back home and get work in his Spanish village.

He looked at his small room, knowing he would never be spending another night, and to his surprise, he was a little sad to be leaving. His room was a modest conversion, in a farm outhouse, which nested above a garage for some of the smaller farm vehicles. It was two rooms. One of which had in it, a bed, sofa, TV, bookcase, kitchen area and small log burner which he now lit. The other room was a shower room, with a shower, sink and toilet. It was cosy, warm and quiet and Bambi felt comfortable there.

He worked five long days a week and a half farm day a week, which was still a seven-hour day. He had never missed a day's work, never turned up late nor ever had a hangover or any other reason to not be working at one hundred per cent, and as a result had been a brilliant worker, even if he sometimes came across as fairly naïve and simple. He was without question a beneficial addition to the farm for the Harrington family.

John and Sarah Harrington were a hard-working family with three young children, Richard, Jenny and Jack, who were quiet, polite and unobtrusive. He ate dinner with the family each night and one day a week, joined John in the local pub for an after-dinner pint or two, but never more.

The Harrington family knew him as Ferran Dacosta, who was from a small village in Northern Spain near Donastia San – Sebastian. He was always polite and engaging in broken English, with a northern Spanish accent. He had relayed his cover story to them a few times about how he lived with his mother and sister in Spain. His father had left the family when he was young and he was raised by his mother.

Tragically, his sister had moved back two months before he had come to the UK after her husband had unexpectedly died from a heart attack. His sister learnt shortly after the death of her husband that she was pregnant with their first child. In his role of Ferran, he told the family about his deep religious beliefs, without preaching to them. He told them how he believed the unborn child was a gift from God after the tragedy the family had encountered.

He talked of his joy about helping his mother and sister raise the child and helping him or her develop into a kind and giving child. He talked about how he wanted to be back in Spain for the birth. The Harringtons always listened with genuine interest and kindness about his family. Bambi actually liked them and early on had decided that he wouldn't kill any of them. Unless he had to of course.

They believed that he spent his days off following his childhood passion of camping and fishing around the Sussex area. Occasionally, this was true for the sake of appearance, but more often than not, he maximised the use of this time by setting up his operational plan, which as far as he could tell at this point, was time well spent.

Bambi took out a brand new disposable phone with a sim card that he had bought this morning and had never used, and called a number he had memorised.

A gruff voice answered his call.

'Hello.'

'Hello, Mr Cohen, this is Pete from Galaxy Insurance. I hear you have unfortunately been involved in a car accident recently?'

'Who told you that, Pete?'

'It was indicated to me by our system. Is this the case, Mr Cohen?'

'No, it's not. Good bye.'

Bambi hung up the phone, took the battery and sim card out, snapped the sim card, then threw all the parts into the log burner fire.

The phone call had triggered two events, by using those exact words in the conversation. The first was confirmation that the remaining money owed would be transferred to Bambi within the hour. The person on the end of the phone had seen the news, so already had confirmation of the killing. The second was that the Harringtons would be receiving a phone call in ten minutes' time.

He made himself a strong black coffee, sat down in his chair with his coffee and a chocolate bar – he figured he'd earned it after his hard work - and switched on the TV. All channels were only talking about one event from today. A few minutes later he heard Sarah Harrington's voice calling out.

'Ferran, Ferran, are you there?'

'Mrs Harrington, are you ok? Is there problem?'

'Yes, yes, I'm fine, your mother just called.'

'Is she ok, can I talk to her?'

'Yes, she's fine, she's had to go because your sister has just had the baby. The baby is being monitored, but everyone is fine. It's a boy.'

'But my sister isn't meant to have the baby for another four weeks?'

'I know, Ferran. That's why they are monitoring the baby, but there is nothing to worry about, all is ok. Congratulations.'

'Oh, thank you, God.' Bambi then used his hand to draw out the shape of the cross against his body.

'I must go and see them.'

Bambi and Sarah continued their conversation as they made their way over to the main farmhouse to use the internet and look at flights for him to Spain. There was one that night at 9.15pm from Gatwick. He was already well aware of this, but acted happy that this bit of fortune had occurred, and he made sure to book his own flight.

The Harringtons promised to give him a lift to the airport in just under two hours' time.

He used that time to pack his meagre belongings, which took all of ten minutes, then the rest of the time, he spent meticulously cleaning his room to wipe away any forensic evidence indicating he had ever been there. He used a cleaning spray that he had mixed with extra bleach to wipe down the surfaces and a thick industrial bleach down the sink and toilet to annihilate any stubborn DNA that he may have left behind. He had always been sure to be careful about leaving his mark within the main farmhouse. Even if he had slipped up, the fact that Mrs Harrington was an obsessive cleaner, and a continuous set of farmhands and lodgers who worked at the local vineyard went through the house, would make it almost impossible to isolate what DNA or fingerprints were his.

At the airport, it was an emotional farewell and only part of it was Bambi acting. They had embraced him as part of the family and shown genuine kindness towards him. He rarely let people into his life and hadn't let the Harringtons into his, but they had let him into theirs and he had liked that.

This wasn't something he was going to dwell on though,

he'd already had a long day and still had a long way to go and needed to make sure he remained alert. He was flying into Bilbao, where he would rent a car and drive to Lisbon in Portugal - an eight hours' drive. From there he was flying to Sao Paulo in Brazil which was close to ten and a half hours. In Sao Paulo he had arranged a safe house, where he was planning on lying low and disappearing for two or three months, until he felt safe and had decided where he would go and settle for a period of time.

He wasn't yet willing to congratulate himself on a good job, but so far everything had gone to plan and this part ahead was the easy part of his journey. He was feeling good.

3

May 11^{th,} 6.30am

Ignatius Winter was woken by the alarm from his phone. He had to change the alarm sound; it was too annoying. His head was throbbing and his throat was arid. Only twenty-four hours ago, he promised himself he wasn't going to drink again until he got another job. The money from his last job was almost gone, and two months before he had budgeted. That was why he was waking up at 6.30am for the past ten days. So that he could go and look for work.

He slid out of his small double bed into his cramped bedroom and as he turned, he banged his knee on the radiator. He paused still and gritted his teeth and scrunched his eyes. Today had not started well.

He opened his bedroom door into a small hallway. On the right was his front door, on the left was a small but modern bathroom and straight ahead was an archway into the combined sitting room and kitchen. He walked through to the kitchen and put the kettle on. He took a mug from the dishwasher, which was still dirty but it would do for now.

Straight from the coffee tin, he poured the last bit of coffee into the mug, then added some cold water from the tap, so that once the kettle had boiled, he could drink it straight away. He half-leant, half-sat against the kitchen counter as he looked into his sitting room. Furniture wise, it consisted of a second hand TV, a second hand two-seater sofa and about a twenty-second-hand coffee table. On the coffee table were some empty beer bottles, a half empty bottle of red wine and some cocaine residue.

He gave a shrug, realising he'd have to tidy it up later, then added the now boiling water to his coffee along with two sugars. Whilst sipping it, he had a look in his cupboards. They were pretty bare, but not as bad as his fridge, which consisted of ketchup, hot sauce and four cans of Heineken. He'd need to stop at the supermarket.

He finished his coffee, and wiped down the counter top. He needed to start somewhere, so headed to the bathroom to get ready. He looked in the full-length mirror on the back of the bathroom door. He was thiry-nine years old and lived a hard life, but he looked good. He was 6ft and a trim eighty-four kgs with dark blonde hair and a couple of days' stubble. His face was too weathered and he had lived too much of a hard life to be good looking, but he definitely had a rugged handsomeness, which attracted a lot of women.

He showered, took a couple of Ibuprofens, then dressed in brown boots, blue denim jeans and a plain black T-Shirt, and went out the front door of his ground floor flat in Balham in South London and headed to the Sainsbury's by the station. Ignatius wasn't the sentimental type, but if he'd known that he'd never spend another night in this flat, he would have taken a bit more time to take in the place that had been his home for the last couple of years. In the supermarket he filled his basket with bread, bacon, orange juice and coffee which would suffice for now, so he headed to the check-out.

The cashier was already looking too happy for Ignatius, so he got out his phone and pretended to be engaged in a WhatsApp conversation. As the cashier was scanning the items, he looked at Ignatius.

'Did somebody have a heavy night?'

Ignatius looked up from his phone briefly. 'What?'

'Oj, bacon, coffee. It's a classic hangover cure, when someone has had a few too many the night before.'

'You a doctor, are you?'

The cashier looked a little wounded by the brusqueness. 'No, sorry, sir. I was just making conversation.'

'How much do I owe you?'

'Eight pound seventy, please, sir.'

Ignatius handed over a ten pound note and stood in silence whilst he waited for his change.

As he walked out the exit of the Sainsbury's, Ignatius saw a sight of absolute beauty in front of him. The woman was probably in her late twenties, with long blonde hair, a perfectly made up face and was wearing yoga trousers and a tight fitting sports crop top. She had the figure of an Olympic beach volley-ball player and was chatting on her mobile, whilst struggling to load her shopping into the small boot of a Mercedes SLS AMG convertible coupe.

Ignatius jogged over towards her.

'Please, allow me, Madam.'

The woman gave a slight nod indicating she was ok with it.

Ignatius loaded her bags into the boot and said.

'There you are, have a lovely day.'

The woman gave a forced demi smile before turning her shoulder on Ignatius and continuing her phone conversation.

He walked away smiling, thinking, I may have my faults but

I'm actually a good guy.

A few cars down, this interaction had been witnessed by a woman of similar age with two young kids in tow. She also was struggling to load her bags, but mostly due to the fact that the two young lads were using her as a climbing frame. She was a large woman and it was clear that the kids climbing on her was uncomfortable and might explain why she was wearing loose fitting clothes and no make-up. She was, however taking it with good grace.

'Come on guys, if you keep climbing on Mum, we won't be able to get home and have pancakes.'

She smiled and ruffled the hair of the nearest child, and as Ignatius is almost parallel with the car, she looks at him.

'Excuse me, sir. I'm sorry to bother you, but might you also be able to help lift my bags into the car? I seem to have two cheeky monkeys using me as a climbing frame.'

Without breaking stride, Ignatius looked to his left with an exaggerated frown on his face.

'Do I look like your bitch?'

The woman was momentarily still shocked by his words. Ignatius carried on walking whilst chuckling to himself. On reflection, maybe he wasn't due for sainthood anytime soon.

Ignatius walked out of the car park, still smiling and crossed the road to a Starbucks. The queue was quite long but there were only a few tables occupied. In the corner, he noticed a man sitting by himself in trousers, shirt and jacket, reading a Guardian newspaper, whilst sipping an Espresso in a takeaway cup with a supermarket bag for life by his feet. The man continued reading his paper without acknowledging or looking at him. Why would he?

Ignatius stayed in the queue for thirty seconds, then sighed, giving the impression of impatience and a man who is too busy and important to queue for coffee. He edged out of the queue and left the Starbucks. He doesn't need any coffee anyway, he just bought some, and he's already got what he needs.

As he walks out of the shop, rather than turn left and head home, he takes a right and heads down the street, with a smile on his face. The day was picking up. He'd just got himself some work.

Every morning between 7.30am – 7.45am Ignatius would visit a well-known brand coffee shop. Which shop, depended on which day of the week it was. If there was a man sitting alone reading a Guardian newspaper, it meant that there was a job request. If it was a normal coffee cup, the job details were to be exchanged via a dead drop, if he was drinking from a takeaway cup, the details were to be exchanged electronically. The bag for life indicated the timeframe. Today's bag for life, showed a job for today.

Ignatius walked towards one of the few internet cafés remaining. On route he browsed the shop windows. On the unlikely chance he was being watched, he didn't want to seem to be rushing anywhere and raise a red flag. He window shopped at a kitchen store, checked out some rental properties on display at an estate agency and had a look through the window of the new fitness studio, Dog House fitness. He made a note to himself to make sure that once he had some money again, he would go in there and do some classes. It looked great and the instructors looked even better.

Once inside the internet café, he was relieved to see that he was the only customer. The owner of the shop was a bit of a beast. He had what Ignatius placed as a Latin complexion but was the size of an ox. It seemed he was a very frequent visitor to the gorilla pit in the gym; the part of the gym, that lacked the engineering of the latest machines, but was cramped full with metal. He also noticed the owner was wearing clearly tailored trousers, some fine Italian leather shoes, a cashmere jumper and a Rolex watch.

On his hands and above the neck line of his jumper, were visible tattoos, that Ignatius couldn't be sure, but thought, were gang affiliated He suspected there was more to the owner's income, than renting out computer time by the minute. That suited him just fine. The owner was unlikely to be someone to talk to or volunteer information to any authorities.

The café was a rectangular room with one of the short ends of the rectangle being street facing. The monitors for rent were set out in a horseshoe pattern around a central till point. Ignatius chose a monitor on the far side of the horseshoe with a peripheral view of the street and the confidence of not being over looked.

He chose his screen and his first action was to change the screen zoom from one hundred per cent to sixty per cent. He had to work hard to read what was on the screen at this zoom. There was no danger of any passing glimpse being able to take in any information.

He opened the internet and logged into his email account. He wasn't inundated with emails, but the email he was after was in his inbox. He clicked the email and opened it up. On the screen, he saw an offer for a five-star holiday to a Greek island at fifty per cent off the usual price, a remote-controlled helicopter at sixty per cent discount and a sofa for forty per cent off the store price. He was reading an email from a popular deal website which he got daily. The helicopter looked cool, but rather than clicking on the deal for more information, he scrolled to the bottom of the page, passing a range of other seemingly unmissible deals.

He got to the bottom of the page at the disclaimer notice. He started counting until he got to the sixth letter e in the notice. He carefully moved the mouse until the cursor was pointing into the semi-circle at the top of the letter e. He clicked the mouse button three times and waited. The screen changed and displayed a page telling him:

There is no Internet connection

There is something wrong with the proxy server or the address is incorrect.

Try:

- Contacting the system admin
- Checking the proxy address
- Running Network Diagnostics

ERR_PROXY_CONNECTION_FAILED

He quickly went along to the fifth e and once again put the cursor in the semi-circle of the e and clicked three times again. Had he not done this within ten seconds, the page would have reverted back to his email inbox and he'd have to wait another thirty minutes before he could try again.

An almost blank page appeared with only two boxes. One for a username and one for a password. He typed in his username and twenty-three-digit password. Once these were accepted, he was taken to a shadow internet site that was hosted in Bangkok, or Nevada or New Delhi, or wherever the hosts of the site decided to allow any trace to end on that particular day.

Once on the site he logged into another email account that could only be accessed via his new internet host site and put in the username and sixteen-digit pass code. He went straight to the draft folder and opened it up. They communicated by saving the emails to drafts for the next person to read, so that there was no electronic trace, even on this highly secure server.

Ignatius opened the only message in the draft and read the instructions for the job offer. Three quarters of the way through, it seemed like a fairly typical job. He was to extract a secure digital memory card using whatever means necessary, then via a strict set of directions do a 'brush past' handover, which Ignatius felt was a bit cold waresque. But he was to get paid four thousand pounds sterling for the day's work, so he was willing to go along with the clients archaic wishes.

He finished reading the email and looked to the bottom of the email for the address he was meant to go to and incentivise the owner of that property to hand over the memory card. Once he read the address, he sat back in his chair, put both his hands on the back of his head and sighed.

'Huh.'

Surely the address wasn't just a unique coincidence? He'd need to deal with that later, for now he had work to do. He ripped a sheet of paper from one of the pads by the side of each computer and took out a pen from one of the perforated metal cups by each pad. In unusually small handwriting, he wrote something on the pad, something he was hoping he wouldn't need to use.

He memorised all the other details required for the operation then deleted the draft email and wrote his own draft email to confirm acceptance and to give details of the bank account he wanted his fee to be paid into.

Ignatius shut down the computer, then picked up the note and headed to the till counter. The owner was behind the reception style desk which had a computer screen and keyboard on one side and on the other side, an old till that seemed out of place compared to the modern equipment in the rest of the shop. Behind the till and computer was raised shelving. The owner was looking at his screen with his right hand on his wireless mouse. Ignatius spoke whilst the owner was still looking at the screen.

'Hi. I'm here to pick up the memory card that was sent to you. The password is Greenwich docks.'

The owner kept looking at his screen.

'The thing is, I haven't received all the money I'm owed for it yet. So if you want the card, I'm going to need five hundred quid.'

'I don't have five hundred quid and the money owed to you is between you and whoever sent it. Can you just give me the package?'

The owner now looked up and spat out.

'Five hundred quid or get out. Don't make me ask you again.'

Ignatius slowly put the note he had written onto the raised shelving so it was facing the owner. He didn't say anything. The owner made eye contact. Ignatius just nodded at the note.

With his right hand still on the mouse, the owner used his left hand to straighten the note and leant his head down to read the small writing. Confusion engulfed the face of the owner as he looked up at Ignatius. Before he had time to process his thoughts, Ignatius had used both of his hands to grab hold of the back of his head, then with a fierce aggressiveness he slammed the owners head against the raised shelving behind his desk.

The address printed on the email to extract the memory card, was this very property that Ignatius was currently in, and the writing on the note simply read, 'This is gonna hurt.'

The sharp edge of the shelf opened an inch-long gash above the owners left eye brow. It was already bleeding heavily and he was dazed, flirting with concussion from the impact. Before he had time to regain his vision or footing, Ignatius had made his way around the side of the desk and grabbed hold of the owner and with a controlled coldness muttered in his ear.

'Don't overthink this, there is no way out of this situation for you. I need the memory card. If you get me the card now, that's the only pain you'll feel. If not, I have no objection to hurting you a lot more.'

'Ok, ok. I don't even know what's on the card, I'll go and get it.'

All the bravado from the owner had shattered.

Ignatius used his right palm and slapped it against the owners left ear, then used his left fist to punch the right ribcage, like a professional boxer working the body.

The owner was on the floor, fear flooding his eyes.

'You said you wouldn't hurt me anymore, if I got the card.'

'I know. I'm such a liar. Get it quicker.'

The follow up attack wasn't just a case of quenching a violence thirst, but Ignatius wanted to make sure the man was completely submissive and under his control, just in case he was thinking of getting ideas of re-igniting his tough guy act.

His jobs didn't usually require violence, but he was willing to serve it if necessary and he was quite good at it. Actually, he was one of the best in the world at it.

36

4

Ignatius was born and raised in Holt in Norfolk, a very English small market town, twenty-three miles from Norwich.

He was from a working-class family. His father was a builder and his mother was a teaching assistant. He had four sisters and one brother; he was the fourth of six children.

His childhood was unremarkable. They didn't have a lot of money, but they didn't need it. His parents loved him and his siblings, and they were surrounded by countryside and woodland, which they used as an oversized playground. Despite this, his upbringing was dull. Holt, as beautiful part of the country as it is, wasn't renowned for its entertainment for the younger generation.

He didn't go abroad until he was seventeen and used money he'd saved up from holiday and weekend jobs to go away with school friends to Spain. It had a big impact. He stayed in school to finish his A-Levels and got very average grades of CCD, which were still enough to go to university if he had wanted. He didn't know what he wanted to do, but he did know he wanted to see more of the world than Holt and he didn't want to academically study any more.

It had not been a path he'd considered before, but a chance encounter with the older brother of a friend, who was serving in the Army as part of the Royal Norfolk Regiment, put the Army as a possibility in his head. When Ignatius had an idea in his head, he would follow it to exhaustion; one way or the other.

After extensive research, he applied for the Paratroopers and was accepted to take part in their selection process. Quite simply, he cruised it. It turned out that the Army and Ignatius just fit one another. He was a brilliant soldier, a clear cut above his peers within an elite, regular army unit. After four years as a Paratrooper, based in Aldershot, but with multiple foreign trips as a member of the British Army, he knew there was still something that was missing.

A year earlier whilst he'd been posted in Afghanistan, he'd come across a member of 22 Special Air Service – SAS. The SAS is a special forces unit of the British Army which was founded in 1941 as a regiment. The unit undertakes a number of roles including covert reconnaissance, counter-terrorism, direct action and hostage rescue. Much of the information and actions regarding the SAS is highly classified, and is not commented upon by the British government or the Ministry of Defence due to the sensitivity of their operations.

He'd of course heard of them, but he'd never been up close and personal with anyone from The Regiment before. He was fascinated. The guy he met in an armoury at Camp Bastion in Afghanistan had a sense of calm and muted confidence about him. Ignatius loved soldiering, but he had become fed up with some of the parts that came with the role. A month before his tour, the base received a visitor from a senior member of the royal family and his part in the visit was painting burnt grass green. He just didn't need that.

Once he'd finished his tour in Afghanistan, he'd become obsessed with joining the SAS. Everything he did, was with the thought of 'will this help me become one of the best soldiers in the world?' He applied for the SAS and was accepted on the selection course. One hundred and seventy-four men started the course. Ignatius got down to the final six, before he was failed or RTU'd -Returned to Unit- at one of the last hurdles, after he attacked an interrogator during Survive, Evade, Resist, Extract training.

The selection course is considered the hardest course in the world, in any field. Hence the saying in the army, selection equals rejection. The course had lasted for approximately six months and as Ignatius had done five and a half months of the course, he had got a good view of life within the SAS. He liked what he saw. No one was shouting demands and making you jump through hoops, you had a task and you had to get it done, whatever it took. As a result, you had a group of autonomous, highly trained and hard-working elite soldiers, leading the world in military operations.

You only get two chances to pass SAS selection, so he knew the next time was all or nothing. He knew in his heart he would have to leave the army completely if he failed again. It was SAS or nothing.

Normally, if you fail, right at the end of selection, they only make you do that particular part of the course again. However due to the nature of how Ignatius had failed, there was a question mark over his temperament, so he was made to do the entire selection course again to test his resolve. This included another month running up and down the Brecon beacons, two months in the jungle, and three months doing a variety of specialist training and tests.

On Ignatius' second attempt at selection, there were one hundred and sixty-two men who started the course. Eight passed and Ignatius was one of them. He was soon assigned to

22 SAS, D Squadron, Mobility Troop.

Within the SAS, there are four troops: Boat Troop, Air Troop, Mobility Troop and Mountain Troop. Each has their own areas of expertise which they focus on, as well as the standard requirements for every SAS soldier such as hostage rescue and reconnaissance.

Mobility Troop focus on basics: mobility - getting heavily laden vehicles over all kinds of terrain, navigation, logistics, maintenance and repairing of vehicles and use of heavy support weapons. On top of this expertise, Ignatius had an aptitude for languages and demolition, both of which he became an expert in; speaking three additional languages and within control, being able to blow open, up or apart anything he wanted, given the right materials. His personality wasn't everyone's cup of tea, but anyone who was asked, wanted him by their side in a firefight.

He served in the best fighting regiment in the world for almost seven years before he was recruited to join the UK's Secret Intelligence Service, which is most commonly known as MI6. He was an MI6 officer for another seven years before he was relieved of his role after a specific incident.

MI6 are predominantly tasked with intelligence gathering and don't hire hitmen as such. In the exceptional circumstance that the UK government wants someone killed, that must be done with a Class 7 authorisation. This requires a sign off by Operations Directors, Management Board, the Foreign Secretary and eventually approved by a judge. A couple of years before, deemed one of the biggest threats to British security, was an Iranian nuclear physicist by the name of Amin Khan. He was one of the top nuclear physicists in the world, but his politics were strongly anti-west.

MI6 had intelligence which suggested that Amin Khan had aligned himself with an extremist terrorist group and they were planning a devastating attack on London. With the skills that Khan had, the suggestion of the nature of the attack was evident. MI6 decided that Khan must be eliminated and they choose their best man for the job.

Ignatius killed Khan and managed a clean exit. However, it later transpired that unknown to him, there had been no C7 authorisation and the Foreign Secretary was furious at an operation of this nature without his approval. His ego demanded that someone was accountable, even though the operation was a success and it eliminated a serious and real threat to British security. Quietly and with no thought for him as a person, Ignatius was chosen as the man who would take a level of accountability and despite his years of service, he was released from his position.

Still, to this day, he was bitter about the whole affair. He understood that many of his operations were deniable and if he had been caught, he was unlikely to receive any support.

However, to carry out a clean operation after following orders, then to have his life ripped apart, purely to massage someone's ego, was not ok to him. He had spent the last couple of years taking work where he could with little direction in his life.

He worked to live and now that meant to drink, go out and have a good time. He was never the most subtle of characters and this episode had only exaggerated this part of him. It took a lot for him to trust someone, and he typically found life easier if he kept people at a distance. He was lost, and a life that once had purpose and direction was now the opposite. He was vengeful and was gradually spiralling deeper and deeper into bitterness.

5

The shop owner handed over the card without hesitation saying to Ignatius, 'I don't want any more problems with us.'

Ignatius looked at him with a smirk.

'I've had no problems.'

As Ignatius walked out the shop he said, 'Oh, and in case you hadn't realised, I'm not paying for the time.'

Despite his demeanour, Ignatius left the shop with a cloud of unease building up over him. He needed to start dictating the game rather than reacting to it. He had a lot of work to do and little time to do it.

He walked home and got dressed in his full civilian battle rattle. He put on a different pair of jeans, boots and a shirt that was a size too big for him and finally a summer jacket.

His jeans had a built-in elasticated holster at the back, so he could carry a gun and run, jump and move in any desired way, without any concern for the gun falling out. His boots he had sourced from an old Israeli Mossad contact and were made with a Kevlar weave and had two hollowed heels. One he used to store the memory card that he had wrapped in aluminium foil for additional protection, and the other he used for a small Swiss army knife as well as an out of date MI6 identification.

It wouldn't stand up to any exhaustive inspection as it was now decommissioned, but it might help evade a lesser inspection. His shirt would cover any indication of a weapon lump at the back of his jeans. His summer jacket was lined with a Faraday cage. A Faraday cage causes the electric charges within the cage›s conducting material to be distributed so that they cancel the field›s effect in the cage›s interior, which effectively meant, that any electronic equipment couldn't be traced or accessed whilst within his jacket.

It could be used for several purposes. Today he was using it to block signals to his phone including incoming phones calls, WIFI, GSM, 4G, Bluetooth and even NFC - Near Field Communication. Ideally he would leave his phone behind, but the risk versus reward analysis that he made most operational decisions by, meant that the reward of having his phone and all it offered on him, was bigger than the risk it carried of having it on his person.

Finally, he went to the door to his bedroom and opened it. The door was an oak effect laminate. He removed the just shy of two inches wide side panel and pulled out a slightly smaller rectangular cardboard box within the frame. This carried his Sig Sauer P226 handgun with extended twenty round magazine which chambered 9mm ammunition.

He wished for more time, but wishing for something wouldn't make it real, so he dismissed the thought and headed out to help give himself as much time as possible. On route out, he glanced over to his coffee table in the sitting room. The empty bottles were still there. He'd love a beer now. He walked to Balham station, took the northern tube line to Bank, then transferred to the DLR line and took that to Greenwich. Along the route, he implimated multiple counter surveillance techniques and was as confident as was operationally reasonable that he wasn't being followed.

Ignatius still had his reservations, but when didn't he before a covert operation? There were still two hours before he needed to take any action, so he picked his spot within the second floor of a bar, and surveyed his surroundings whilst drinking a pot of coffee.

12.00pm arrived and he had seen no suggestions of an ambush. He did his risk versus reward analysis again, and decided to board a sightseeing boat on the river Thames, that did multiple daily tours between Greenwich and Westminster.

He considered his position from the other persons' scenario and realised they wouldn't attempt a brush past until they were exiting the boat. So Ignatius had no expectations of contact until they were at Westminster. He could only control what he could control so he took a seat and embraced the persona of a sightseer. He wasn't tasked with initiating the contact so he had to wait anyway. He did a field assessment of the passengers and considered his contact could be any one of three likely suspects.

Almost an hour later as they were approaching Westminster, he was fully alert and expecting contact any minute. He could see two of his likely suspects, but wasn't sure where the third candidate had gone. He let it go. He could only control what he could control.

As they were about to dock, he heard what was unmistakeably to his trained ear, a flash bang in the distance. It was out of place. It took another eight minutes before the passengers were able to leave the boat and as Ignatius was starting to move, there was already a vast Police presence and they were starting to organise some levels of structure.

He didn't know what was happening, but he did know that he couldn't be caught with a weapon and a chip that contained

God knows what. So as he disembarked from the boat, he checked his exit points. To the left was a crossroads including Westminster bridge, where the traffic both on foot and by road was at its heaviest, and it still seemed to be the least organised. He headed in that direction and during the confusion he managed to exit the perimeter the police were clearly trying to set up, without encountering any authorities.

The cloud of unease he had been feeling had now turned into a storm. One that he had no intention of getting caught up in. He needed a reality check. There had been far too many coincidences for him not to somehow be a part of whatever was occurring. It was time to go dark.

He made his way to Westminster underground where he took the Jubilee line north to Baker Street, then the Circle line east to Euston Square, where he left the underground and walked to Euston Station. From there he took the Northern line to Highgate, then walked through Highgate woods following a path that took him to Muswell Hill Broadway. He eventually turned up at an old SAS colleague's house for safe haven and was greeted as any brother in arms would greet another.

'What do you want? Thought you were dead?'

'Hey, Tank. I need to lie low for couple of days.'

'Upstairs, first room on right. Piss off the missus, I'll drop you. Eat my cheesecake, I'll kill you.'

Ignatius made his way upstairs and took the first right into an immaculate spare room with a modern en suite. Maybe Ignatius should have married a lawyer also.

He needed to make sense of the situation. Still suffering from a nasty hangover, he took another shower today and let the flow of water hit him, as hot as his skin would allow. He checked the cupboards and used a spare toothbrush and toothpaste to brush his teeth.

Back in his room, he got dressed again, before heading downstairs. There was no sign of Tank or his wife, so he went to the kitchen and opened the fridge. There was a half-full two litre bottle of lemonade. He emptied the remaining lemonade, then filled the bottle with water. There was a pizza box with half of the pizza left on top of the fridge, so he grabbed that- it wasn't cheesecake, so why not?

Ignatius carefully climbed the stairs, not because he was physically exhausted but the mental see-saw of the day so far was becoming more and more cryptic in his head. His laboured walking was more about mental concentration than actual exertion.

For lack of knowing what else to do, Ignatius lay on the bed, eating cold pizza and put the TV on. Every channel was covering the same story. He didn't know how or why, but he knew there was trouble ahead.

6

May 12th

Sahira Basha had just finished Salah, which is one of the five essential pillars of Islam. She had finished Dhuhr prayer, the prayer time nearest to noon. Today's prayer time had started at 11.53am and she finished two minutes before midday.

She left the mosque and was momentarily blinded by the increasingly warming sun. She put on her sunglasses that to most eyes were modest, along with her high-necked, long sleeved black dress. The only thing unusual about her outfit was the price.

Her sunglasses were black Louis Vuitton at almost seventeen hundred pounds and her dress was a Gucci crepe jersey dress at thirteen hundred pounds. These were ably partnered if not overshadowed by a twenty-two thousand pounds Gucci hand-bag. She had exited the Mayfair Islamic centre mosque which was near both her home and gym, where she was now heading.

She took her heavily encrypted phone out of her handbag and saw two messages waiting. The first message was confirmation of receipt of a large sum of monies she had earlier transferred to help towards a cause in the name of Allah. The second was a direction for her to make contact immediately.

She groaned to herself. She hated missing her daily workout. It was the reason she stayed as trim and fit as she did, and was thus capable of using her body to advantage when needed. She turned around and headed back to her apartment to access the relevant equipment she needed to make contact.

Five minutes later, Sahira arrived at the outside of her building. She briefly admired the Search for Enlightenment sculpture that faced Hyde Park and the Serpentine lake as she headed up to her Penthouse at One Hyde Park. The apartment block was built in 2007 at a reported cost of £1.15 billion. As well as residential properties within the complex, there are retail units that are occupied by the likes of Rolex, McLaren Automotive and Abu Dhabi Islamic Bank.

Sahira moved in 2012 after her father's company had bought one of the Penthouse apartments for one hundred and ten million pounds. The penthouse at one Hyde Park boasted amongst other perks, a stainless steel ozone pool, an entertainment suite, a golf simulator, and a spa run by the adjacent Mandarin Oriental hotel. There was also a temperature-controlled wine cellar, a car cleaning and valet service and basement parking.

She took the private elevator up to the front door of her penthouse, entered the penthouse main, removed her shoes putting them on the rack, then walked bare foot across the heated marble floor to what was originally a pedicure and beauty room.

Sahira had adapted the room into her communications room with state-of-the-art computer and surveillance equipment, such as to cause jealousy with many FTSE 100 companies. Whilst she was waiting for the equipment to boot up and run anti-hacking software, she picked up her phone and dialled 0. The Mandarin Oriental hotel also provided a room service option to the apartments. Sahira ordered herself a wild salmon salad with sesame mustard dressing and room-temperature sparkling water.

It took another seven minutes for all the diagnostics to be completed to ensure that it was impossible for her to be hacked or traced. She then picked up the phone and dialled a number that had long been etched into her mind. After three rings a voice answered.

'Hello?'

'This is Sahira Basha. Passcode: Delta. Charlie. Whiskey. 1. 4. 0. 9.'

There was a pause whilst the voice recognition software, confirmed it was her voice and her passcode was verified.

'Afternoon, Miss Basha. Please confirm today's password.'

Sahira, checked her watch, as the password varied depending what time of day it was.

'Green avocado.'

This was another level of security to help confirm that it was indeed her and more importantly to confirm she wasn't under duress.

'How can I help you, Miss Basha?'

'I need a secure connection to Thames House please.'

'Are you logged into a secure station?'

'Of course.'

'Thank you, Miss Basha. A secure connection has been enabled.'

The line went dead and Sahira connected to the system at her office at Thames house in her role as an Intelligence officer for MI5.

MI5's role as defined by the Security Services Act 1989 is, 'the protection of national security and in particular its protection against threats such as terrorism, espionage and sabotage, the activities of agents of foreign powers, and from actions intended to overthrow or undermine parliamentary democracy by political, industrial or violent means.'

MI5 is not part of the Home Office but does work under the statutory authority of The Home Secretary.

Sahira's parents were nationals of Saudi Arabia and although she had spent a lot of time there visiting family and enjoying the land of her heritage, she was born and raised in the UK. Her father owned one of the largest oil companies in Saudi Arabia as well as multiple other highly profitable companies across the globe. He spent more time in residence in the UK than he did anywhere else in the world, including his homeland.

She was educated at a private girls' school in Cheltenham in the South West of England, and despite offers from both Oxford and Cambridge, she studied at Loughborough University and got a 1st class degree in Engineering and IT. This was followed by a masters in the same disciplines. She chose Loughborough, partly for its excellent engineering department but mainly due to its reputation as the leading sports university in the UK. She had represented England in football at age group levels up to University and had always wanted to represent the Women's Great Britain football team at the Olympics. Despite her unwavering dedication to this cause, she had fallen just short of the required standard and had been heartbroken when she realised she wouldn't be considered for the 2008 Great Britain Olympic squad.

Her heartbreak was short-lived though, when she was approached and recruited for a role within Britain's Security Services graduate scheme. Her academic prowess as well as her physical capabilities were a large part of the reason she was an attractive prospect, but also the fact she had high level contacts - via her family - in the middle east; and she spoke fluent Arabic. As part of normal rotation on her graduate scheme, she took roles within both MI6 and MI5 and at the end of her graduate training, she was given the choice of a position within either service.

She had no preference for either organisation, but chose MI5, predominantly due to favouring the boss there. She had no need to work at all, due to her family's incredible wealth, but she had always been driven by achievement rather than money, so that would never have been an option for her.

This was nine years ago and since then, she fast-tracked through the organisation to become a highly valued asset.

Sahira was currently on her annual leave, something she rarely took, but she had other external projects she was working on at the moment and needed time to focus on this highly valuable work for Allah. After the events of yesterday, she had liaised with her partners on these projects, and they had all decided that she should offer her services and make herself available to assist the current situation as it could be useful for them all in future.

She had called in to the office yesterday after the event, but had been assured she wasn't required and they would let her know if that situation should change. Evidently it had changed, as she had an email from her boss, letting her know he wanted her to come in to the office and help in the investigation. He had called her earlier but couldn't get through – it must have been during Salah, so in the meantime, he sent her the latest update of the situation report. She read through the report, including next action points and realised that if she hurried, she had time to make the next briefing.

She logged out and shut down her computer, then grabbed a pair of black pumps and a black Gucci jacket and rushed to her private lift outside her front door. As she hastened to the lift, she almost knocked over the waiter who was bringing up her salmon lunch. She'd completely forgotten about that and apologised to him, saying she had to hurry out, but to bill it to her account and she was happy for him to have it instead. She knew he wouldn't, but it was going to be wasted, so she thought she should at least offer.

The briefing, rather than take place at MI5 headquarters, was to take place at the MOD headquarters in Whitehall on the fabled 4th floor. She suspected the briefing was taking place at Whitehall rather than Thames House or Vauxhall Cross - the MI6 headquarters - due to a political argument, well above her pay grade, as to who would be running the investigation.

After passing through security, Sahira made her way to Historic room seventy-nine which was formerly part of Cromwell House and dates from around 1722. It is a completely panelled room with decorated modillion cornicing, featuring elaborate carved architrave and an ornate carved pine chimneypiece.

Sahira had made better time than she expected, so poured herself a peppermint tea and took a seat in the room to wait for the briefing. Gradually, selected officers made their way into the room followed by the big deals within the Intelligence community, including The Director General of MI5, Matt Sayer and Director General of MI6, Tim Wyatt.

Shortly after them came the big deals within UK politics,

led by Prime Minister Mary Henshaw and flanked by Home Secretary, Tom Forrester and Foreign Secretary, John Maguire. As the political A-Team entered, the room stood up out of respect.

As Sahira stood, she could see a Chinese contingent hovering outside. To Sahira's surprise, the Chinese contingent also entered the room led by the Chinese President, Li Jintao. Less surprising to her was the fact that Li Jintao had three members of his own security team with him. She didn't blame him.

7

Mary Henshaw waited for the room to settle, which due to her usual commanding, dignified presence, only took a matter of seconds. She then addressed the room.

'As you are all aware, along with the rest of the world, yesterday the Chinese Minister of National Defence, Xu Hua was assassinated on the terrace of the Houses of Parliament. Make no mistake, I see no difference to this assassination, as I would if it had been a member of our own Government. You attack one of our closest allies, you attack us.'

Sahira was thinking, 'one of our closest allies. Really?' But she understood this was about political positioning above any investigative necessity.

Henshaw continued.

'Yesterday afternoon, I called an emergency session of COBR and for reasons that will soon become apparent, we have elected for the investigation to be run by MI5. This investigation will be done with full transparency with our Chinese colleagues. Everything I know, they will know. I thank you upfront for your hard work. Now let's go and get this person or people and let the world know, the UK will not tolerate terrorism in any form. Thank you.'

The Prime Minister, along with her Chinese counterpart left the room and after a few seconds of silent contemplation, the Home Secretary, Tom Forrester stood up.

Tom Forrester was a career politician and very much from the historical political stock of private school, first class university, with a wealthy upper class family. The only difference being, he was very popular, with both the public and his colleagues. He didn't rely on contacts or money but on hard work to reach his position within the government. Like his Foreign Secretary counterpart, he had a unique character that endeared him to the general public. Whilst the Foreign Secretary was a huge film and cinema fan, Tom Forrester was a fan of cartoons and always had been. He had a vast collection of famous cartoon pictures, some copies but many originals. He was famed for always wearing a cartoon T-shirt under his shirt, even when sitting on the front benches.

Today wasn't a time for levity so he focused on the group.

'What I'm about to tell you, needless to say, doesn't leave these four walls. The Prime Minister told us that she will share everything she knows with the Chinese. I'm sure you know that she is a woman of her word and intends to keep that promise. Which is why, in the COBR session yesterday, she asked us to keep her somewhat out of the loop. She wants overviews and updates, but nothing with any granular detail. Specifically, nothing that could compromise any of our intelligence or protocols. This means, the only people with access to the ongoing investigation, are the people in this room and as always, not everything will be shared with everyone. Is that clear?'

There was an obedient silence.

'Good. Now, although Five will be running point on this, Six will give all the support they require. There will be no jurisdiction bull on this. Ok. Matt over to you, let us know where we are.'

Head of MI5, Matt Sayer stood up and nodded to one of his

officers who was standing by the door. The officer slipped out of the room. Sayer had a remote in his right hand and pointed it to switch on the sixty-inch screen that had been wheeled in the room before the briefing.

'The face you see on the screen is Ignatius Winter. He is ex SAS and ex MI6; he is our prime and only suspect.'

Sayer checked he had everyone's attention. He needn't have bothered. 'We know that Xu Hua was killed with a 7.62x51 NATO round from a L129A1 rifle. This is a British made rifle, popular with UK Special forces. Initially, we believed the shot had come from a building directly across the river, due to multiple reports of a loud bang coming from this building.'

Sayer pressed a button on the remote which altered the screen giving an aerial view of The Houses of Parliament, and across the river, multiple buildings, one of which was highlighted in red.

'However, our forensic investigation, showed the trajectory of the bullet originated from seemingly the river.'

Sayer changed the screen again. 'CCTV footage shows that this sightseeing boat was passing at the time of the shot, and the trajectory of the bullet to the boat is an exact match and we know this is where the shot was fired from. We found gunshot residue within the engine room of the boat, and a circular part of the ship's frame had been cut out and reattached. The bang heard from the building was a flash bang which had been rigged up to a remote sensor and was used as a crude, albeit effective diversionary tactic. A few minutes later, after the boat docked, we have CCTV of Mr Winter leaving the boat.'

Sayer updated the screen to a still CCTV picture of Ignatius disembarking. 'In the confusion of the moment, and the fact that law enforcement at this time were focusing on the building they believed the shot originated from, he managed to get past our police presence. We tracked him to the tube station where he took several tubes, clearly along the way using counter surveillance techniques. The last image we have of him is leaving Highgate station and heading in the direction of Highgate Woods.'

Sayer left a long enough pause for it not to be intrusive to ask a question, and as Sahira had many questions, she took the opportunity.

'Afternoon, sir.'

'Hi, Sahira.'

'Sir, are we working on the theory that Mr Winter is a gun for hire? If so, do we have any leads on who hired him?'

Sayer looked across at his counterpart, The Director General of MI6, Tim Wyatt.

Wyatt was sitting back in his chair, twisting a pen through his right hand. There was a momentary pause, almost as if he hadn't acknowledged the question, but just as the silence was becoming awkward, he sat forward and engaged the room with his eyes.

'Since Winter and Six departed company, we know he has been doing hire work, for want of a better phrase. Various jobs, but nothing on this level and nothing that we've felt obliged to involve ourselves with. We don't believe this was a mercenary assignment.'

Wyatt paused again, clearly pondering his wording for his next part. 'In 2008, Ignatius Winter led a Special Forces team to intercept a North Korean kill squad, who had been dispatched to take out a unit in the Chinese 80th group army based in Shandong.'

Sahira looked puzzled.

'Sir, China are North Korea's closest ally. Why would they act on a Chinese army unit and why were British Special Forces involved?'

'We don't know what North Korea's motivation was, but we believe that elements of the Chinese government were involved and aware of the operation. Due to the fact that China and North Korea are allies, they reached out to our government and asked for support. The higher-ups in Westminster, decided that we were glad to help, hence our involvement. The operation didn't go to plan. They were betrayed and instead of one kill squad, there were five, and they ambushed the SAS team. The whole team were killed apart from Mr Winter, who managed to escape, but not after killing most of the ambushers and being badly injured. He spent three months in a NATO hospital.'

Wyatt paused to reposition himself in his chair. 'It has never been officially acknowledged, but it is widely accepted that it was Xu Hua who betrayed our team.'

Sahira had to acknowledge that his motivation for killing Xu Hua was high.

'Sir, why did Xu Hua betray us?'

Wyatt sat back in his chair and started twisting his pen again and just said,

'Foreign Secretary.'

John Maguire stood up to address the room.

'We don't know and China has never admitted it was him. They've in fact actively denied it, but from the best we can tell, it was down to self-interest on his part.'

Maguire, then changed his tone. 'I understand there might

be some distaste based on what we just heard, but the fact remains. This was an assassination of an ally, a foreign dignitary on UK soil and it is our job to bring the assassin to justice. It seems highly likely that the person is Ignatius Winter, so we need to find him and take him into custody as soon as humanly possible.'

Sayer picked up the thread.

'To this end we have brought in 22 SAS Squadron Sergeant Major Andrew Atkin-Berry, who served with Winter for ten years in both the Paras and SAS.'

Sayer called out and the MI5 officer whom Sayer had acknowledged earlier came back into the room with Atkin-Berry.

The officer, Ezra Larholt once again introduced Atkin-Berry to the group, then began a formal, clearly pre-planned speech.

'Squadron Sergeant Major, thank you very much for your time. As I'm sure you are aware, what we are about to discuss is highly classified and mustn't be discussed with anyone outside of this room.'

Atkin-Berry visibly rolled his eyes but remained silent.

Larholt continued, 'Perhaps you could help us with this matter.'

He then made a show of looking at Atkin-Berry to engage him. Atkin-Berry looked bored.

'I don't know what THIS is, who YOU are or WHAT you want?'

Larholt looked embarrassed, which pretty much represented how the rest of the room felt. Not to be put off Larholt continued.

'Perhaps you could begin by telling us about Ignatius Winter?'

'He's a prick.'

'Ok... well thanks for that. I think we were hoping for more detail.'

'All right. He's a massive prick.'

Larholt was still showing a rumour of embarrassment but also now some anger.

'Squadron Sergeant Major, may I remind you, that this is a highly......'

Before he continued, Sayer jumped in.

'Ezra, thank you very much for arranging for Squadron Sergeant Major Atkin-Berry to be with us today. I think we can probably share with him the information we have, bearing in mind his position and service.'

Sayer then outlined all the information about the assassination including the role they believe Ignatius played.

Atkin-Berry pondered this momentarily before he spoke.

'Right, I wasn't expecting that. Firstly, please just call me Andy. It's easier for us all. So, you believe that Ignatius is behind this all?'

'It's our best, current working theory. You seem hesitant with it?'

'He's definitely capable of pulling it off, but I'm not buying the whole revenge thing. If SAS soldiers spent time taking revenge on people who try to screw them, they'd be constantly hunting people down, most of whom are within our own government. But even more than that, I don't think Ignatius would have even known Xu Hua was behind it. You guys don't exactly share all that stuff with us.'

'So, you don't think Mr Winter did this?'

'I honestly don't know, it doesn't add up for me, but I haven't seen the guy for at least a couple of years and I don't have the information you do. If he did do it, good luck catching him, he will know how to disappear. Mainly though, be careful. Trust me when I say this, when he's fighting, he has no mercy, pity or empathy.'

No one had anything relevant to say, so Larholt tried to regain some level of self-pride.

'Ok, well thank you for your time today, Andy, we appreciate your input.'

Atkin-Berry, looked at him.

'That's it? We couldn't have done that on the phone rather than make me take a six-hour round trip from Hereford?'

No one answered, so Atkin-Berry walked to leave.

Just before he left, Sahira called out.

'Andy, one more quick question. Is there any reason outside of personality clashes that you don't like Mr Winter?'

'I never said I didn't like him.'

Atkin-Berry, then turned and left the room.

The rest of the meeting was predominantly taken up with discussing action points and who had ownership and responsibility for each one.

8

May 13th

Ignatius had spent the entire previous day watching Netflix on Tank's TV and eating his food, for lack of knowing what he should be doing now. He didn't know what, if anything, he was dealing with. Tank's wife had got up early the previous morning as she was away with work for a couple of days and had luckily been too preoccupied with last minute packing to know that it was Ignatius who was staying there. Tank had called her to say that an old army friend was in town for work and at the last minute had to stay over so he'd said he could crash there for a night. She just replied, 'Ok sweetie, I'm meeting the girls for drinks in a bit, so will probably miss you guys, but have fun catching up.'

Ignatius was now eating a bacon sandwich and watching the final episode of a box set on Netflix. There was a sudden crash as the front door slammed against the wall.

He jumped of the couch, whilst drawing his Sig Sauer and taking a defensive position, covering all breach points. A few seconds later, Tank burst in the room.

'What the hell have you done?'

Ignatius holstered his weapon.

'What are you on about, Tank. Have you been drinking again?'

'You're the drunk. Not me.'

'Oh, yeah. But I still don't know what you're talking about.'

'Are you serious. Have you seen the news?'

Tank picked up the remote and switched over to the twenty-four hour news. On the screen was a picture of Ignatius. They spent the next fifteen minutes watching different news channels that were all leading with the search for Ignatius for his suspected role in the assassination of the Chinese Minister of National Defence, Xu Hua.

The news broadcaster, finished the segment with, 'If you see this man, you must under no circumstances approach him, but contact the police immediately. He is extremely dangerous.'

Tank looked at Ignatius with an expectant expression.

'You might want to say something now.'

'I am pretty dangerous.'

'Stop pissing about, Ignatius. What have you got yourself into and more importantly, what have you got me into?'

Ignatius outlined exactly what had gone down a couple of days ago from the minute he woke up to when he turned up at Tank's door. Tank believed him and asked.

'Do you know who Xu Hua is?'

'Never heard of him.'

'So how are you part of this?'

'I have no idea, but I know where to start trying to find out.'

Tank and Ignatius spent the next five minutes coming up with an Immediate Reaction plan, before Tank headed out.

Just over thirty minutes later Tank reversed his car as near to the front door as he could and went inside to get Ignatius. He handed him two thousand pounds in cash, which was part of the cash he'd taken out from the bank, as well as a brand new phone he had just brought in cash from a random corner shop.

They both went out to Tank's car and Ignatius looked at him.

'A Range Rover? How much does your wife make?'

'Shut up and get in the car.'

Ignatius climbed in the boot and pressed a button for it to shut. Tank went around to the driver's door and started up the engine to begin their trip to Woolwich where Ignatius had a storage garage that couldn't be traced to him.

The trip was uneventful other than Ignatius absolutely positive that Tank was purposefully hitting every pothole possible as well as taking roads that he knew had speed bumps on them. It hadn't taken too much detective work to figure that out. The fact he heard Tank laugh out loud every time they went through a pothole or over a bump was a bit of a giveaway.

They arrived at Ignatius storage garage. When he opened up, Tank was a bit underwhelmed. The shelves on the side were empty bar a few items, there was a cupboard and dead centre on the garage floor was something covered by a dust sheet.

When Ignatius pulled the sheet away, Tank became a bit more interested. In the centre of the garage was a Ducati Multistrada 1200 Enduro which has 158hp and is considered one of the best, on/off road motorcycles in the world. Ignatius went over to his cupboard and pulled out a set of licence plates and started putting them on the bike.

'They can't be traced to me and won't raise any flags with the police.'

Ignatius offered this bit of information to Tank, despite him not asking. Tank watched for a minute or so before he said.

'I'm off then. If you need me, you know how to get in contact.'

As he was walking out, he picked up a laptop that was one of the few items on the shelving. The laptop was a top of the range Hewlett Packard, and was still in its box as it had never been used before. He looked at Ignatius, 'I'm gonna need this.'

Ignatius just shrugged. He wasn't going to need it in the near future and he didn't really feel he could argue the point.

'Tank, thanks mate. Sorry to get you involved in this.'

Tank raised his right arm as he was walking back to the car and after a few steps, curled his hand into a fist, raising one finger.

9

Ignatius attached what looked like a tom-tom sat nav system on a diet, to the front of the bike, filled up with petrol from a jerry can, then checked the engine and made sure everything was in good working order. Once he was happy with everything, he put some bike leathers on over his clothes, a helmet with a blacked out visor, started the bike and headed out the garage on route to his next destination.

Ignatius pulled up outside the house of two of his ex-colleagues, just outside of Rainham in Essex. The roads were relatively clear and it was under fifteen miles, but it was still partially through London. He was trying not to draw any attention to himself, so it took him around forty-five minutes until he parked his motorbike out the front. He kept his helmet on as he opened the gate on the pathway to the front door. On the gate there was a rainbow painted message. It read, 'Welcome to the Wilsons'.

The front garden was immaculately tended as he walked the path that perfectly dissected the lawn, towards the two-bedroom detached bungalow. On the front door, Ignatius saw a new addition since last time he'd been here, in the form of a hanging wooden sign. 'No home is complete, without the pitter patter of kitty feet'.

Confident, that he couldn't be overlooked from here, Ignatius removed his helmet, then rang the doorbell. A matter of seconds later, Justin opened the door. Most people would be horrified if one of the most wanted men in the world turned up at their door, but Justin might as well not have even known.

'Iggy, darling. We were wondering when you'd be getting here.'

Justin air kissed both cheeks without getting too close.

Ignatius hated being called Iggy, but Justin was one of the few people he let get away with it, without repeatedly hurting him.

'Hi, Justin. I need both your help. Is Ricky here?'

'He is, but I'll warn you, he is being a grumpy bear today. He's in the workshop.'

'Can I speak with you both?'

'Of course, of course. We're playing host to a birthday party today, and I think we can both agree it might be better if you're not seen, so go around the back and I'll open the gate.'

Along the left side of the Wilsons' house was a path in between them and their neighbours. The path led to a park which backed onto the other houses on this side of the road. Ignatius put his helmet back on, but lifted the visor as he felt this would be less conspicuous. The path to the park was surprisingly long. What Ricky and Justin's modest bungalow hid was a big garden, especially in length. At the bottom of the garden, was a converted shed, that itself wasn't far short of the size of the bungalow in square metres. The shed was longer and thinner and side on compared to the bungalow. It was also very differently decorated to the bungalow.

To the right of the shed was a gate built into the fencing that led directly into the park. Justin let Ignatius in through this gate. At the top of the garden Ignatius saw a BBQ smoking away, a gazebo with tables full of food with colours that food had no right having. There were also a scattering of adults and a flood of children in fancy dress running around the top of the garden. Ignatius gave Justin a 'what's going on here look'.

'Our neighbours, Paul and Jenny are having their whole house renovated. It's going to be gorgeous. It's their son Stevie's birthday, so we said we'd host the party for them.'

Ignatius let it be and walked through the door to the shed and walked inside. The shed was one continuous building, split into three rooms. The first room Ignatius walked into, was a workshop on steroids and in the corner was Ricky in a pair of jeans, a New Zealand rugby top, some heavy duty tan welding gloves and a welder's mask. From what Ignatius could tell, he was working on an ornate metal archway.

Three years previously, Ignatius had saved both Justin and Ricky's life, after an operation they were all working on went very wrong. It was via this operation, that Ricky and Justin had met, and two years later they were married.

They were probably the two smartest men Ignatius had ever met. Justin was capable of making computers do things that shouldn't be possible and had worked in Cheltenham at Government Communications Head Quarters – GCHQ. He had designed much of the encryption software that the government currently used and a few others that neither the government nor any other organisation were even aware of being in existence.

Ricky was a different prospect altogether. He had a double doctorate and had worked for many years as part of the Research and Development branch for MI6 at Vauxhall Cross. If you needed someone to design a cigar that shot an arrow into the throat of the smoker, or a beer bottle that exploded in the face of the opener, or a tie that could be ordered by remote control to strangle the wearer, then Ricky was your man. Given enough time and assuming the laws of science weren't completely violated, he could make almost any concept become a reality.

Justin called out to Ricky, who fired down his welding torch and lifted his visor. As he turned and saw Ignatius.

'Here we go.'

Justin had a big grin on his face.

'I told you he'd need our help didn't I, Bear?'

'Yeah, yeah, well done.'

Ricky then focused his attention to Ignatius and shook his hand.

'Good to see you, Ignatius. Why don't you fill us in on what is going on, then we've got some presents for you. Justin said we needed to have them ready for when you turned up.'

Ignatius shook Ricky's hand and told his tale again. He didn't offer any opinions or emotion on the situation. He knew there would be no value in that and he also knew that the Wilsons would help him whether he was guilty or not. Ricky didn't question Ignatius' tale, he just moved forward.

'So, what's the plan, Ignatius, or do we need to make one?'

'Clear my name. Just want to be left alone.'

Ricky raised his eyebrows and gave an ok nod.

'Ok, well let me get your bits. It's going to take me twenty minutes or so to get it all together.'

Ricky turned and although he remained in the same room, at the same time he seemed to vanish into his surroundings as he managed his workshop like a veteran pilot in a cockpit.

Ignatius turned to Justin and held out the digital memory

card he had collected from the internet café.

'I need to know what's on this card. I think this is the key to it all.'

'No problem, give it here, darling.'

They both walked through to an adjoining room filled with electronics. Justin pulled some cords and sheeting unravelled to cover what would otherwise have been exposed brickwork or a plastered ceiling. Justin flicked a switch and lights within the sheets started flickering, making the room look like a cheap mall's Santa grotto.

Ignatius looked around the room confused.

'Should I ask?'

A smile swept across Justin's face.

'It's actually my own design. Not only can I block any infrared, parabolic or other sig int, but it can distort and actively manipulate any electronic signature to make….'

Ignatius cut him off.

'A simple no, would have worked.'

'Uh, oh. Two grumpy bears in one place. Tell the kids to hide their picnics.'

As he was saying this, he was firing up his equipment and snatched the card from Ignatius' hand and placed it in what looked like a miniature card reader. Once the equipment was live, Justin's innate bounce became a tunnel focus. His hands moved like a court stenographer. Multiple screens were spilling lines of code down them. Justin's eyes darted between them all, whilst his hands maintained their level of fury, without him once looking at them.

Ignatius thought he'd become part of *The Matrix*. He positioned himself to ask a question, but before he could get a sound out, Justin had lifted his right hand and pointed his palm towards Ignatius' face. Ignatius wondered whether to break a finger but just smiled instead.

Justin then moved one of his laptops into a padded briefcase, and a microphone near the screen. He motioned for Ignatius to follow him and they left the room back into Ricky's workshop, where he was working on what looked like a mannequin's head.

'Justin, I'm no Bill Gates, but isn't it harder to work on computer stuff when we're in a different room?'

Justin was still in his focus mode and gave his analysis. 'I don't know yet what is on this card but it is encrypted using one of the most secure encryption algorithms in the worlds, 4096-bit RSA.'

'Does this mean, you can't read it?'

Justin held up his hand again. Ignatius thought to himself, 'that's strike two'.

'Of course I can break it. It will take some time the traditional way though, so I'm trying a side channel attack.'

'What the hell is that?'

'A side channel is an attack vector that is non-direct and unconventional, and thus hasn't been properly secured. For example, your pass code prevents me from directly attacking your phone — but if I could work out your pass code by looking at the greasy smudges on your screen, that would be a side channel attack.'

That made some kind of sense to Ignatius, which was a first for him with tech stuff.

Justin continued, 'I am going to try an acoustic cryptanalysis. If you know exactly what frequency to listen out for, you can use low and high-pass filters to ensure that you only have the sounds that emanate from your PC, while the CPU decrypts data. In case you were wondering, the acoustic signal is actually generated by the CPU's voltage regulator, as it tries to maintain a constant voltage during wildly varied and bursty loads.

'What happens, if that doesn't work?'

'It will take longer, but it's doable. I might need to get some outside help though. I'm lacking a few bits of equipment. Do you have a problem with that?'

Ignatius trusted Justin's judgement and knew he wouldn't compromise him.

'Sure thing. No dickheads though.'

Justin smiled but just said.

'I better go and play host for a bit; do you want anything to eat from the BBQ?'

'A burger would be great. Cheers.'

As Justin joined the party at the end of the garden, a group of sevenish-year-olds all mobbed him and were jumping up and down around him. He was clearly a big hit with the kids. Ignatius went back into the workshop and watched Ricky at work. The precision was impressive. After about five minutes of this, Ricky started talking. Ignatius hadn't even been aware Ricky knew he was there.

'Right mate, come and have a look at this. It is a prototype of something Justin and I are developing for our company.'

Since the incident three years ago, when Ignatius had saved both their lives, Ricky and Justin had left the government payroll and had set up their own company, where they designed equipment for the government and private sector companies.

Despite the current, relatively modest surroundings they had done very well out of it. They had just bought a cottage in the

Peak District, on top of a villa they already owned just outside Nice in the South of France.

Ricky handed Ignatius what looked like a smaller version of a supermarket scan as you go scanner, but with a bigger screen on the back of it.

He took Ignatius outside and pointed it at Justin. The screen showed an infrared picture of Justin, with a green dot at his midriff. Rick explained that the dot was where a laser that was invisible to the naked eye was hitting Justin. As he finished explaining this, a phone number came up on the screen.

Rick got out his phone and showed him Justin's phone number. They were the same. He explained to Ignatius that it could read any phone number, including encrypted phones from a distance of up to approximately forty metres and assuming the phone was within a diameter of fifty centimetres of where the laser hit.

So, if the laser was hitting someone's shin, but their phone was in the jacket pocket, then it wouldn't get the number. It could work through some materials such as glass but had a far higher success rate with just air between the parties.

He explained that the phone needed to be within the diameter of the laser touch point for three seconds, so it was a lot easier to achieve this if the person was stationary. It also extracted the code that Justin could then use to easily hack into that person's phone and extract and monitor all the data on it; without it being possible for them to know they had been hacked or were being monitored. All Ignatius would have to do, is press a button on the scanner, allow it time to collect data, and then send this information back to Justin via the scanner.

Ignatius was impressed, but Ricky wasn't seeking approval

and he moved on to the next bit of equipment and began explaining its purpose and how to use it.

After a few more pieces of equipment were explained, Justin walked back into probably the most capable shed in the world and asked Ricky how they were getting on.

'Good, darling, I've got a couple more bits to show him, but I need to tweak them first.'

Justin looked at Ignatius.

'He's a smarty pants, isn't he?'

'He's a frickin' genius.'

'That's my man. Well, whilst he is playing, shall we go and see how the acoustic cryptanalysis is coming along?'

'Sure.'

Ignatius followed Justin back into the room and watched the screen whilst Justin furiously typed on different keyboards. Sometimes it seemed like he was typing on two different keyboards at the same time. Whilst Justin was typing away, the door opened and they both looked up expecting it to be Ricky. Instead, in ran a seven-year-old boy in a Buzz Lightyear outfit, with his arms spread out wide and squealing.

'Look at me, Uncle Justin. I'm a spaceman. I'm fighting the aliens.'

'Well, aren't you the galactic hero, Peter, but remember, we mustn't disturb Uncle Justin, when he's in his workshop,' Justin said smiling.

'Sorry, Uncle Justin. I just wanted to show you I can fly.'

'And very good you are at it, but you go and join the rest at the party and I'll be up soon and you can show me how you're going to defeat the aliens.'

When the young boy had walked in, Ignatius had ducked his

head and looked away pretending he was engrossed in a screen. He was sure the kid hadn't seen his face and even if he had, it was highly unlikely a seven-year-old would have a clue who he was, but he was still pissed off that the situation occurred.

After Buzz had run back to his friends, Justin looked at Ignatius with puppy dog eyes.

'Aren't they just adorable at that age?'

Ignatius stared back.

'I thought I said, no dickheads.'

The next few minutes were an awkward silence, but that was ok for Ignatius. He didn't really do awkward. Soon enough Ricky walked in with some more gifts. Justin and Ignatius used their feet to roll the office chairs they were using, towards the door.

The first gift was a skin mask. This was what Ricky had been working on earlier, on the mannequin.

'Ignatius, I need you to listen carefully with this. This is a living organism and when put on your face, it will absorb into the skin, so there's no way to tell it is a mask, but you need to look after it, or it will die and won't work.'

'Like from Mission Impossible?'

'No, not like from Mission Impossible. That isn't feasible. The mask won't move with your face. What it will do is change the contours of your face. Your cheek bones will be higher, it will widen your eyes, protrude your eyebrows, lengthen your nose. You will look like an entirely different person and more importantly, it will completely fool any facial recognition software, which is where any search will predominantly be carried out.'

'Sounds like Mission Impossible.'

76

Ricky ignored him and carried on.

'You can wear it for up to three days and it will feed off the natural nutrients in your skin, but it will need refreshing in the solution I will give you, for twelve hours every three days.'

Ricky held up a tub of cream.

'This cream will help extract it from your skin. A pea-sized amount around the circumference is ample and it takes about fifteen minutes to work.'

'Got it. Skin, solution, cream.'

Ricky then held up a bottle of moisture cream.

'This will change your skin pigmentation and don't even ask me if it's like fake tan. Wherever applied, it will evenly spread across the whole organ that is your skin. It is very subtle, but will change your appearance enough to give a Mediterranean rumour to your complexion, which I'm sure is not the search brief your hunters are looking for.'

Ignatius was impressed and somewhere inside him, he might even have been grateful. As they were chatting about next moves, an alarm sounded on Justin's computer.

Justin used both legs to kick off the wall and roll himself back over to his main monitor.

'Clever bastards,' he said after reading his screen. He looked up at the others. 'They have manipulated the voltage regulator to disguise the sounds that emanate. This is a dead-end. We're going to need to do this the old-fashioned way.'

Ricky looked at Justin.

'I didn't think anyone had ever broken 4096-bit RSA before.'

'That's because I've never bothered trying before.'

Ricky walked over to where Justin was sitting and stroked his head giving him a kiss on the top of the thinning red hair.

'How long do you think this will take?' Ignatius asked.

Justin kept looking at his screen typing away whilst he answered.

'I'm sorry, I don't know. It will take me a few days in between everything else, I would have thought.'

'Ok, thanks. I'll run down some other leads in the meantime.' Ricky jumped in.

'Ignatius, I don't want to ruin your fun, but have you considered handing yourself in and letting all this be figured out, without having to run from every law and security person on the planet?'

'Yeah, it did occur to me that some humans might do that, but I have a few issues with that. In case you don't remember, I'm not exactly flavour of the month within the intelligence community. The resources it would have taken to pull this off are immense. Do you honestly think there wasn't help from someone high up somewhere?'

Ricky gave a nod accepting that fact.

'If I hand myself in, we both know I'll disappear. Even if there was any doubt that it was me, the easiest thing in the world is to blame me. It is in everyone's interest for this to be resolved and go away. I don't think our government, or any other, would fight too hard to clear my name.'

'You did make a lot of friends when working there.'

This time, it was Ignatius' turn to give an accepting nod to the cheap shot. Justin cut in and asked Ricky a question with so much tech jargon, that Ignatius wasn't sure if he was speaking English or Klingon. He had heard the two of them speak Klingon to each other enough times, followed by them chuckling away at one of their crap jokes to each other.

Whilst they were chatting, Ignatius walked over to the door that led to the garden. He was pondering his current dilemma whilst lazily flicking his foot at the cat flap. Bloody thing was broken. He knew how it felt. It mirrored his current life.

He meandered back over to Ricky and Justin.

'Your cat flap is broken.'

Ricky looked at him as if he'd just broken into his house on Christmas morning and taken a piss on the tree.

'What do you mean, it's broken? Stuff doesn't break in this house.'

'It doesn't open. I was nudging it with my foot and it didn't budge.'

Ricky's face flushed with relief. 'It's not broken. It's a microchip cat flap. It only opens when it gets a signal up close from the microchip that's in one of our cats' collars. How have you never heard of these before? Even the Flintstones know about them.'

Justin jumped in.

'Don't tell me, you've never had a cat before? They're purrrfect.'

Ricky and Justin giggled whilst Ignatius sighed.

'I have had a cat before actually. I was on a deniable mission in South Korea. It was a bit tough for my palette.'

'Iggy, you're terrible.'

Ricky brought the subject back to the matter in hand.

'What are you going to do now? You said you have other leads?'

Ignatius laid out his next plans of action to them both. For the first time in a while, Justin looked up from his computer.

'Can we help in other ways?'

'Guys, not many people would help me out half as much as

79

you have. I don't want to take the piss.'

'Do you have any money?'

'An old mate gave me some loose change. I'll figure something out.'

Ricky went over to a wall picture and looked at it up close, whilst placing both hands against the picture.

Within the picture was micro technology that was an iris scanner, as first security checkpoint. The second checkpoint was a pulse reader in both thumbs and the final checkpoint was an x-ray of the hand and measurement of the bones within the hand.

Every person's bone make-up in the hand is on the same unique scale as fingerprints. Once all of these were confirmed by the computer, a six-inch-thick steel door detached itself from the reinforced concrete wall.

Ignatius took a guess, that some of the technology and designs in that safe would one day be worth in the tens of millions. Ricky however, pulled out a wad of cash totalling four thousand pounds and handed it to Ignatius.

'Loose change won't get you far. Take this.'

Ignatius took the cash and gave a weak smiled nod to him. There was even a hint of guilt within the smile. He had no doubt that would pass soon, though.

10

Sahira was in the sniper's nest, standing slightly bent over and taking in the entire surroundings, before she focused on specific parts.

The boat had been commandeered by the authorities as soon as they realised it was involved in the assassination, and it was now docked in a navy yard of undisclosed location, being guarded twenty-four hours a day by armed guards.

The forensic team had been through the whole boat and taken as much forensic material as possible, which was a lot bearing in mind the nature of the boat. Realistically, Sahira knew they'd need to get very lucky to find anything of forensic value in the boat.

The hole that Bambi had cut out of the metal frame was exposed and Sahira made her way over to the area, so that she could occupy the same space as the sniper had, who she believed to be Ignatius Winter.

As she walked towards the hole, she almost lost her footing which was some feat, considering the grip pattern on the flooring. After a couple of minutes lying where she believed the sniper had laid, trying to get in his mind at the time of the shooting, something occurred to her. What a complete waste of time the last couple of minutes had been.

She put both hands down, to push herself up and once again she felt a slipping sensation. She realised this time, she hadn't lost her footing, but the panel beneath her had slipped, which was strange for a panel that was screwed into the floor. She stood up and used her foot to push the panel back and forth and realised it was loose.

She checked and all the screw heads were in place. She asked one of the navy guards there overlooking her inspection if he had a screwdriver on him. He didn't but gave her a knife. She wedged the knife under the panel and used another panel as a fulcrum to lift. The panel lifted easily. She looked underneath and realised there were no screw bottoms. The screw tops had been stuck on as a visual manipulation.

Sahira climbed under the panel and there was a low level of water in the hull. She called the Navy guard over.

'Petty Officer, should there be water at the bottom of the boat?'

'No, Ma'am, but sometimes there can be minor breaches, that over time slowly let water into the hull. It's not uncommon in older vessels.'

Sahira looked around the boat at the pristine equipment. 'This boat looks new.'

'Yes, Ma'am, maybe it was a fault in the building of the ship?'

'Wouldn't that be picked up, when the boat is inspected before it's passed to be water worthy?'

'Yes, Ma'am, but sometimes the fault isn't apparent if it's minor, until after it has had a minimal amount of wear and tear. It would be picked up at the standard inspections, so would never cause a major incident.'

'Petty Officer, please get me the owner of the boat on the phone.'

'Yes, Ma'am.'

The guard spoke into his radio and a minute later his phone

rang. He answered and briefly spoke into it, before he handed it over to Sahira.

'Hello, who am I speaking to?'

'This is Mark Finch. I am the owner of the boat. I was told you need to speak to me?'

'Yes, Mr Finch. Thank you for your time. This is Sahira. I'm with the Home Office. I need to ask you a few questions about your boat if that's ok?'

'Of course. What do you need to know?'

'There is about two inches of water in the hull of your boat and across the length of it. Do you know why that might be the case?'

'No, no I don't. The boat just underwent its safety inspection and everything was fine. There shouldn't be any water in the hull.'

'When did it have its last safety inspection?'

'I'm just checking now.'

Mark Finch was in front of his computer and brought up the records.

'April 8th was the last inspection. It passed with flying colours, there wasn't even any indication of wear on the vessel.'

'Thank you, Mr Finch. Please remain contactable, if I have any further questions.'

'I will be on this phone.'

Sahira hung up and considered this information.

'Petty Officer, I need a full forensic team here immediately.'

'Yes, Ma'am.'

Within the hour, a full team of forensic officers were outside the boat in white overalls and waiting further instructions. Sahira stood in front and addressed them. 'Thank you all for coming so quickly. We're all aware of the relevance of this boat. There was a loose panel in the sniper's nest that led to the hull. The hull had water in it that shouldn't be there. I need to understand why it's there.'

The team looked at Sahira with a mixture of confusion and of 'what the hell is this crazy woman on about'. She picked up on it. 'Look, I know it's thin, but bearing in mind the significance of what's happened, I just want to make sure we cover all bases.

The team leader, Des Itoje, looked at her briefly then turned to the rest of the group.

'Right all. You heard her. Every inch of this boat gets inspected. I want to hear if a paint stroke is out of place'

He then started dishing out the technical breakdown of the search and assigning different teams to different parts of the boat. They moved like a synchronised swimming team to their areas and began the search.

After approximately twenty minutes, Sahira was beginning to think that she was chasing a dead-end. She went through to the small kitchenette just off from the dock yard and poured herself a cup of boiling water. From her handbag, she took out a bag of jasmine tea and put it in the water. Jasmine tea wasn't highly sought after within the navy.

As she strolled back out to the yard, there were two forensic officers waiting for her, the team leader and a young woman. The young woman was beautiful with flawless skin and a mass of dark bushy hair which was on display now that the hood of her white overalls had been pushed back. She was looking down as she began talking.

'Hi, Miss, uh...'

Sahira jumped in.

'Just Sahira is fine.'

Intelligence service officers only ever used first names; sometimes, even their own.

'Ok, hi Sahira. We found a panel that has been replaced and, in its place, a new panel put in, one that can be opened up as an escape hatch.'

Sahira's eyes lit up. 'Show me.'

The three of them walked over and the young woman showed Sahira the hatch and how it worked. Sahira had to admit, there was no way you could tell it was there by visual survey alone.

The young woman volunteered. 'It must have been put there when the boat was out of water for inspection, but after the inspection had taken place.'

Sahira took a second to look at the young forensics officer. She was impressed. She had no doubt she would have a successful career.

'What's your name?'

'It's Heather. Heather Sillwood.'

Sahira looked at Des. 'Des, I know you've got a million things going on right now. If it's ok with you, I'm going to use Heather as my point of contact for the time being?'

'Fine by me.'

Sahira focused back on Heather.

'Heather, great work. I'm going to need you again. Please can you email this address - she handed her a white card with a generic email address and her phone number on it – with your direct contact details.'

Heather took the card with a smile. Sahira continued, 'I'm going to head back to the office. Please, can you continue the search and see if anything else pops up. Anything out of the ordinary, please call me immediately, Heather.'

Both Des and Heather gave confirmation of the request and went back to work.

She climbed into her BMW Nazca C2. Only three were ever made and Sahira was the lucky owner of one of them after she bought one at auction in 2016 for the cool price of £1.4 million. The car was originally made in 1992, but she had updated the interior to include built-in sat nav and bluetooth.

Once she had cleared the dockyard and was on the road, she dialled the boat owner again. He picked up on the fourth ring.

'Mr Finch, it's Sahira from the Home Office.'

'Hello, Sahira, how can I help?'

'Where did your boat have its inspection and who undertook the inspection?'

'The boat undertook its inspection at Tamesis Dock and as always was undertaken by the Environment Agency.'

'Do you know who at the Environment Agency undertook the search?'

'Bear with me.' Finch checked the paperwork. 'It was signed by a Ben Cooper.'

'Thank you, Mr Finch.'

Sahira hung up and dialled her office. When she was connected to the relevant department, she requested CCTV footage of Tamesis Dock for the 8th and 9th of April, before the boat left the dock. She also requested a background check on Ben Cooper from the Environment Agency.

It was another hour until she was back at her desk in the office. She had a message to call back regarding the CCTV and the Environment Agency officer. She picked up her phone and dialled the Analysis department.

'Hi, it's Sahira from International Counter-Terrorism.'

'Hi, Sahira, we have the information you want.'

'That was quick, great.'

'I'm afraid we don't have much. The CCTV had been disconnected at the times you requested and there was nothing suspicious about Ben Cooper's background or any unusual activity on his bank accounts.'

'Thanks. Can you send me Mr Coopers' address? I think I'll still go and have a chat with him.'

'That's what I was about to tell you, Sahira. I'm afraid that won't be possible. Mr Cooper was found dead in his apartment on April 11th. He was hanging from a beam. The coroner ruled suicide.'

Sahira said her thanks and hung up. There had been a lot of new revelations, but it didn't change anything or realistically give any new beneficial information to the investigation. She planned on checking in with Sayer before heading over to Ignatius Winter's flat to have a look around.

11

Sahira made her way to Matt Sayer's office feeling deflated. They had plenty of circumstantial evidence against Winter, but nothing concrete. She had no idea that an annoyance which was coming her way, would end up being the best bit of luck within the whole investigation.

When she was in Sayer's office, she was dismayed to see that Ezra Larholt was also there. She didn't really know what Larholt did there, but to quote Squadron Sergeant Major Atkin-Berry, she thought he was a massive prick.

All she knew about him, was he used to have his own recruitment firm and now was here. As far as she could tell, he was Sayer's bitch.

Sayer asked about the investigation. She updated him on what she'd found. He was skimming through some paperwork, whilst he asked what her thoughts were on the latest bits of news.

'I don't know, Matt.' He insisted on his staff calling him Matt, even though they often still referred to him as 'sir', especially if they'd pissed him off. 'Winter is a highly trained and skilled operative. It makes sense he'd have another option as an exit strategy, but it seems a bit strange that he'd go to the effort of a diversion with the flash bang and then walk right into the epicentre of law enforcement. Also, how did water get in the boat if he didn't use that exit strategy?'

Sayer pondered this. 'Yep, I agree. There are some anomalies.

Keep cracking on.'

'Will do. I'm about to pop over to Winter's flat and have a look around.'

'Hold that thought. I need you on something else this afternoon. We've had a potential major security breach. It's a high-profile, big deal thing. I need you there, Sahira.'

'Matt, I really wanted to crack on with the assassination investigation.'

'Normally, I'd agree, but this could be a potential threat against the PM. I need a top person on it.'

Larholt's eyes lit up and he jumped in.

'Matt, I agree with Sahira, her time would be best spent on what she's doing. Maybe I should check this one out?'

'Thanks, Ezra but I really need you on something here. Actually, could you go down to Technical Operations and Surveillance now and chase the report they're meant to have for me?'

'You got it, Matt. I'm on it.' Larholt bounded out the room as a man on a mission.

Sayer looked back at Sahira.

'Sorry to throw this at you Sahira, but please can you do this for me. I can't have that moron going over there.'

Sahira smiled.

'Of course, Matt. I got to ask, why the hell is Larholt here?'

It was Sayer's turn to smile now.

'I know you will keep this to yourself, so I'll tell you. His father has very high level ties within the CIA and they have been incredibly useful over the years, so we need to keep him happy and therefore, we're stuck with Larholt. Tim Wyatt and I argued over who got him, so one night we got drunk and had a game of poker. I lost, so he's with us. I'm not even meant to have a report from Tech Ops, but should keep him busy chasing it for a while.'

Sahira was happy to know recruitment standards hadn't dropped.

'What time do you need me on this thing, Matt?'

'I said you'd be there for 4.00pm, so soon.'

'Ohh, 4.00pm. That's usually a little later than I care to work.'

Sayer chuckled. 'Funny. Get there for 4.00pm and report back directly to me on this one.'

'No problem. Where am I going?'

'Battersea Power Station.'

Sahira arrived at Battersea Power Station at 3.45pm and was greeted at the entrance by two security guards.

They were clearly not part of her organisation but part of the Power Station's crew. She knew that there would be another level of more discreet security checking happening by her people. But the security guards were a good deterrent, and it was often useful to keep the venue staff involved as they had an insight into the structure that others wouldn't. They seemed reasonably aware and competent and Sahira got through the checkpoint fairly quickly after showing relevant ID.

Sahira parked her BMW away from all the other vehicles in the vast structure as the last thing she needed was to get blocked in. She headed over to what had clearly been used as a staging area and introduced herself to a police officer who was standing up, filling in some form of paper work on a trestle table. He got on a radio. After a short wait, a tall man with short dark, heavily gelled hair whose shoulders could be measured in square footage, rather than inches, and a woman who was taller than her, but still looked short next to the man and had dark slicked back hair, walked over.

Sahira guessed she was mainly muscle. They simply introduced themselves as Simmonds and Peters. Simmonds the man and Peters the woman, and were part of the Prime Minister's close protection team.

Peters was in charge and she substituted any small talk for getting straight to work after Sahira had introduced herself.

'Thanks for coming, Sahira. How much do you know?'

'Let's assume nothing.'

'Ok. Here's where we are. The PM is hosting a charity event here tomorrow evening. As always, we sent a team to do a security check and risk assessment. When it was operating as a power station, there were a number of pipes that led from the building into the river. Whilst checking these pipes, we found that one of the grates that prevents the pipe from being used as an entryway had been purposely cut open. We immediately sent a team of divers into the river and they have recovered a number of bits of sophisticated diving equipment that has been abandoned into the river, right below the grate. Within that equipment was an Oceanic OCI personal wrist dive computer. We have sent that to tech, to see if they can get any information from it. We should have results soon.'

This was a genuine, high probability threat and she understood why Sayer had insisted on her getting there right away.

'Does the PM know?' she asked Peters.

'She does, and we have asked her to cancel, but she insists that a lot of work has gone into this event and it will raise a lot for the charity, so it has to go ahead.'

'Have there been any other security breaches at all?'

'None, but we are going over every inch again, now as we speak and we have amended our security protocols for tomorrow. We have secured the pipe, we will have boats patrolling the river before and during the event and we will have SBS - Special Boat Service - divers in the river patrolling, all day tomorrow.'

Sahira knew she was dealing with competent professionals and knew that they wouldn't moan about the PM not cancelling; which, from a security perspective would be by far the preferred option. This team would get on with the job in hand and ensure the PM's safety. She didn't have much to offer so she said,

'Let me know if there is anything additional that we can do. I will speak with the office again, but we haven't received any chatter about an attack and none of the actors who we would place as likely suspects for any attack, have been flagged as mobilising any form of assault.

Please let me know as soon as you get the information back from the dive computer and if it's ok with you, I'm going to have a look around?'

'Knock yourself out.'

They all shook hands and went in separate directions.

Sahira spent the next hour walking around the vast structure and couldn't see anything else out of place, but she could hardly do a search of any merit. She was feeling uneasy though. Surely there would be some chatter or some other intel of an attack, however minimal. There had been nothing.

After another ten minutes, a member of security came up to her to let her know that Peters wanted to see her. Sahira made her way back to the staging area, where Peters was standing and clearly waiting for her, whilst Simmonds was speaking with some team members and relaying orders to them.

Peters told Sahira what had been found on the dive computer. The tech team had taken all the data from it, which included GPS positioning. The device had only been used once. It was used from Westminster to the Power Station at 1.06pm until 1.31pm on May 11. Sahira gave Peters a knowing look. Peters responded verbally.

'I know, right. The time and date of the assassination. Maybe this has nothing to do with the PM after all.'

Sahira nodded whilst responding.

'I think this was used by the assassin as an escape after the assassination of Xu Hua.'

Peters pondered this momentarily before replying.

'It does seem too much of a coincidence, but I wouldn't be doing my job if I didn't proceed as if the threat against the PM is still very real.'

God, she was good.

Sahira agreed with her and they swapped direct contact information and agreed to share any bit of information that might help the other one, until the event was over tomorrow night. The place was still alive with activity, so Sahira headed back over to the security guards by the entrance.

'How often do you two work here?'

Both guards looked around startled whilst sitting in their hut as they hadn't heard her approach.

'Both Dougy and I are employed by the company that own the Station. We do the day shift and another crew do the night shift. We do the week and others do the weekend,' the guard nearest to her responded.

'Were either of you working on May 11?'

'Sure, we both were. It was the day that Chinese guy got blown up.'

'Close enough. Did either of you notice anything strange that day. Anyone on site who shouldn't have been, maybe.'

'Love, there were over a thousand people on site that day. There was a big lunch going on. Comings and goings all day.'

Sahira was about to ask another question, when the security guard continued, 'But to answer your question, nothing unusual. The staff were all good as gold, not always the case with these student types when they're working here. I remember it well as Dougy loves to complain, and the only thing Dougy could complain about that day was about how he almost got run over by the Deliveroo guy.'

Sahira smiled to herself. She had almost knocked into a guy delivering food to her the other day. She asked a few more questions to find out who the catering company had been that day and if any other contractors had been on site. Just as she was walking away, she turned around again. 'You said it was a lunch?'

'Sorry, love?'

'You said on the 11th, it was a lunch?'

'That's right.'

'Why was a Deliveroo guy here then, if there was already food here? Do the staff order their food?'

'I don't know, hadn't really thought about it to be honest. The catering company are diamonds. They also feed their staff, even send food out for us. It makes no sense for the staff to order food. They weren't here that long, the event didn't go on for very long and the cost of getting food in, would probably be most of what they'd earn.'

Sahira was fully engaged now.

'Do you remember what time you almost got knocked over by the Deliveroo guy?'

Dougy spoke for the first time.

'I don't remember exactly but it must have been between 1.45 to 2.00pm.'

The timeline fit.

'Do you remember what time the Deliveroo guy arrived?'

This time, it was the first security guard who answered again.

'That's the funny thing. Neither Dougy nor I can remember seeing him arrive.'

Sahira got both their contact details and gave a number for them to call if they remembered anything else strange from that day and headed to her car. She needed to get back to the office. In the car she called the office and got them to transfer her to the relevant person at the Deliveroo offices.

She was worried they might be reluctant to share the information, but she needn't have been. They were happy to help. They weren't breaching anyone's privacy and they wanted to be helpful. The information she got from them, went a long way to confirming her suspicions. Deliveroo had no orders whatsoever to be delivered to the Power Station that day.

On route back to the office, Sahira spoke with Sayer over a secure line. She outlined everything she'd found out to date. Sayer let her know, he would put pressure for the forensics from the original search to be returned as soon as humanly possible, and she was to be in the office for 7.00am tomorrow morning to meet with him and the Home Secretary, and run through everything again. He left her with the words, 'Sahira, we have

just opened up a complete shit storm.'
He had no idea yet how much of one though.

12

Ignatius was sipping his coffee whilst keeping an eye on the internet café across the road. He had shaved his head with a razor and put on his disguise whilst at the Wilsons. He hadn't recognised himself in the mirror, but now was as good a test as any. No one had even given him a second glance; it seems like it worked.

He now had to wait until the internet café was empty. There were three people in there. How much of that was legal trade, Ignatius wondered? The café was packed with what he assumed was post work trade and there was a moment of jealousy within Ignatius, wishing that his life was simple once again, without having to run for his life. At the table next to him, there were two guys who Ignatius placed in their early twenties. They were talking about women they know. The guy nearest the window said, 'I am definitely going to tap that this weekend.'

He then held out his fist for the other guy to pump. Whilst doing this, Ignatius saw that the group of customers who had been in the internet café were leaving, so he got up to head over the road.

'Dude, I'm not giving you a fist pump. That's my sister you're on about.'

The first guy didn't seem to care and kept his fist up expectantly. Ignatius made his way to the door and on his way past the two men he gave the first guy a fist pump. He'd earned it after all.

Ignatius walked through the door of the internet café. The owner was walking towards the door and as Ignatius walked in the shop he said, 'Sorry, we're closed.'

'You're not anymore. You can shut in ten minutes when I get what I want.'

The owner looked like he was about to cry. Clearly his nerves were still a bit frayed from the other day, but even so, his reaction seemed over the top.

For Ignatius, the key point that he was taking out of the situation was the fact that he hadn't been recognised. If this guy didn't recognise him, no one would.

The owner's left side of the face was deeply bruised and he had butterfly stitches above his left eye. Ignatius didn't have the time to flirt with him today as someone could walk in at any moment, so he got straight to the point.

'I need to know where the memory card came from.'

The owner did a good job of looking confused.

'What memory card?'

'You know exactly what memory card I'm talking about…'

Ignatius was about to carry on talking, but he saw the owner's eyes flash past him. He spun around to see two men pointing guns at him and the owner. He didn't think before he reacted. The man nearest to him was too close. Ignatius hands moved like a whip and he dismantled the gun in the man's hand. The slide at the top of the barrel was in Ignatius' hands and he used it to stab the man's throat. The man dropped to the floor grabbing his neck and grasping for air.

The second man was slow to react and he was only just starting to bring his gun up towards Ignatius. Ignatius poked both his arms forward, so they were between the man's body and his arms. He then opened up his arms like chicken wings, so that the man had no control nor any opportunity to fire his weapon. He went to headbutt Ignatius, but there wasn't the room to get up any power and the move had been foreseen and both foreheads met limply in the middle of the space between them.

Ignatius tilted his head to the right and then sunk his teeth into the tip of the second man's nose and bit until he felt his teeth touch again. The scream was feral, but that didn't discourage Ignatius who pushed the man back and used an overhand right to crash his fist into his jaw. As man two fell to the floor, Ignatius spat out a mouthful of blood and flesh.

He searched both men who had assault equipment on them, but no phones, wallets or identification. Ignatius used the handcuffs he found on the men to secure them to metal piping in the shop. Whilst he walked over and locked the door to the café he turned the sign to indicate they were closed.

'Who are they?' he asked the owner.

'I don't know. They came into the shop, about fifteen minutes before you. They had just asked about the memory card, when three customers were coming in. These two,' the owner nodded at the restrained men, 'managed to slip into the store cupboard, out of sight before they were seen and told me they'd kill everyone if I said anything to give them away.'

'Fine, I don't have time to explain, but the memory card that was taken from you the other day. I need to know where and who it came from?'

The owner told the tale about how he'd received an email, telling him that he was going to be sent a memory card and he was to hand it over to a contact at the right time.

Ignatius stared at him, slightly disbelieving. 'And you just agreed to do this from an email from someone you didn't know, with no idea what was on the card, and hand it over to someone else who you didn't know?'

The owner looked apologetic.

'I'm kinda known as a guy who can do small favours on the side, under the radar.'

That explained his expensive clothes.

'How were you supposed to know whom to hand the card over to?'

'I was told the guy would come to me. He definitely did that.'

Well, that was true and also reassuring that the owner still hadn't clocked who he was.

'Show me the email.'

Ignatius got Justin on the phone and updated him. Justin told him what to do. 'A friend of mine needs access to your computer, you need to do what he says.'

'What? I can't do that. There is information on lots of different clients on here. Dangerous clients, who would be angry if they knew I'd let someone else see their information.'

'More dangerous than me?'

The owner took a look at the two restrained men on the floor in all types of pain and saw the blood pooling on the floor and a man with half a nose. He dipped his head in what was a clear indication that he thought, they probably weren't as dangerous as this man. He also accepted the fact that they weren't here and he was.

Ignatius put Justin on speaker phone who gave directions on what needed to be done at their end.

Justin was using Freshservice Service Desk software to access the computer and once he had access, the screen of the

100

computer seemed to change as if someone was flicking through a picture book. In no time at all, Justin said, he had everything he needed and hung up.

Before he left, Ignatius said to the owner,

'I'm sure you've been caught up in all this unknowingly, but I can assure you, this is not something you want to be part of. If I was you, I would disappear for a couple of weeks at least. Your life may well depend on it.'

Ignatius emptied the magazines of the guns from the two men and put them on the floor, out of reach from them. He had a layer of super glue on his fingertips and palms, so his prints wouldn't be on them. He said to the owner, 'I'm going to give you thirty minutes before I call the police and tell them about two armed men being here. It's up to you if you want to hang about to answer their questions or not. I would advise, you're not here and if and when the police track you down, you claim you were never here when they were and it was a robbery. It's your call. One bit of advice I'll give you for free. They will plead and bargain for you to let them free. I can promise you with a hundred percent certainty, if you do that, they will kill you.'

Ignatius didn't know if the owner would take notice and didn't care that much, but he had at least warned him.

Ignatius headed to the supermarket for the supplies he would need for the next few hours or days or even longer, depending on factors outside of his control.

He bought eighteen packs of crisps, twelve Mars bars, six sandwiches, some toilet roll, some bin bags, a blanket, a tooth brush, some antibacterial gel soap and four 1.5 litre bottles of water as that's all he believed he'd be able to carry on top of his other equipment.

He made his way to his location by circling the building in a wide arc and gradually decreasing it. On his third arc, he spotted the surveillance team. He wasn't concerned though as they weren't watching the building he was going to enter; they were watching the building he was planning on surveilling.

Ignatius went to the back door of the building and had a look at the ADT Pulse security system. He wrote down the serial number for the system. He knew it was a good system, but however good it was, it was no match for what Ignatius was about to throw at it.

He pulled out his phone and first of all made an anonymous call to the police about a robbery in an internet café. At the very least, he hoped this would slow down the men, if not put them out of commission completely.

He then dialled a memorised number. Justin answered on the second ring. Ignatius told him what he needed and Justin told him he'd call him back in five minutes.

When he called back, he told Ignatius that he was ready to disable the alarm on his say, and he let him know that the loft wasn't alarmed, so he could move freely in there without fear of triggering any alarm. Ignatius told him to do it now. Justin tapped his return key and the alarm was disabled. Ignatius then got out his Kronos electric lock pick gun and made short work of the back door.

The building was a mid terrace house that had been converted into three different offices for small companies. Ignatius made his way up the staircase on the left of the house to the top floor, and once again made short work of the door lock with his electric pick.

Once in the room Ignatius took in his surroundings. It was a small architect firm proudly announcing themselves via a glass sign as Gaul's Halls. The name annoyed him and also rang a bell in his head. He'd deal with that in a bit, but first he did a quick search of the office to see if there was anything in there that might be of use. After he found nothing useful, he had a great idea.

He opened the filing cabinet, which had six separate files with different names on the top; clearly clients. He took the paperwork out of the files, mixed them all together and returned them to folders randomly. He then went into the small kitchenette and took off the top of the half-filled sugar pourer. In one of the drawers was a pile of salt packets, which had clearly been collected from many takeout working lunches. He opened about fifteen of them and added them to the sugar pourer and buried the empty sachets at the bottom of the bin, under a pile of other rubbish and stirred the contents of the pourer with his finger.

For now, that would do and should help teach them a lesson for annoying him. The reason the name rang a bell, is that they had made complaints about Ignatius before. After one of Ignatius' money earning excursions, he had returned to his flat covered with a fair amount of blood and looking filthy. The firm had complained to his landlord. Apparently, it wasn't a good look to prospective clients of theirs, who had also witnessed this. It had resulted in Ignatius, very nearly being evicted.

He made his way to the latch in the roof and stood on a chair to push it open into the loft. He took off his large rucksack he'd borrowed from Ricky and put it up in the roof. He then returned the chair to its original place.

He walked back to the open latch and jumped up, gripping his fingers on the edge. He pulled himself up into the loft and was pleased to see there was boarding on the floor and it wasn't just an exposed wooden frame with fiberglass insulation. He went over to the Velux window and took in the view. It was an ideal viewing point for the front of his flat.

There was plenty of old office equipment stored up there. He shifted a heavy filling cabinet across the hatch, so it couldn't be opened from below, and set about making the loft his home for the near future. He had time now to set up the equipment he would need, as Ignatius knew that no one would be investigating his flat at night in the dark, so he didn't have to worry about keeping watch for the time being.

He took out the blanket and folded it up into a makeshift pillow then set his head down. He'd learnt long ago in the army to get sleep whenever you can.

13

Sahira's alarm woke her at 4.30am. She had always been an early riser, but even for her, 4.30am hurt. It was a struggle for her to slide out of her 1200 thread count, Egyptian cotton bed linen and four poster mahogany bed.

She stepped onto the heated marble flooring and walked to the kitchen where she cut a fresh lemon in half and squeezed one half of it into a mug in the copper sink to avoid the juice going over her worktops. She then put the mug under her Heatrae Sadia Aquatap, which would pour boiling or chilled water on demand.

Whilst waiting for the lemon drink to cool down, she went to the bedroom, got her bag for the day ready and put on her swimming costume with a tracksuit over that. She sat down and turned on the news whilst she finished her drink.

It was still dominated by details of the assassination, so she switched it off and sat and finished her hot lemon in quiet. A few minutes later, she left the penthouse and took her elevator down to the garage. She had a double glass fronted garage which also had heated flooring. As well as her BMWs, she also had a Range Rover SV Autobiography, that she decided to use today.

She left her complex and headed just over a mile away to her gym, which had private parking for Platinum members. She had decided a while ago not to use the gym facilities at One Hyde Park as she felt obligated to speak with any neighbours, which meant her workout would take twice as long.

Once in the gym, she swam fifty lengths, before she did a light weights workout, spent ten minutes honing her skills on the heavy bag and finally a thorough stretch. She then had a shower before she put on her work clothes and headed to 2, Marsham Street in Westminster, which was the Home Office and residence of the office of the Secretary of State for the Home Department; or more commonly known, the Home Secretary.

Her meeting this morning was to be held in Tom Forrester's office.

Sahira was in the office for 6.30am, so as she still had time before the meeting, she made calls concerning several aspects of this case she wanted to chase up. She was happy to hear that she would be getting the results and information she was after this morning.

She also had another project that Sayer had given her, so she took a card out of her bag and dialled the number. It was taking a while for the phone to be answered and Sahira wondered if she was calling too early. She was just about to give up when she heard the female voice at the other end of the phone.

'Hello, this is Peters.'

'Hi, it's Sahira. I'm sorry, I haven't called too early, have I?'

'Oh, hey, no, not at all. Both Simmonds and I have been here since four this morning.'

Sahira gave a knowing nod.

'I just wanted to call to see how it's going over there. Have you found anything else of concern?'

'Not at all. We've also had no further intel from you guys, suggesting any attack is likely, but we've doubled security and changed the timelines of tonight's schedule, so we're confident that we can handle anything that comes our way. But I must admit I'll be a lot happier when tonight is done with.'

'I get that. Well, you've got my number, give me a call if there is anything I can do.'

'Thanks. Catch you later.'

Sahira hung up and tapped her phone against her chin. She was completely convinced now that this incident was nothing to do with the PM's charity dinner and everything to do with the assassination. Still, she'd keep a close eye on events today, just in case.

Matt Sayer turned up with about fifteen minutes to go until the scheduled meeting. He was wearing a dark blue pinstripe suit, white shirt and a red tie. He wore suits well, but Sahira realised that she didn't think she'd ever seen him without a suit. They had a great working relationship and got on well enough and often shared a joke, but Sayer made a point of not socialising with his staff.

Sahira wanted a drink, so asked Sayer what he wanted and headed to the café on site to get her peppermint tea and his black coffee. She got back at five minutes to seven. Sayer wasn't there, but the door to the Home Secretary's office was ajar, so she knocked and was invited in.

She didn't realise they'd be there, but wasn't overly surprised to see head of Six, Tim Wyatt and the Foreign Secretary, John Maguire, who was carrying a large rectangular object still in its brown paper wrapping. Tom Forrester was on the phone, but gave Sahira a friendly smile and wave. He was wearing suit trousers and a shirt that was three quarters buttoned up. Under his shirt Sahira could see the top of Goofy's head on his t-shirt.

She passed Sayer his coffee.

'Thanks, Sahira. Two sugars?'

'Sorry, sir.' She always called him 'sir' in front of others in formal situations. 'I forgot you're a sugar man.'

'No problem, my wife keeps telling me that I need to give up the sugar anyway,' Sayer smiled and said.

Forrester finished the phone call and said,

'Sorry, that was the PM. She wants me to update her over lunch on the current threat level, nationally and also for tonight. She also asked if you were able to attend, John?'

'Sure.'

Before he continued, Forrester looked at the package by the side of Maguire.

'Hey, it finally came.'

Maguire's face widened to a Cheshire cat grin.

'It certainly did. A mint condition, original poster from the film Days of Thunder.'

He tapped the poster as he said it.

Maguire was a huge film fan generally but he was especially a fan of all Tom Cruise films. Sahira really liked the quirks of both the Home Secretary and Foreign Secretary. It gave them a human touch that, in her opinion, had been lacking in some previous holders of the post.

Forrester looked genuinely happy for him, but there was work to do, so he focused on the group as a whole.

'Matt, where are we with the security for tonight's event?'

'We have doubled the security for tonight, changed our usual protocols and expected activity timelines, but for reasons that will soon become apparent, we have reason to believe, no attempt will be made at all.'

He took a quick pause. 'Sahira, why don't you update the group on what you found out yesterday?'

Sahira recounted in an efficient but detailed manner the events that had taken place yesterday. She finished more boldly than Sayer thought she would and even more boldly than she thought she would.

'I don't believe Ignatius Winter is our assassin.'

Sayer gave her a 'Really? You went for that?' expression. Wyatt sat back - stone faced - twisting his pen is his hand. Forrester and Maguire held eye contact with each other.

It was Maguire who broke the silence.

'I don't see it. Like you said, he was bound to have a second exit strategy. The water could have got in the boat from one of a thousand places and the dive equipment is a coincidence, or worse than that, a decoy to lead us away from an attempt on the PM tonight.'

Sahira replied, doing her best to hide frustration.

'Sir, there would have been other indicators if something this big was happening tonight. We've had no chatter. None whatsoever. None of the likely actors have raised any red flags outside of usual activity and there have been no further security breaches, which we would have seen if they were making an attempt on the PM.'

Maguire was still looking at Forrester and raised his left hand before Sahira could continue.

'We're wasting our time chasing ghosts. We need to make sure the PM is safe. That one hundred per cent has to be our focus. Following that, we need to take care of Mr Winter.'

The wording caught Sahira of guard. 'Take care of.' She hoped she was reading too much into that.

Forrester stood up from his desk and walked over to the wall, where he adjusted a picture from a scene in the Lion King movie before he spoke.

'Matt, have we got all eventualities covered for tonight?'

'Yes, sir.'

'Have we got enough personnel working on it?'

'Yes, sir.'

'Ok, great. Sahira, what are your next moves?'

Sahira ran through her plan for the day and what avenues she would be following.

'Forrester pondered this, whilst straightening a picture of Danger Mouse that didn't need the adjustment.

'Fine. I'll give some rope for these leads to be followed up for now, but if anything comes through about tonight, you are to drop what you're doing and assist with that. Tonight is the priority.'

Sayer answered for Sahira.

'Of course, sir, we'll make sure you get hourly reports throughout the day.'

Maguire was clearly holding down levels of annoyance and was getting angry.

'May I just remind you all, that it is in everyone's interest that the Chinese incident resolves itself as soon as possible. Not for it to be dragged out or any doubts to be cast on our handling of it.'

'I agree John, but let's see where this next part of the investigation takes us and reassess from there,' Forrester responded.

Maguire clearly wasn't satisfied, but The PM had given directions that the investigation was to be led by Five and therefore Sayer and Forrester, so he couldn't do much about it for now, so he focused on what he could control.

'Tim, I want you to make sure that all support necessary is available for tonight.'

'Done.'

Forrester eased the tension in the room by changing the subject back to Maguire's poster. Sahira took the cue and asked.

'Do you need me any more, sir?'

Forrester looked to Sayer to reply. He didn't want to supersede his authority in front of his own staff. Sayer gave Sahira a smile and said,

'No thanks, Sahira. Good work so far, go and crack on.'

'Yes, sir.'

As Sahira was walking out, Sayer was smiling as he said to her,

'Oh, and Sahira, once again, thank you for my coffee and honestly, don't worry, it's no big deal about you forgetting the sugar. I'm not someone to hold a grudge. I'm not a petty man.'

Sahira looked at him with confused amusement.

'Ok, sir. Thanks.'

'No problem, oh and one more thing. Could you take Larholt with you this morning, I think he'd be an asset to your investigation?'

Wyatt smirked.

Sahira gave him an exaggerated exhausted look whilst saying.

'Of course, sir.' If the Home Secretary and Foreign Secretary hadn't been present, she would have still done what he asked out of respect for him, but also given him the finger.

14

Sahira and Larholt pulled out of the parking garage in Westminster in Sahira's Range Rover SV Autobiography.

'Nice wheels, Sahira. Personally, I've never been a Range Rover man myself.'

'Is that so?'

Before Larholt could continue, she outlined the plan for this morning and then headed towards Muswell Hill, whilst turning the radio up. The drive was just short of ten miles, but with the morning traffic, it took them an hour and a half. When they arrived at the location, Sahira was planning on running through a quick briefing with Larholt, but before she had time, he'd already got out the car and headed towards the front door. She caught up with him just after he had rung the bell.

The door opened and the large man standing there just said, 'Yeah?'

Larholt, jumped in before Sahira had time to even flex her lips. Usually she would have preferred Larholt to not speak at all, but she didn't mind now as it would give her time to fully watch and analyse the man's behaviour.

'Mr Williams, my name is Ezra and this is my colleague, Sahira. We are with the Home Office. We need to speak to you about Ignatius Winter. May we come in?'

Tank stared back at the man and woman.

'No, you may not.'

Larholt looked pissed off, that his attempt at authority was shut quicker than a winter's day door.

'Mr Williams, we know that you have met up with Mr Winter in the past few days.'

Tank didn't react to this and simply said,

'I haven't seen Mantress in a while.'

Larholt, flicked through his pad quickly.

'We have no mention of Mantress here. Is that a call sign of some sort?'

Sahira scrunched her eyes and pinched the top of her nose whilst Tank said,

'It's a nickname, genius.'

Sahira had let this go on long enough, so she jumped in.

'Mr Williams, we know that Mr Winter was in the area the other day. We know that you two served together previously and we just wondered if you'd by chance seen him in the last few days. It's very important that we speak to him as soon as possible.'

'Like I said, I haven't seen him in a while.'

'Do you remember exactly when was the last time you saw him?'

'No, I don't.'

Sahira knew this guy wasn't going to give away anything, so she had to play her trump card, however weak the trump card was.

'The other day, you took twenty-three hundred pounds in cash out of your bank. May I ask what that was for?'

If Tank was surprised by the fact that his bank records had been looked at, he didn't show it.

'Not that it is any of your business, but it was a present for my wife. Her birthday is coming up and I saw an ad in a local shop window for a present I knew she'd want. The seller wanted cash.'

'May we see that present?'

'Wait there.' Tank left the door open and they both saw him walk to a cupboard at the side of the stairs and pull out a cardboard bag with an intricate design on it and string handles. He walked back to the front door with it and unlatched the transparent plastic buckle. From the bag he pulled out a top of the range Hewlett Packard laptop, still in its original box with an envelope sellotaped on top with his wife's name written on it.

Sahira, could sense Larholt was about to say something, so she jumped in.

'Sorry to bother you, Mr Williams,' she handed him a card and continued, 'please call us if you hear from Mr Winter. It really is very important that we speak to him as soon as possible. Have a nice day.'

Tank shut the door without saying anything else. He saw the two MI5 officers walk back to a nice Range Rover, then turned and walked back to his kitchen with the laptop in hand. When he was in the kitchen, he tore the empty envelope from the laptop box and ripped it into small pieces before putting them in the bin. He made a mental note to himself to return the laptop to Ignatius at some point. He also made a mental note that he needed to buy his wife a birthday present. It was her birthday tomorrow, after all.

He went over to his safe, opened it and took out a phone, put a battery and sim card in and texted the only number on it. 'What a lovely summer day. I've just seen two deer run through the garden.'

He removed the battery and sim card from the phone and

put them all back in the safe and locked it. He walked back through to the sitting room and continued eating his scrambled eggs whilst watching a replay of last night's football game.

Geographically speaking, they hadn't done things in the most efficient way, but Sahira had wanted to get to see Mr Williams before he headed to work, which she knew was at 10.00am.

They headed to Balham to look at Ignatius Winter's flat to see if that brought up anything of value. When they arrived at the flat, there were two policemen stationed outside the door along with crime scene tape to ensure that no one tried to gain entry. They had decided that, should Ignatius or anyone else who shouldn't, try and get entry to the flat, they would almost certainly do so at night. So they would position police outside during the day, to ensure there was no forensic contamination from any curious members of the public. But at night, there would be an undercover surveillance team to watch the house in an almost attempt to invite entry.

Sahira and Larholt both put on forensic coveralls before entering the flat. An experienced and skilled Forensic team had already done a full sweep of the flat, gaining fingerprint and DNA samples. There was nothing that they believed would give any further evidence of the assassination in the form of a laptop, or phones, or hidden cubby holes with incriminating paperwork. Sayer had instructed that the flat be left in the exact condition they had found it, until his investigators had a chance to look around.

They spent forty-five minutes searching around the small flat and Larholt was frustrated with not finding a smoking gun. Sahira wasn't sure what type of smoking gun he was expecting to find.

Sahira felt the search had been productive. The lack of evidence to her was as important as finding the evidence. She was confident they were chasing the wrong man. What professional got drunk and took cocaine the day before they carried out an assassination? All there was left to do was to find out who did carry out the assassination and why?

Sahira's next move was dictated to her, when she received a call from Heather Sillwood, telling her that forensic results from the first investigation of the boat had been returned. Heather asked if Sahira wanted the results over the phone. Previous experience had taught Sahira, that you lose something in translation over the phone, when you take in a lot of technical evidence.

Sahira called over Larholt and they got back in the car and headed to Thames House.

When they arrived there, Sahira suggested that Larholt went to update Sayer. There was nothing new to update, but she knew he'd take the bait and disappear. She then walked to reception and collected her guest, Heather Sillwood. Heather had a laptop with her along with some printouts.

Sahira showed Heather to a meeting room in a limited part of the building where approved visitors were allowed to go, and offered her green tea. When she returned to the room, Heather had set up the laptop and put the printouts in what seemed like some type of order.

'So Heather, tell me what we got.'

'Ok. Well the main part of the boat was as we expected, of no forensic value to this case. The foot traffic is just too high which leads to multiple cross-contamination. The engine room was a better source for us. It is cleaned weekly and was cleaned the day before the assassination, so the only people we know of, who were in the engine room between it being cleaned and us having access were two engine mechanics for its daily checks and the assassin.'

Heather paused briefly whilst she arranged the relevant paperwork in front of her. Sahira felt no need to fill the silence.

'Unfortunately, the assassin' – Sahira appreciated, that unlike many others, Heather didn't automatically refer to the assassin as being Ignatius – 'didn't leave any DNA or fingerprints, they definitely knew what they were doing, but they did leave the next best thing.'

'What's the next best thing?'

'A stone and some mud.'

Sahira looked at Heather for any hint of a joke. Heather was not joking, so Sahira kept quiet to let her continue.

'For the analytical determination of elemental concentrations in the stone found we used the following methods: laser ablation – inductively coupled plasma – mass spectrometry, neutron activation analysis and x-ray fluorescence analysis.'

Sahira looked at Heather with an 'are those words English' expression. Heather got the point.

'Sorry. The main point being, the stone we found is Horsham Stone.'

Heather took a quick pause before she carried on – 'So Horsham stone is a type of calcareous, flaggy sandstone containing millions of minute sand grains and occurring naturally in the Weald Clay of south-east England. It is also high in mica and quartz. The rock extends in an arc-like formation for several kilometres around the town of Horsham from which it takes its name.'

Sahira perked up, thinking she was starting to understand the significance.

'So, you're saying that this stone is unique to this area?'

'Exactly, so we know that the assassin was either from, or had spent time in and around the Horsham area and realistically, very recently.'

'Couldn't the stone have come from one of the mechanics?'

Heather nodded agreement.

'It could have, but I contacted both mechanics. Neither has ever been to Horsham or the surrounding areas in their life, so we know it must have been the assassin.'

Sahira liked this woman a lot. It wasn't her job to chase up the mechanics, but she appreciated the fact she had. She was going to keep her close to this investigation. Her pleasure was short-lived though as she came back to the reality of the situation.

'Horsham and its surrounding area is still quite a large region. It's great that we've shrunken the net, but I fear it might not be enough.'

'That's where the mud comes into play. To analyse the mud, we used…'

Heather had caught the expression on Sahira's face, which was that of someone who was about to be confused, so she adapted her speech.

'Well, it doesn't matter what we did, what matters is what we found, which was high trace levels of pesticides in the mud, including Meptyldinocap, which is a recent dinitrophenol fungicide that's an effective tool against mildew and mould on grapes and their vines, as well as gourds and watermelons.

In the area where Horsham stone can be found, the only place that would use these chemicals is a vineyard. The only vineyard in this area is Mannings Heath vineyard, which is a small village on the outskirts of Horsham.'

Sahira was fixated with every word Heather said.

'Does this help narrow your search?', Heather finished off.

'Heather, you're a star. I could hug you. Please stay contactable in case I have any other questions.'

'Of course, glad we could help.'

Sahira escorted Heather out of the building as was protocol and then headed back to her desk and made a call.

She spoke to the analysis department and asked to speak to the person who had been tracing Ignatius Winter's movement timeline. After a brief but informative conversation the Analyst confirmed what Sahira had suspected.

They could say with relative certainty that Ignatius Winter hadn't been in or around Horsham in the last month, and there was no evidence he had been in that area even further back. But they couldn't be completely sure as the granular detail of his movements were decreased the further back they went.

Sahira made one more request to them for immediate attention and asked how long it would take them to get back to her. She was assured she would have the information by the end of the day.

Sahira walked to Sayer's office but he wasn't there. His new Executive Assistant, Ian Parslow, told her that he was across the river at Vauxhall Cross, having a meeting with Tim Wyatt, but he wasn't sure when Matt was due back.

Sahira didn't want to waste any more time. Just before she headed to her car, she gave Peters a call to check that everything was in order for the PM's charity event tonight, as she was aware it had been made clear to her that tonight's event was the priority. Peters assured her that everything was in order and there was no need for her to stop by.

Sahira began her drive to West Sussex. She had just finished updating Sayer over the phone, when she pulled off the A24 dual carriageway and headed the short distance to Mannings Heath Golf club, which also was where the Vineyard was situated.

She entered the idyllic Tudor mansion set in 500 acres of beautiful parkland. She identified herself to the polished young man overseeing the reception desk. It didn't take long for the estate manager to shepherd Sahira into his room.

Sahira began asking about his staff, but focused on the staff that would be out in the vineyards, and who had worked there for at least two months and left recently.

It matched the profile of the assassin that the team at Thames house had put together, in that, the planning for the job would be meticulous. She wasn't arguing with them there. Although the FBI were still considered the leaders in criminal profiling and rightly so, the MOD profiling team in the UK were producing some excellent results and Sahira had faith in them.

After a couple of hours, multiple calls back to the office to run background checks and expanding the parameters, she still didn't even have a profile of someone who would likely commit a burglary; let alone assassinate a world leading politician. The closest she got to a criminal, was the golf course apprentice who a couple of years before, had been caught smoking pot in a local park. She was beginning to give up on the Vineyard staff.

'That's all the staff you have, no one else works at the vineyard?'

The manager was nodding his head when he suddenly

stopped and had a thought - an expression that wasn't lost on Sahira.

'What is it?'

'Well, this year, the agency staff were quite thin on the ground and our head groundskeeper had his appendix out, so we asked a local farmer to help us out sometimes, but we've known them for years and they're a lovely family.'

'Who are they?'

'John and Sarah Harrington.'

Sahira thanked the manager for his time and hurried out to the car park and began the short drive to the Harringtons' farm.

Both Sarah and John were about and welcoming. Sahira was sitting at their long oak kitchen table drinking herbal tea, whilst asking them some questions about the work they'd done on the Vineyard.

On the short drive over, Sahira had called the office for a background check on them and she just knew they were not involved.

John checked his watch and gave Sahira an apologetic look.

'Sorry, I really have to get back on the farm. It's not been the same since Ferran left. You never appreciate something until you lose it, right?'

'Ferran?'

'Yes, Ferran was with us for about six months. He only just left to go back to Spain, because his sister had her baby.'

'Do you remember when he left?'

'Sure. It was May 11th. It was the day the Chinese minister was assassinated. I remember watching the news, when his mother called to tell us about the birth of his nephew, ' Sarah jumped in.

'Do you know where he went?'

'Sure, we gave him a lift to Gatwick, let me just check the details.' Sarah opened a few drawers before she took out a note-pad with some writing on it. 'It was the 21.15 from Gatwick to Bilbao.'

Within two and a half hours a full forensic team were down at The Harrington's, paying special attention to the rooms 'Ferran' stayed in. The manifest for the flight had been tracked down and no one under the name of Ferran Dacosta was booked on that flight. Sahira would have been more surprised if there had been someone by that name on the flight. It would take a while to do a full background check on each passenger.

It didn't take that long to track the address that 'Ferran' had given to the Harringtons and realise it was a false address.

15

Ignatius woke up at 5.30am, but he'd still had a good night's sleep and felt rested even if it wasn't the most comfortable bed he'd ever used. There had once been a time when he could sleep on a desert floor with bombs going off in the background and still feel comfortable. But he was pushing forty now and would much rather have a bed to lay his head on.

He stretched out as best he could in his adopted room, went through his morning ritual, then sat down and ate half a sandwich. He wanted to eat and drink only what was needed to keep his body alert, so that he wouldn't need to use the toilet that much.

He took up vigil by the Velux window at approximately 6.30am. He saw two policemen arrive at the flat to guard the scene at 7.00am, but they were of little interest to him. He was expecting that.

It wasn't until near 10.00am that he saw his first visitors; unfortunately he wouldn't be home to entertain. There was a man and a woman who had turned up. Ignatius had been with the Intelligence Services long enough to know that these two were also with them. The woman was Middle Eastern and clearly in charge. He had to admit that even from a brief viewing of her actions, he was impressed.

After forty-five minutes or so, they both left the flat and he was waiting. He pulled out the supermarket scanner look-alike gadget that Ricky had given him, pointed it at her midriff and held it there for a few seconds. As Ricky had demonstrated on Justin, her phone number appeared on the screen and some computer coding that meant nothing to him, but he knew Justin could pull out all sorts of information with it.

Ignatius sent these details to Justin, via the computer within the scanner. He did the same with the man who was with the Middle Eastern woman.

Throughout the day there were also three more forensic officers who went in the flat. They were there for a couple of hours and came out with bags of material. Another man went in alone, who Ignatius was confident was a senior police officer of some kind and was only in the flat for around ten minutes; and another man and woman, who Ignatius couldn't place. He wasn't sure who they were with and more annoyingly, neither was carrying a phone on them, so he couldn't extract their data, like he had with the others.

The staff in the office below had long left, as had the policemen guarding the door to the flat. Ignatius was thinking about calling it quits for the day, when, he caught movement in his peripheral vision. As a Special Forces soldier, he had long learned not to ignore this. He pulled out a detached rifle, telescopic sight and used it to look through the window of his flat and saw there were men inside.

They were Chinese and they were pros. They didn't give him much surveillance opportunity. With what he could make out, he thought there were three of them.

His flat backed onto a builder's yard and since the Chinese hadn't entered through the front door, they had clearly waited until all the workers at the yard had left for the day and entered via that route. It seemed the Chinese were clearly doing their own investigation on the side and they were also using professionals.

The builder's yard was very well secured with state-of-the-art surveillance, which made sense considering the cost of building equipment. The Chinese had obviously managed to beat the surveillance and structural security and would have done so without leaving a trace. Ignatius tried to use his scanner to extract some information from them, but there were two sets of windows between him and them, and they kept moving out of sight inside the flat, so he wasn't able to get any data.

Ignatius felt that he had seen as much activity as he was going to. But to be sure, he planned on staying for another couple of days' surveillance for the sake of due diligence and, more to the point, he didn't have anywhere else to go. He could try a hotel but despite his complete faith in Ricky, he was still nervous about someone, somehow, seeing through the disguise.

All this changed when he received a call.

He had changed his phone from silent to vibrate, once the last of the office staff had left for the day and he now felt the shaking in his pocket. He took the phone out and saw the number on the screen.

'Hey.'

'Ignatius, get here now.'

Ignatius hated it when Justin called him Iggy, but the fact he hadn't now felt disconcerting.

'What's going on?'

'Not on the phone, get here right now.'

'Uh, ok. Let me just pack up my stuff here and I'll head over.'

'Just pack what you need, you don't need a clean exit, you won't be going back. We've got bigger things to worry about.

I've disabled the alarm though, so you can get out quietly.'

The line went dead as Justin hung up after his last words.

Ignatius took the phone away from his ear and stared at it for a couple of beats, before shrugging to himself and putting his phone back in his pocket. He wasn't going to worry yet about what Justin had dug up. He could only control what he could control.

Despite what Justin had said, Ignatius made sure he had a clean exit and left no trace of himself. Years of training were hard to ignore. He was just checking the pictures he had taken on his phone, to make sure everything was in the same place, when a thought occurred to him. Justin had said, 'We've got bigger things to worry about.'

It had been a long time when he hadn't just been his own army. He was surprised to realise how much he appreciated the support.

Ignatius fired up his Ducati and began the twenty mile journey to the Wilsons.

He parked around the corner and walked the rest of the way, with his helmet off, this time. As he was walking up the garden splitting path, Ricky opened the door to greet him and they shook hands.

'Justin has been pacing about waiting for you.'

'How bad?'

'Bad.'

'Ok, where is he?'

'Workshop.'

Ignatius and Ricky both walked down the garden to the converted shed and made small talk about rugby. Ricky liked to think he had some New Zealand Maori blood. Ignatius was pretty sure that just because Ricky had dated some rugby players before, it didn't make him an All Black, but let it go.

When they entered the shed, Ignatius said hi to Justin and asked,

'What's going on?'

Justin, didn't acknowledge the greeting, swivelled his office chair around, so that he was facing both Ricky and Ignatius.

His usual playful demeanour wasn't in sight. He looked troubled and said,

'It's Bambi.'

Ignatius looked at Ricky who gave a nod.

'What? Bambi's behind all of this?'

'I don't know if he's behind it all, but he's definitely involved.'

'How can you possibly know this?'

Justin settled back in his chair and took a sip of red bull before answering.

'Remember a few years ago when the German Vice Chancellor was assassinated?' The question was rhetorical. 'There was a behind-closed-door deal with the German Intelligence service that we would assist them with the search for the assassin, so I was temporarily seconded to the Bundesnachrichtendienst. We managed to trace the source of the hit to a rogue, senior Mossad agent. Under interrogation, he gave information that there is no way he would have known if he wasn't behind it. He brokered a plea deal and as part of that he had to spill all. He admitted to hiring Bambi. It is the only time we've ever known for sure that a hit was carried out by Bambi. However, before he could give us any information of real value, the Mossad agent was found hanging in his cell. Officially it was a suicide but very few people believe that is true. We weren't given enough

127

information to locate Bambi; not even close actually. We were however, given some correspondence between them. I managed to sneak a quick look at those.'

Both Ricky and Ignatius gave each other a knowing look before Justin continued.

'The encryption that Bambi used to disguise the source and location of his correspondence was bespoke coding. Coding is like DNA and if you know what to look for, it's unique to every individual.'

Justin paused but not for effect. He looked scared.

'The correspondence that the internet café guy had about the memory card, well, let's just say that it is an exact DNA match.'

Ignatius knew Justin well enough to know that he wouldn't come with this information if he hadn't done a full due diligence. He looked at both Ricky and Justin who were watching him expectantly. He didn't have much to say.

'Well, there we are.' He needed some time to think this through.

Justin was still looking worried and needed to change the topic for his own sanity.

'Do you want me to run you through the results from the scanner?'

Ignatius removed his hand from cupping his chin, and before Justin had time to start going through the results, Ignatius spoke again,

'Let's do it. Why did he use the same encryption again?'

'What?' Justin answered.

'Bambi, why would he use the same encryption coding, when he knows it's been discovered before?'

'He doesn't know it has been discovered. In fact, no one

does but us. When I broke it down and analysed it, I shared the details with GCHQ hierarchy. They took the decision not to share this with the Germans. It wasn't anything malicious, but it has always been suspected, though never proved, that a senior member of German Intelligence was also involved in the assassination. The decision was taken that we wouldn't share this information, until we could be sure that it was one hundred per cent secure audience.'

Justin looked apologetic for this, but he needn't have bothered. Ignatius actually looked somewhat chirpier as he replied.

'So, Bambi wouldn't know that we know he's involved?'

'I guess not.'

'That's something at least. Talk me through the scanner results?'

Justin gave an ok nod.

'So, the first number you captured belongs to Sahira Basha. She works within International Counter Terrorism and reports to head of JTAC. Did you cross paths with her at all?'

'No, I didn't. What does JTAC stand for again?', Ignatius answered.

Justin looked at him, surprised.

'What did you do when you worked at Six? Did you make any friends? It stands for Joint Terrorism Analysis Centre. This is where Sahira reports, which isn't unprecedented but I guess is unusual. Usually, people in her position would report to the Deputy Director General. However, going through the information on her phone, she is reporting directly to Sayer on this one.'

It was Ignatius' turn to look surprised.

'She's reporting straight to the DG. Why?'

'Iggy, it's about time you realised how big a deal this is. I'd be surprised if she wasn't reporting directly to Sayer.'

'Ok, fine. Anything else on her?'

'She's clearly very highly thought of and here's the main part. She might be having doubts it's you. She's been on a bit of a journey chasing other leads and is asking a lot of questions about your guilt.'

This news was a huge relief for Ignatius momentarily, until he gave himself a reality check. His face was still all over the news and he knew that the evidence they currently had wouldn't be enough for most within the intelligence community. A suspected assassin who went on the run immediately and turns up with information that no else has seen, and puts doubt on his guilt. It probably wouldn't carry much weight.

Justin then went through the other information that Ignatius had gathered, which was that of Larholts and also Jenny Schaltz, who was the Director of European Network of Forensic Science Institutes within the Metropolitan Police Service. The information that Justin had gained from her phone, showed that due to the high profile of this case, she had visited the site to ensure that any forensic work that was carried out, was satisfactory. It seemed it exceeded satisfactory whatever that meant in the forensic world.

Ricky had been quiet throughout all of this, but he now felt the need to introduce himself in the conversation.

'Ignatius, what are you going to do? I mean, it's Bambi. This is a lot to take on.'

Ignatius had been thinking this through, but he didn't have a full answer. He only knew of two courses of action he had to take, so answered Ricky with them.

'Look guys. You have been brilliant. I would be screwed without the help you've given me so far, but the stakes have been raised higher than I thought possible. They've already been knocking on Tank's door and it's only a matter of time before they come knocking on your door. You need to distance yourself from me. If you don't, you'll ruin everything you've built here.'

Justin shook his head like a wet dog.

'Iggy, we wouldn't even be here if it wasn't for you.'

Ignatius argued back, but it was no use. Ricky and Justin were not going to take themselves away. Ignatius had meant what he said, but he was also secretly very glad that he had them on his side. The argument was finished with Ricky saying,

'Oh, and Ignatius, stop this moral high ground stuff. It scares me when you're not being your usual prick self.'

Ignatius smiled and said,

'Yeah, no problem.'

After a few minutes silence Justin asked,

'Any other genius plans you have that we can shut down?'

'I need to reach out to Five. I'm not going to just hand myself in, because I still don't trust that they don't see me as the easy solution. Then finally, I'm going to find and kill Bambi.'

Ignatius waited for the objections to fly his way, but just heard from Ricky with no hint of sarcasm,

'Good plan. Count us in.'

16

Sahira hung around for an hour after the forensic team had arrived, but realised that she wasn't going to be able to offer much help on the farm. She got in her Range Rover and headed back to London. She had hoped to avoid the worst of the traffic, but she wasn't in luck and spent much of the time crawling along. She had already called Sayer to arrange an update. He said they would do it tonight, whatever time she arrived, and that Wyatt, Forrester and Maguire were also going to be attending.

Just as Sahira was coming into London, she got a call with the results she had requested earlier. She asked the forensic team to hang about until she was in the office and that she would come straight to them.

Sahira was back in the office just after 7.00pm and headed to a room that, on top of multiple computer monitors, had a wall completely wallpapered with screens. She was being eagerly awaited by Ashish Khan, who was head of the Forensic Image team.

Previously, they had only searched the CCTV for passengers who boarded the boat at Greenwich and left at Westminster, shortly after the assassination. The result of this CCTV imaging had accounted for all the passengers and given them Ignatius, who up until now, everyone assumed was the assassin.

After the information that Sahira had come across in the last couple of days, she called Ashish this morning and requested that they also had a look at customers who had boarded at Westminster and taken the return trip option. Ashish was now showing a picture of a man who boarded at Westminster, but there is no imagery of him leaving the boat at all.

Sahira knew in her heart that she was staring at the actual assassin. Sahira asked if they'd be able to get an identification via facial recognition software.

Unlike fingerprints and DNA, which do not change during a person's life, facial recognition has to take into account different factors, such as ageing, plastic surgery, cosmetics, quality of image, effects of drug abuse or smoking, pose of the subject.

The man on CCTV had managed to make the forensic imagery team work hard for a good enough image of his face to use the software with any reliability, but they did find a clear enough image eventually. However, no match was found in any database they had access to, and following the international attention this case was receiving, many foreign countries, whether they were close allies or lesser so, had opened their databases for identification search purposes.

Although it was not possible to be positive, it was Ashish's opinion that the man was wearing a sophisticated masking system and would likely look very different now. She asked Ashish for a high resolution printout of an image of the man's face and then thanked him for his work and staying later to accommodate her. She promised to buy him a coffee from the onsite café soon, as a thanks.

Sahira had plenty of work she could get on with but she had already taken the piss a little bit, by visiting Ashish and keeping the British leadership of Intelligence waiting. She felt her best course of action would not be to volunteer that information to them.

She made her way to Sayer's office. His executive assistant had gone for the day, so Sahira knocked on the office door and heard Sayer's voice calling her in. She walked into the office and saw the four key people sitting in chairs formed in a wide jagged circle in the centre of the room.

Sayer and Wyatt were still both in suits and looked like they had just walked out of a Saville Row tailors. Forrester was in jeans, t-shirt – although Sahira couldn't see the cartoon character on it, as his shirt was buttoned almost to the top- a shirt and jumper. Maguire was the same, except no t-shirt and his jumper had been substituted by a woollen cardigan, something that seemed out of place in May.

Forrester, Maguire and Sayer were drinking a Macallan, forty-year-old, single malt scotch whiskey, which had a warming autumn russet colour to it. Wyatt was sipping a glass of sparkling water. They were all smiling and Sahira was fairly sure the conversation had been social rather than security.

As Sahira walked in the room, Forrester stood up and went to get an extra chair from around a nearby coffee table and added it into the loose circle for Sahira to join. Sayer offered her a drink and Sahira held up her water bottle whilst smiling, indicating that she was ok.

The DNA of the room changed back to intelligence. Sayer asked Sahira to update them all. Sahira gave a detailed update on what she had been doing and what she'd found out. Maguire was the first to speak after Sahira had finished.

'It seems we're spending a lot of time chasing this thread of a different assassin and no time on finding the man who is the most likely assassin, and even if Mr Winter didn't actually pull the trigger, do you honestly expect me to believe that he wasn't involved? Are we supposed to believe he just happened to be on a sightseeing tour and then ran off for an entirely different reason?'

'No, sir,' Sahira answered, 'Mr Winter is still our main priority. All the Forensic Image searching is focused on Mr Winter and him only. He has just disappeared, sir, and we've had no credible sightings. He may even be out the country for all we know.'

Maguire looked somewhat appeased but he still wasn't fully satisfied.

'Have we spoken to any of his contacts at all who may be helping him?'

'Yes, sir, but they either haven't seen him or are helping him and not telling us.'

'Can we put pressure on them to be sure?'

'We have done, but we have no evidence that he has contacted any of them and these people are not the type who scare easily.'

Maguire acknowledged this point and finally asked,

'Do you not think that Mr Winter is our man then?'

Sahira, paused before she answered.

'Sir, I'm convinced he didn't pull the trigger. As to whether he's involved, I have no idea. A big part of me believes he was set up, but the problem with that theory is, I can't see anyone else who has a motive for such a high-profile assassination on Xu Hua. I appreciate that every senior political figure has enemies, but our background checks on the Chinese minister didn't show anyone with the capability and motive for such a public event.'

135

There was a pause as Forrester and Maguire held an eye contact. Forrester spoke,

'That's not strictly true.'

'Tom, are you sure?' Maguire asked.

'John, we need to read her in, so she has the best chance of getting to the bottom of this.'

'Tom, what we need to do is find Winter and make this whole thing go away.'

Forrester pyramided his hands covering his mouth.

'Sorry, John, I believe it is necessary.'

Forrester stood up and walked over to the open globe, picked up a pair of prongs, added three cubes of ice to his tumbler, took out the bottle of Macallan, unscrewed the top and poured a generous portion over the ice. With his back still to the group he began,

'May 2013 in the Sichuan province in Southern China, thousands of witnesses saw a strange spiral shape in the sky which was obviously not a natural occurrence. No one knew what was going on and the images were soon posted online and within a matter of hours, they had gone viral. The internet went crazy and even some reputable Chinese media suggested that it was evidence of extra-terrestrial life. Due to the increasing speculation, Chinese officials had no choice but to respond.

They did so, by claiming that it was the after effects of a rocket launch for a weather satellite, saying that it was part of a routine upper atmosphere admission to sample things such as cosmic radiation and ultra violet rates. The US government then decided to involve themselves and tracked and analysed launch data. What they found alarmed them. A conventional weather satellite launch reaches an altitude of approximately five hundred miles. This launch went up eighteen thousand miles, almost forty times higher and exactly where the A-team of American satellite capability orbit. A military analyst who studied satellite imagery of the launch found a surprising detail, in that, it wasn't a traditional launch site but a military vehicle was present at the space launch site. What is known as a TEL - A Transporter Erector Launcher. The fact that one of these was present, leaves no doubt that the Chinese military were involved in this launch. This launch was inconsistent with a science mission, it seems in all likelihood it was a test of an anti-satellite weapon. Should that be the case, and China has managed to produce an anti-satellite weapon, the consequences are very far reaching and there is a huge shift in the balance of power. The American's most advanced military satellites are now within the reach of the Chinese, who could eliminate them, should they choose. We all know that space is the key to military power and it seems the Chinese might now hold that key. The man behind all of this is Xu Hua and due to a lot of convoluted reasons, it is firmly believed that if he disappears, so does this entire programme. I hate to say it, but Xu Hua's death has been of huge benefit to many countries.'

Forrester stopped talking and looked up at the group. Sahira was still trying to process the full extent of this information and she had no doubt that her face revealed that. She looked at Sayer and Wyatt, but couldn't get a read on whether this was new information to them or not.

Briefly, she hoped that one day she'd have learned that skill as well as they had.

'Sir, as troubling as this might be, surely it is the Americans who therefore have the best motive to disincentivise Xu Hua?'

The tip of Forrester's hand pyramid had now reached his forehead.

'Yes, that is certainly a possibility, but we also have a motive ourselves. Possibly a stronger motive.'

Forrester went silent but no one filled it, so he continued,

'I won't go into the details of how, but we had some inside sources that have allowed us, to date, to piggy back on these American satellites for our own military and intelligence benefits. If the Chinese continued with this line, it is possible that the Americans would do a deep dive into all their satellites and might realise what we have done. This not only would mean we lose a huge intelligence source, but would at best, severely and probably irreparably damage our relationship with our closest and most important ally. At worst, it could be seen as an act of war.'

Sahira immediately understood that motives don't get much bigger than that.

'So now that Xu Hua is dead, does this all disappear?'

'It does seem that way, but if it isn't a revenge killing and is seen to be some other reason, then it might start people asking a lot of awkward questions.'

'So there's a good chance that Winter is innocent?'

'We don't know that,' Maguire jumped in. 'He had just as good a reason to kill Xu Hua, and so far the best evidence I've seen is that Winter did this. Winter worked for us for a long time and I've seen his file. I can assure you he's not innocent.'

Frustration overtook Sahira.

'With all due respect, sir, the best evidence I've seen is that it wasn't Winter who killed Xu Hua, but everyone is determined to make it look like it was.'

Sayer somehow managed at the same time, to seem calm whilst also giving Sahira a look saying 'are you high?'

'Miss Basha, we are just outlining the facts to you. We want you to get to the bottom of this, but it is important that you also understand the sensitive nature of this case. The world has its eyes on us and we don't want to air our dirty laundry, the same as any other nation.

Just make sure that whatever you find is contained to this group, and then the relevant people will make the choice as to how this is displayed to the world.'

'Yes, sir.'

'Thanks, Sahira,' Sayer said. 'That's all for now, keep up the good work.'

As Sahira left the office she got on her phone to Peters, who told her that everything had gone smoothly at the dinner and although it was going to carry on for a while, the PM had done her bit and left about fifteen minutes ago with no incident.

At this time of night, Sahira knew the PM was likely back at 10, Downing Street now, where she was very safe. She asked Peters why she hadn't gone with the PM.

'I've been the liaison on site for the past couple of days, so have stayed to oversee the security for the remainder of the event. Any potential aggressor against the PM, may not know that we changed her schedule at the event to run earlier, so there's a chance that there might still be some happenings here,' Peters said.

'Well, let's hope not. I hope you don't get home too late.'

'Thanks, Sahira. I've appreciated your help on this and I'm sure I'll see you soon.'

It was nearly 9.00pm when Sahira had reversed her Range

Rover into her glass fronted, two port garage. She took the lift up to her penthouse and decided to treat herself after a long day. She ordered a facial and head massage from the beauty salon in The Mandarin Oriental.

They would come up to her flat and carry out the treatments. She had barely eaten all day and despite being hungry earlier, she'd gone past hunger now, but knew she had to eat to ensure she was fuelling her body, so ordered food for after her treatments.

Roast halibut and green sauce with braised chicory, parsley, pepper, onion and eucalyptus from Dinner restaurant by Heston Blumenthal.

Much later, Sahira stripped off and went under her hot amazon rainforest shower and let the water pour down on her for a long time, and with every stream of water, she felt more relaxed. After her shower, she put on a grey cashmere dressing gown and a towel over her hair. She made herself a hot lemon drink and took it through to her bedroom.

She hung up her dressing gown and towel and climbed naked into her white silk sheets, which had been freshly put on the bed today by her housekeeper.

She read her book for only about ten minutes before she felt sleep creep up on her. She put her book on the bedside table and turned the lamp off. She was sure she'd be asleep as soon as she rested her head back down on the pillow. Her head settled down and she was the least awake a human could be before sleep, then her phone rang.

Lazily she felt for her phone in the dark, and put it to her ear.
'Hello?'
'Is this Sahira Basha?'

'Yes. Who's this?'
'It's Ignatius Winter.'

17

Sahira was instantly wide awake. She sat up fully and was suddenly very aware of how naked she was, even though she was alone, and the person she was speaking to was on the other end of a phone. She put her light on and walked over to put her dressing gown on, whilst replying, 'I must admit, I wasn't expecting this call.'

'I didn't do it', Ignatius replied.

'Why did you run then?'

'I knew something wasn't right and I've learned to trust my instincts on these things.'

'Ok, well, let's say that I believe you, which I'm not saying I do. What do you want from me?'

'I know who the assassin is and I need your help finding him.'

'Ok, well come in to Thames House and we can discuss it and help you out.'

Ignatius rolled his eyes even though he was currently alone in his room in a Bed and Breakfast, on the outskirts of St Albans in Hertfordshire.

'Don't take the piss. If I want to hand myself in, I don't need you for that.'

'Ok, Mr Winter. Well, what makes you think that I won't take you in as soon as I see you?'

'I'm the only one who knows the identity of the assassin' – he wasn't under any circumstances going to admit to Ricky and Justin's involvement - 'and I'm only willing to share what

I know, if we do this my way. I'm not convinced that it wasn't you lot who set me up.'

Sahira let a silence linger which tempted Ignatius to talk more. The more he talked, the more information she would get. He didn't bite and the silence went on long enough for her to wonder if he was even still on the line, so she made her move.

'Ok, fine, but if you want our help, at some point, I will need to read others in. I'm not going to just go off the grid for someone, who as far as I'm concerned might have assassinated the Chinese Minister of National Defence.'

'Fair enough, we can discuss that when we meet, but if you tell anyone else before we meet, I disappear. Where are you going to be tomorrow?'

'At the moment, I'll be in the office tomorrow, trying to find you.'

Ignatius ignored this.

'I'll call you tomorrow with a time and place, and you know that I'll know if you share with anyone the fact we've talked, or if you try to bring a team with you.'

'Mr Winter, why do you want to meet me?'

'Because you're leading the investigation, no other reason than that.'

'Ok, well ignoring how you know that for now, how do I know that you're not going to kill me as soon as you see me, so that the whole investigation is interrupted?'

'You know that I won't for a few reasons but mainly because, if I wanted to kill you, I would have done so this morning at 10.30am, when you were at my flat.'

Ignatius hung up.

Sahira felt a bit of a chill overtake her. She felt exposed

knowing that she had been watched. Her mind was also racing. She needed to decide how to play this. She was confident though that he meant her no harm.

He had worked at six for long enough and would know that harming her wouldn't disrupt the investigation at all. She'd be replaced within an hour and the new person would be fully up to date within an afternoon. She had also read his files. He wasn't necessarily someone she'd want as a friend, neighbour or even acquaintance, but she didn't believe he'd cause someone harm for no reason.

There was no point trying to force an answer in her head now. Her best bet was to try and get as much sleep as she could, and make a decision with a fresh mind.

Three hours later she was still wide awake, so went through to her computer room and read over again, every bit of information she had on Ignatius Winter.

18

Jerry was sitting in his office in his large town house. He'd just finished dinner with a friend in a local restaurant and was now at home alone as his wife and kids were visiting her mother and father. He was sitting behind his desk in his study sipping a glass of red wine. His study was his fortress of solitude that, over the years, he had spent making into a room that was perfect for his needs. He was usually at his most relaxed and comfortable in his office, but right now he was very uncomfortable.

He was reading over the transcript of the phone call that Sahira Basha had just received. It was very troubling, especially what Ignatius Winter had said about knowing who the killer was.

He had gone to great lengths to ensure he couldn't be linked to the event, but nothing was ever one hundred per cent guaranteed, so he had to make sure this latest development didn't disrupt his past six years' work. He had read up enough about Basha, to know that she would take the opportunity presented to her, and that she would agree to meet with Winter.

Jerry went over to his safe, which was a cliché in the sense that it was behind a picture on the wall.

From the safe he took out an encrypted phone with voice distortion software. He turned on the phone and waited for a minute or so until the phone was up and running and all the apps had time to load. He made a call that he had hoped he wouldn't have to make. The person on the other end answered after three rings and he got straight to the point.

'We have a major problem, but with that problem there is also a solution. Ignatius Winter called Sahira Basha tonight to arrange a meeting. He claims to know who the killer is.'

There was a momentary pause as the person on the other end of the phone was thinking how to respond. They responded exactly how Jerry wanted them to.

'What do you need us to do, sir?'

'As troubling as this is for me to say, I need you to kill Basha and Winter.'

Jerry could feel the hesitancy transmit through the receiver.

'Sir, I understand the seriousness of the situation, but Basha is a serving MI5 officer. If she is killed, it will cause huge waves and more problems for us.'

Jerry was expecting this response.

'If you do exactly what I say, we can make it look as though Winter killed Basha and then disappeared. No one will doubt that he can disappear with his background, and it will effectively show his guilt for the assassination and then this will all be over. We'll kill two birds with one stone.'

Jerry could sense there was still hesitancy, but he felt he had done enough to mitigate most of it.

'Ok, sir, please let me know what I need to do and I will make sure that it is done?'

Jerry was pleased now. He had managed to get this person on board, which was vital and, as troubling as Winter's claim had seemed earlier, the situation might just work to his advantage. He took a moment's breath before he explained exactly what needed to be done and how it was to be done. There needed to be a level of flexibility to the plan as he didn't yet know where Basha and Winter were going to meet, but that was a minor detail.

After he finished the call, he poured himself another wine, sat back and allowed himself some momentary pleasure as he believed he had tied up all the loose ends.

19

Sahira had managed to catch sporadic sleep throughout the night, but all in, she'd be lucky if she got more than three and a half hours good sleep. Her workout this morning was adapted to reflect her mood and she spent most of it bullying the heavy bag. She walked in the office with only one thing on her mind: Ignatius Winter.

When she got to her desk, there was a brown envelope waiting for her, and her heart sank. She opened it and it was as she thought. A colleague of hers had promised her some tickets to watch her beloved Chelsea play Arsenal tonight.

She used to have a box at Chelsea, but with work she almost never went so felt obliged to free it up for another fan. She now knew there was next to no chance she would be watching this match. She spent the morning between forensic imaging and analysis, seeing if there had been any hits on Ignatius Winter; there hadn't.

How he had managed to avoid being caught on any cameras was beyond her. She had to admit, he was good. There were a few leads for her to follow though. When Ignatius had worked for Six, he had built some close relationships and she planned on visiting those people, starting with Richard and Justin Wilson.

It was just after 3.00pm when her phone rang. She looked at the screen and saw that it was from an encrypted phone. She knew who it was and answered.

'Hello, Mr Winter.'

'Verulamium Park in St Albans for 5.30pm. Park at the Waffle house and enter via the northern most entrance that is just across the road.' Ignatius paused slightly before finally asking, 'Will you be coming?'

'Yes, but I'm not promising anything other than hearing what you have to say initially.'

'Fine. See you later.'

Ignatius hung up and looked over to the park entrance where Sahira would be arriving. Since 7.00am this morning he had been doing reconnaissance around the park to ensure he had options for any eventuality he could think of.

He didn't know Sahira but his instincts told him that she was trustworthy and would come alone to hear him out. The same instincts that told him it was a good idea to take the job he was offered on May 11th, which is exactly why he was being so diligent with his preparations.

Sahira did a quick search on her maps to see exactly where she would be going. She realised that at this time of day, with the traffic, she might need all the time left just to get there. This is exactly what Ignatius had wanted, because it would give her no office time to try and put a trap in place. Sahira gathered her bag and keys and headed straight for her car. She wanted to give herself as much time as possible at the location to try and recce the area before she entered.

Thirty minutes after Ignatius had called Sahira, as planned, Ricky gave him a call and Ignatius answered immediately.

'Hey, Ricky.'

'Hi, Ignatius. So far, no calls and she doesn't have any other transmission devices on her person.'

'Ok, thanks.'

Ricky was sitting in his car, in the car park in Westminster where Sahira had parked her Range Rover this morning. Justin had access to her phone because of what Ignatius had sent him from the surveillance of his flat, and had passed this information on to Ricky. Earlier on Ricky had used an RF Bug Hunter all over her car to ensure that the car wasn't emitting any radio frequency.

Though some bugs do conceal their radio frequencies altogether, or may be turned off during a sweep, so Ricky also used a non linear junction detector which helps detect semiconductor electronics. There are objects on this type of sweep that can produce a false positive, so the owner of this information needs to fully vet and understand whatever turns up. Ricky was probably in the top ten in the world for this, so was definitely the right man for this job.

Sahira arrived at the Waffle house opposite the park at 5.10pm and quietly cursed to herself. She had wanted to have as much time as possible but that dream was over. She had nothing better to do, so figured she might as well enter the park now. She crossed the road and entered the park via the entrance exactly as Ignatius had instructed.

As she walked up the path towards the lake, she saw that the foot traffic was congested, which she suspected is exactly what Ignatius Winter had planned. Her phone rang.

'Hello?'

'You're early.'

'I didn't see the point in sitting in my car for fifteen minutes.'

'Ok. You're approaching the lake, walk along the path and then cross the arched bridge, walk up towards the café and on the left in the middle of the field, you'll see a Roman mosaic and hypocaust. Go to that and I'll call you when you're by the entrance.'

The Roman mosaic and hypocaust is an ancient under floor heating system and is a marvel of Roman engineering and an example of the first indoor heating systems installed in Britain.

It is covered by a mosaic and is thought to have been part of the reception and meeting rooms of a large town house, built around 200 AD. The floor is covered by a small modern building which was purpose built for viewing the attraction. Within the building is also a walkway which is raised above, and then dips down to the level of the mosaic and hypocaust, and rises again for a further bird's eye view. The raised part of the walkway has a square panel of glass flooring to enable visitors to see directly under the walkway which had also been excavated.

It took Sahira just over ten minutes to reach the entrance. As she approached, she instinctively scanned the proximity around her. The building was right in the middle of the park and was surrounded for a few hundred metres each side, by well kempt and mowed grass. She only had to wait a matter of seconds before her phone rang again and she answered.

'Hi.'

'There's no point looking for me, you won't see me.'

She hadn't expected to when she'd looked around, but let the point go.

'What now?'

'Go into the building and under the raised walkway, behind a pot, is a phone. Go and get that and walk back out when you have it.'

Sahira entered the building on the part of the walkway that

was already raised. A couple of feet in front of her there was the glass flooring. She stepped over and looked through it. Under the glass flooring she saw the excavated floor with multiple pots. Great. She spent the next ten minutes walking around the mosaic, taking her time, reading the information signs that gave the history of the flooring as well as information about the excavation.

She was waiting for the room to be empty so that she could hop off the lower walkway and across the mosaic to go under the raised walkway and check the multiple pots to see which one was hiding the phone. Finally she realised that at this time of day, she wasn't going to get an empty room, so she thought 'screw it' and jumped over the railings of the walkway onto the mosaic floor.

She found the phone after looking behind six or seven pots and getting multiple looks by members of the public, but she had correctly relied on innate Britishness, that no one would say anything. She stepped outside the room and the new phone rang immediately and she answered straight away.

'Yes.'

'Ok, go back to your car now.'

'Seriously? Ok, fine. Then what?'

'Then drive back to your flat.'

Sahira was doing her best to not show the anger in her voice.

'I thought the point of this, was for us to meet up and chat?'

'It is.'

'Ok. So when are we going to meet up then?'

'At your next location.'

'The next location is my car.'

'I know. I'm in it.'

152

Ignatius hadn't sent Sahira to the park for no reason. He needed to check that she wasn't being followed and making her drive through London, a brief stint in the countryside and then the one-way convoluted streets of St Albans would ensure that Ignatius would know if she was being followed, as he had a friend checking these details for him.

Overnight, Ricky had let himself into the mosaic building and installed a body scanner under the raised walkway, so that they could also check Sahira. Ricky had called him to let him know that Sahira was clean, which was when Ignatius had let himself into her car.

As Sahira was approaching the car, she could clearly see a male figure sitting in the driving seat. She was thinking, 'this better not be some alpha male crap that he's trying to pull by insisting on driving'. When she got in the car, the first thing she said was,

'You're not Winter.'

'Yes I am. It's a disguise.'

'Prove it?'

'Not now', Ignatius said. 'Can I have the keys please?'

Sahira gave Ignatius the keys, in for a penny in for a pound she thought, and he started driving. She knew Ignatius was an expert with vehicles after serving within the mobility troop of the SAS.

It was somewhat reassuring to see that the man driving was an expert and that it wasn't some alpha male stunt he was pulling but rather, he was implementing pretty much every counter surveillance driving technique that she knew; and many more she didn't know.

She gave him ten minutes of focus, during which time he

hadn't said a word. She finally broke the silence.

'So, who was it then?'

'Have you heard of Bambi?'

Sahira looked at him sceptically.

'Yes, I've heard of him. You want me to just believe that it was him, do you?'

'No. I'm going to prove it to you, but we need to use a secure system, which is why we're going back to your penthouse, so we can use your system there.'

'How do you know I've got a secure system there?'

'Does it matter?'

'Yeah, it does to me,' she said.

'I don't care what matters to you. I care about clearing myself.'

'Are you always this easy to get along with?'

Ignatius didn't answer but just focused on his driving. After a few minutes, Sahira tried a new tack and they spent the rest of the journey with Ignatius telling his version of the story from the past few days that he was willing to share.

Sahira also shared certain parts of her investigation, which she felt might help in them forming an alliance of sorts. They arrived back at Sahira's penthouse just after 7.00pm and pulled into the garage. Before the ignition had been fully shut down Sahira said,

'I'm not leaving this car, until you prove that you're Winter.'

Ignatius could see she meant that, so he took out the cream, put a pea-sized amount on his finger and applied it by tracing the circumference of the mask. After five minutes or so, Sahira could see that what looked like his skin seemed to be pealing away from his face like two identical poles of a very weak magnet. She made her decision then.

'Ok, it seems you might be telling the truth. Let's go up to the flat for you to finish your routine.'

When they got up to the flat, Ignatius couldn't believe the luxury he saw. He knew from his briefing with Justin that she had a fancy flat and lots of family wealth, but this was a whole other level. He was still taking in all the furnishings, when Sahira told him,

'Help yourself to what you want from the kitchen. You've taken your face off, I'm just going to do the same.'

She left the room giving him a friendly wink to try and make him feel at ease and hopefully help make him share more information with her.

Ignatius saw her wink and thought 'Hello... She's definitely flirting with me.' He was feeling good about himself and had a look in the fridge. He took out a bottle of water and some carrot sticks. He'd have preferred a beer and crisps, but he'd make do with this.

He sat down on a Tufty-Time leather sofa and took out the solution that Ricky had given him, so that he could give the mask its twelve hour refresh. He was sipping his water when Sahira walked back into the room. She was wearing some cotton trousers, a small white t-shirt and a hoodie that was open.

Ignatius was, for the first time, focusing on her as a woman and realised she was beautiful. He looked at her and said,

'Hey, you look nice. Before we crack on with work, why don't you have a bit of a rest and sit down.' Ignatius patted the seat next to him on the sofa.

The only thing going through Sahira's mind now was, 'Oh, dear God, no!' She looked Ignatius in the eye and said,

155

'Before we carry on, there's something we need to take off the table.'

'Oh really, what's that?' Ignatius answered.

'My arse! I'm not interested, so can we please just get on with work and figure this out.'

With these words, she turned and left the room and went to set up her computer equipment.

After a few seconds, Ignatius, feeling a little discomfited, got up from the sofa and followed her through her palace into her high tech computer room. Sahira was keen to move on from the incident in the other room so made small talk with him.

'Your complexion is darker than I was expecting from the photos I've seen.'

'Oh, it's just fake tan. Anyway, I thought you said we needed to focus on work.'

'Great', she thought. 'I'm dealing with a child'. She swallowed a sigh and said,

'Ok, show me this proof then.'

Ignatius pulled out a new memory card that Justin had given him.

Pretty much every business in the world, will at some point, have to do a presentation of sorts. Whether that is to clients for business, to banks for loans or to employees to share information.

Ignatius was aware that the presentation he was about to give was likely for his very survival, because if he didn't get Sahira on board, he'd be in a lot of trouble.

Justin had put together a straightforward presentation on the memory card, which described the story behind Bambi's involvement, which was easy to understand and most of all, easy for Sahira to verify when she dug up the previous evidence that GCHQ had on Bambi. She was one of a few people who could get access to this.

Sahira sat back in her chair and took the hairband out of her hair and tied it back in a bun again as it kept coming loose. She looked at Ignatius who was still staring at the screen but not looking at it.

'Ok', she said. 'Assuming that this all checks out and Bambi is involved, it doesn't necessarily mean that you're not also involved?'

Ignatius massaged his temples.

'Really? It shows that he was setting me up with the memory card with nothing on it?'

'It shows that he was sending you a memory card. I agree that it suggests you were being set up, but it's not definitive proof.'

'So, you still think I was involved?'

Sahira wasn't sure if this was a smart move on her part but she went there anyway.

'Tell me about 2008 in Jinan?'

Ignatius gave her a hard stare.

'If you know enough to know it happened, you know what happened.'

'Do you know how you were ambushed?'

'We weren't exactly working at Disneyland. These things happen.'

Sahira, briefly paused but knew she needed to say this.

'It was Xu Hua who set you and your team up!'

Ignatius was having a flashback. He was now seeing his brothers lying dead in the street.

'I'm glad he's dead then. If I'd known about it, I would have

157

killed him myself, but I didn't know and I didn't kill him.'

Either he was a brilliant liar, or he was telling the truth. Sahira, decided that it was time for her to put all her cards on the table.

'Ok. To answer your question then, no I don't think you were involved with the assassination.'

Ignatius gave a small smile.

'Well, thanks for letting me know that from the start and making all this a lot easier. So how do I clear my name?'

Sahira ignored the tantrum part of his speech and answered his question.

'We need to find Bambi.'

Ignatius knew this was true and sat in silence, mainly because he had no idea how they would go about doing this. After a short while, they discussed what the best next moves were. Ignatius didn't want Sahira to tell anyone about the meet, but she managed to convince him that Sayer could be trusted and she wasn't willing to keep it from him anyway.

He had little choice but to agree. He got her to agree to give him a lift back to his vehicle which was near St Albans, then asked if he could use her internet to do a search. Ignatius had no intention of staying in a hotel of any sort. He'd need to keep his mask off for the night, so couldn't risk being recognised. He planned to go feral and spend the night in a wooded area near St Albans.

He did trust Sahira he thought, but he didn't want to take any risks, so he did multiple searches of Bed and Breakfasts near Slough in the Thames Valley. If she was going to hand him in after he left her, they would start with checking what he had searched on her internet and would then focus the search on accommodation in the Slough area.

Whilst he was doing this search, Sahira took a phone call.

When her phone rang, she looked at the number and her heart sank. It couldn't have come at a worse time.

The call was about the money she had paid in the name of Allah. She knew that the person calling had almost no opportunity to make a call, so she had to take it, otherwise it could be another week before she heard again; and that was unacceptable. She couldn't leave the room for fear of spooking Ignatius, so she answered and said,

'Hi. Sorry, can't really talk now as in the middle of something, how's everything going?'

The voice on the end of the phone responded.

'We got delayed, but the foundations are now in place and it is full steam ahead.'

Sahira smiled at the news and said,

'Ok, that's great news, well done. Update me again when everything is ready.' She then hung up.

Ignatius looked at her and asked,

'Everything ok?'

'Yes, all fine, just an old friend from University calling for a catch up,' Sahira answered.

Ignatius wasn't sure he believed her, but he knew the Intelligence Services' protocols and knew she hadn't sent a hidden message while she was speaking, so he let it go.

Ignatius collected his rucksack and stood waiting awkwardly by the door that led to the hallway with the lift.

He had never been a wordsmith nor one for small talk. Sahira was getting frustrated with her hairband which kept coming loose in her hair, so she had pulled out a washbag from her gym bag and was using four or five metal hairclips to put her hair in place. She had given it a chance, but it didn't listen, so now she'd restrain it properly.

Whilst pulling out her hairclips a miniature spray deodorant can fell out of her bag. Ignatius saw it and asked,

'Can I borrow some? Don't want to show my face in a shop buying some right this minute.'

'All yours,' Sahira said.

As she said this, she launched the can out of the side of her hand towards him, like a baseball pitcher trying to teach someone a lesson for hogging the plate.

Ignatius only just caught it, using razor sharp reactions, which stopped it from hitting him square in the face. He gave her a 'what the hell' look, but she was focusing on the clips in her hair and wasn't looking, so the look was lost on her.

He couldn't tell if it was a passive aggressive act or she just had a rocket hand.

'Thanks', he muttered

He had his rucksack in his hand and decided he was best served keeping his wits about him, so he would put the deodorant on when they were in the car driving to St Albans.

They made their way down to the garage in silence. The garage structure was empty and they headed towards Sahira's glass fronted double port garage. Sahira pressed a button on her key fob as they were approaching and the doors slid open. They had both stepped into the garage and were just about to split and make their ways to separate doors of the car, when they both froze still.

Standing in the garage, were a man and woman who were both pointing guns at Ignatius and Sahira.

Sahira seemed stunned and Ignatius was the first to talk.

'I know you. You two were both at my flat looking around.'

Sahira looked at Ignatius, surprised, then back at the couple and said,

'Who are you then? You're clearly not protection for the PM.'

Simmonds and Peters stared back. Simmonds was wearing a tight black t-shirt under which his huge chest slowly moved up and down, some jeans and trainers, and Peters was wearing black trousers, a blouse and a thin nylon jacket. Like last time, both had their hair clearly slicked back with gel.

What is that all about, Ignatius was thinking?

Peters answered Sahira's question.

'No, we're not. When the cut grate and equipment in the river were found at the power station, we were sent to take charge of the situation and manage it as best as possible, which isn't easy with Five poking their nose in as well as everyone else.'

Sahira wasn't sure if she was actually after sympathy for this and asked,

'So, what are you doing here, pointing guns at us?'

Peters responded again.

'We're managing the situation. This is far more important than either of you, I'm afraid.'

She tossed Sahira some handcuffs that had a solid metal frame between both wrist holders and warned Sahira.

'We will kill you here if you mess us about. Put them on him', she nodded towards Ignatius.

Ignatius was weighing up the situation. They were both carrying a Glock 26, which is the usual weapon issued to plain clothes and firearms officers of the Met Police.

They were both holding the weapon in a relaxed but firm

stance. They weren't gripping too hard unnecessarily, which can cause arm lock and shaking fairly quickly, which could lead to erratic shooting, especially if accompanied by adrenaline.

So, they knew how to handle and use their weapons. Ignatius made that 1-0 to them.

Sahira came towards him with the cuffs and he gave her a small nod to say, do what they ask.

After he was cuffed, he was ordered to stand against the car with his cuffed hands on the roof. Simmonds readjusted his position, so that he could cover both Ignatius and Sahira as Peters approached and cuffed her.

So, both Peters and Simmonds had weapons and both Ignatius and Sahira were handcuffed. Ignatius conceded that was 2-0.

They were made to stand against the car with their hands on the roof and were then searched and Ignatius' rucksack was taken off him along with their phones, wallets and anything else in the pockets.

Ignatius now made it 2-1.

When they had first entered the garage, the bonnet of the Range Rover covered enough of Ignatius for him to have been quickly able to slip the miniature deodorant can in his pants. He didn't know how that was beneficial yet, but the fact that they didn't discover it during the search meant that he felt they deserved a point.

Whilst Peters kept her gun trained on them both, Simmonds walked out of Sahira's garage and was gone all of thirty seconds before he turned up outside in a plain black BMW. Simmonds got out the car and walked over to Ignatius, who gave him a 'how you doing' nod before asking Peters,

'So, does Shrek talk, or is he not the social type?'

Both of them ignored him. Ignatius was manoeuvred into the backseat of the car, behind the driver's seat, with a little more aggression than was required. Simmonds strapped the seatbelt on, then he went and did the same with Sahira putting her behind the front passenger's seat. As she was strapped in she looked remarkably cool to Ignatius, but he still gave her a reassuring smile.

Peters got in the driving seat and Simmonds in the passenger seat, and they began their journey. Sahira felt that she had kept her mouth shut long enough.

'So, are you going to tell us what's going on here?'

Peters kept her eyes on the road whilst responding,

'It's nothing personal, Sahira. I respect you, but you've taken the wrong path and you seem to be under the illusion that helping a traitor to this country is the best thing to do.'

'He's not a traitor, he had nothing to do with the assassination and we can prove it.' She let the last word linger as the realisation of the situation hit her, 'but you don't care about that, do you?'

'Sahira, we are going to do what we can to protect this country'

Sahira almost spat out her response.

'So, you're now going to torture us to find out what we know and then kill us.'

'We know what you know, Sahira. We're not going to torture you, we're not savages.'

Up until this point, Ignatius had sat there in silence and almost seemed bored by the whole experience, but Peters last words had caught his attention.

They may not be savages, but he sure as hell was.

2-2.

They were heading north out of London on the A10 road, but where they were going wasn't being shared with Sahira or Ignatius. Thirty minutes into the journey, Simmonds lit up a cigarette and gave one to Peters who also started smoking.

'Since I'm gonna die anyway, any chance I can have a smoke?' Ignatius asked.

Simmonds looked at Peters who gave him a 'why not' shrug.

Simmonds threw back a cigarette that Ignatius picked off his lap and put in his mouth. He then said,

'Can I have a light, please?'

Simmonds fumbled in his pocket and then lit the lighter and moved his hands towards Ignatius who was ducking his head towards the flame to light his cigarette.

Had Peters and Simmonds been truly capable professionals, they would have known not to allow a meaningless request from a captive to happen, and they would have also realised that when they searched Ignatius, there were no cigarettes in his pocket nor any lighter or matches. A smoker would almost definitely carry some indication of their bad habit.

Just before Ignatius was about to light his cigarette, he whipped up his hands holding the deodorant can in them. He had slipped it out of his pants whilst Simmonds was getting the lighter out of his pocket.

Ignatius sprayed the can over the flame creating a handheld flame thrower, which he used directly in Simmonds face as he was leaning over with the lighter.

Simmonds' natural reaction was to pull away as quickly as he could. This was a mistake though, as the jerking reaction only locked his seatbelt and kept him wedged in position.

He was screaming and the skin on his face was blistering. Ignatius moved the flamethrower to his hair, and with the dried gel it was effectively a crispy wick and lit instantaneously.

Ignatius then moved the flame thrower over to Peters who had been caught between trying to control the car at fifty mph and help Simmonds.

When the flame hit her, her velvet jacket caught fire and spread quickly and her hair also lit like a candle, scorching her scalp.

Sahira hadn't been a pure spectator during this. Her reaction time was very impressive. As soon as she saw Ignatius make a move, she had grabbed a hairclip from her hair. She couldn't unlock her cuffs due to the solid metal between the wrists, so she went straight to work on Ignatius' cuffs, which was tricky with his arms moving, but she had still managed to pick the locks and release his hands very quickly.

Ignatius now had his hands free and grabbed Simmonds gun out of his holster whilst he was still thrashing about. Peters had lost all sense of calm as the skin on both her head and the back of her neck was melting. Ignatius saw what was coming, so used both his hands and released Simmonds' and Peters' seatbelts, whilst he sat back in his seat.

The car had slowed to about thirty-five mph but had now veered off the road and crashed into the front garden wall of a house along the A10, opposite a Travelodge near Enfield.

Sahira and Ignatius suffered a whiplash effect from the crash, but the seatbelt saved them from any real damage. Simmonds' and Peters' seatbelts were free but still half covering their frames, causing the effect of contorting their bodies on impact, so they were thrown about in the front of the car. This had a huge concussive effect even though it wasn't fatal. The one bit of luck for both the front seat torches. The flames were extinguished in the commotion.

Ignatius moved quickly in the aftermath of the crash and managed to get the keys from Simmonds and unlocked Sahira's handcuffs. They opened Sahira's door and both climbed out onto the side of the road. They had to move quickly. Ignatius went to the front passenger seat window and aimed Simmonds' own gun at his head.

Sahira jumped in.

'Whoa, whoa, what are you doing?'

'They were going to kill us, they are involved in this, what do you think?'

Sahira's voice was commanding.

'NO. We are not murderers. I don't care what they've done.'

Ignatius holstered his weapon and looked like a kid who'd just had his Christmas present taken from him.

He didn't have time to sulk though, so ran around to the driver's window and used a loose brick from the wall to smash the window. He then reached in, grabbed the keys out of the ignition and threw them to Sahira. She opened the boot and retrieved all their possessions, whilst Ignatius searched Peters and Simmonds. He took Peters' weapon as well and both their phones and then turned to Sahira.

'We need to get out of here, there's a crowd starting to form and some are on their phones. First responders will be here soon, we can't be here then.'

They both ran off, leaving Simmonds and Peters semi-conscious, moaning and smelling of burnt flesh. As they were

running across the road, Ignatius thought to himself.
3-2.

20

Ignatius led the escape and ran into the car park of the Travelodge, with Sahira shortly behind him.

Dusk had fallen and Ignatius needed to get close to the cars in the car park to see inside them. He found the right car fairly quickly. The car had clearly just had a valet. There was a shirt hanging on the handrail in the back seat and a folder with a logo on it. There were also some papers next to that with a matching logo at the top.

The car 'shouted company car for a travelling salesman' or something similar, and they were clearly staying at the Travelodge.

It was just after 9.00pm, so Ignatius was gambling on the fact that the salesman would be in the hotel now. It was unlikely that he knew anyone in the area, so he wouldn't be heading out later. He hoped it gave them at least ten hours until it was noticed missing. With his vast knowledge of vehicles, it took him a matter of minutes until he was able to break into the car, hotwire it and disable the GPS. He then stepped out the car and said to Sahira, 'You're driving.' They both jumped in and Ignatius said, 'Head north, back towards Verulamium Park.' As soon as they were out the car park and moving along the A10 he said, 'Give me your phone.'

Sahira looked at him a bit puzzled.

'Uh, ok.'

Ignatius put it on the floor of the car, stamped on it, opened the window of the passenger side and threw the phone out of the car.

'What the hell are you doing?' Sahira yelled.

'Who did you tell about meeting me?'

'What? Hang on, you honestly think I was involved in this? They tried to kill me too.'

'I don't see any injuries.'

Sahira looked over at Ignatius.

'Screw you. You came to me, you dictated where we'd be and when.'

Ignatius paused for a few seconds before saying

'Ok, let's say I do believe you. How did they know where we were?'

'I don't know, my phone is secure. No one would be able to hack into it or track its location. Is it possible you were followed?'

'No, it's not.'

Sahira sensed his tone and knew that he was still doubting her. She had only known this guy for a couple of hours and she was already sick of this arsehole.

The next half hour was silent as they both let their individual thoughts percolate. Ignatius was in two minds. He wasn't ready to trust her but despite what she thought, her phone could have been hacked. Justin had managed to do it.

He got Sahira to drop him of about half a klick from his Ducati Multistrada 1200 Enduro. He didn't want Sahira to know exactly where he had left his bike as he still wasn't convinced by her but he equally didn't want to be exposed in public, even if it was getting darker by the minute.

When he reached his bike and was sure that no one was in

earshot, he pulled out his phone and called Ricky and Justin. Ignatius spoke as soon as Justin answered.

'I need to see you guys right away.'

'We'll be there in forty-five minutes.'

Ignatius retrieved his helmet from behind some crates that were at the back of a takeaway Chinese and then fired up his bike with his rucksack spooned to his back. He headed to a pre-arranged meeting spot with he Wilsons.

The traffic was light and he made good time to an address in Harlow. The street was quiet and off the main road in a typically suburban neighbourhood. Ignatius was beginning to wonder if he had come to the right place when he saw a sky-blue Fiat 500 pull into the street.

Ignatius was sitting on his bike with his helmet on. The engine was running in case they had unknowingly been followed and he had to make a dash.

Ricky and Justin would have seen him, but they got out of the car, ignored him and went to a detached house and let themselves in. Ignatius did a quick loop of the surrounding streets before he parked up and went and knocked on the door.

Ignatius walked into a sitting room that was on the right of the entrance hall and looked at the décor. It was practically furnished rather than done with any thought of homeliness in mind. Justin explained that the place belonged to their biggest client.

They were a large aerospace company based in The United States. They bought this place as somewhere to stay when their staff were over in the UK for business. It worked out a lot cheaper than paying for hotels all the time. It wasn't traceable to Ricky or Justin or any of the other hundreds of subcontractors that the firm did business with.

Ricky gave Ignatius a concerned look and asked if he was ok.

'I'm fine. Why do you ask?' Ignatius replied.

'We just got an alert' – Ricky and Justin still monitored all Police and Intelligence updates, out of a matter of habit as well as business interest – 'that there was an incident in Enfield. A car crash with two burn victims, who were choppered to hospital and both in critical condition. A man and woman were seen fleeing the scene.'

'What about it?' Ignatius asked with more calm than he felt.

'One of the witnesses says she was sure that the man was the one who has been on the news for the assassination of the Chinese Minister?'

Ignatius nodded confirmation. He wasn't trying to hide things from Ricky and Justin but he felt that the less they knew the better off they were.

'I assume the girl was Sahira Basha?' Justin asked.

'It was.'

'Of course, it was. It wouldn't be our Iggy if he didn't complicate the matter tenfold.' Ignatius wondered if he'd actually just been told off.

Justin continued, 'That explains why her phone has died and I can't monitor it anymore.'

'Not exactly. I threw it out of the car whilst we were fleeing.'

'Naturally.' Justin responded.

Ignatius was feeling defensive and said,

'Look, I arrange to meet her and suddenly two Government pricks turn up trying to kill me or both of us. I'm not sure yet.'

Ricky put his arm on Justin's shoulder as if to say, 'I've got this'.

'I don't think she sold you out, mate. We've been monitoring her messages and we scanned her and there was nothing to suggest that she tipped anyone off that she was with you.'

'She must have been followed then.'

'You had Tank check to make sure she wasn't being followed.'

'Well how did they know where we were?'

Ricky went off on a tangent briefly, 'Do you know who they were?'

Ignatius nodded.

'They're definitely government. I think SOCA or Police Intelligence?'

'Based on?'

'They were both carrying a Glock 26 and I saw them both at my flat, and obviously had credentials to get past the police officer guarding it. They were the man and woman who weren't carrying phones when they went around my flat. However, they were carrying phones this time.'

With this, Ignatius pulled out Simmonds' and Peters' phones from his back pocket and threw them to Justin to see what he could get from then.

Justin brought the conversation back on track.

'Iggy, don't be naïve here, as vulgar as this might seem. She is a Muslim woman, who has strong ties to Saudi Arabia through her family, whether by Five directly or outside of them. She would by some be considered a higher risk and very likely, she is being closely monitored. Depending on what tool they're using, it would be undetectable on her phone.'

Ignatius hadn't considered this before. He didn't care about religion, colour, creed, or sexuality. As far as he was concerned, everyone was an arsehole until they proved otherwise.

'So, she didn't sell me out?'

'She didn't.'

'Huh.'

Justin gave an exaggerated sigh which made Ricky smile with a mixture of pride and love.

'Let me guess, Iggy. You gave her the benefit of the doubt whilst reasonably explaining to her your concerns.'

Ignatius didn't know how to look sheepish, but this was as close as he was likely to get to it.

'I'm pretty sure I was cool about it.'

Justin raised his eyebrows whilst giving Ricky a 'what are we going to do about him' look. Ignatius realised he might have got this one wrong.

He started thinking about how he was going to put this right. He needed Sahira if he was going to stand any chance of finding Bambi.

Ricky and Justin told Ignatius to spend the night in the house they were currently in. He was relieved. He wasn't looking forward to sharing his bedroom with the foxes. They left shortly afterwards with an arrangement to chat in the morning.

Ignatius looked through the cupboards in the kitchen and was pleased to find some washing powder. He stripped of his clothes and put them in a hot wash to get rid of the smell of burnt flesh that had permeated his clothes. Experience had told him that it would take more than one wash but it was better than nothing. Whilst his clothes were washing he set about his person and went and stood under an almost scolding hot shower. He scrubbed hard with whatever soaps and sponges he could lay his hands on.

He got out the shower and realised there were no towels

about, so he took a sheet off one of the made up beds and wrapped it around him. There wasn't much food in the cupboards and he couldn't risk being seen whilst he didn't have his mask on. He ordered a pizza and a couple of cans of coke and told the shop to leave the pizza on the mat, and that the money would be under it. He spent the next thirty minutes waiting for his pizza and exploring the house.

He saw someone walk up the path to the house and held his Sig Sauer P226 in his right hand ready to engage if he needed. He wondered whether he might be the first SAS soldier in history, getting ready for battle wrapped in a bed sheet. Luckily the man walking up the path was just delivering his pizza. Ignatius waited until he had left and three minutes later opened the door and took in his pizza and coke cans.

He put his clothes on a dry cycle then sat down on the couch and ate his pizza whilst watching a re-run comedy on TV.

21

Sao Paulo is one of the world's most populous cities with 12.2 million people living in Brazil's vibrant financial centre. In the heart of the city is Catedral da Sé de São Paulo. It is the largest Catholic church in the city of Sao Paulo at one hundred and eleven metres long with a spire height of ninety-two meters. More than eight hundred tons of rare marble were used for the construction, with the inner capitals decorated with sculpted Brazilian produce, like coffee branches, pineapples, and native animals such as armadillos.

With a floor space of six thousand seven hundred metres the cathedral has a total capacity of eight thousand people. Currently, there were no more than fifty people spread out across the whole building.

Bambi had spent the last few days of his few month tenure hiding in plain sight in the crowds of Sao Paulo. He spoke fluent Portuguese and he was not an amateur at fitting in with new surroundings. So far no one had given him a second glance. The people of Sao Paulo lived full, busy lives and weren't interested to second-guess what a random stranger's deal was.

The cathedral was open to the public between 9.00am to 5.00pm, but a well placed five hundred Brazilian Real, the equivalent of around ninety pounds sterling, had enabled Bambi early access to the church.

It was 7.30am now and he was half way down the main aisle on the left side. He was kneeling on a pillow with his hands pressed together in front of his face. Five minutes earlier he had lit a candle at the main altar and was now deep in prayer. Religion had always been a great comfort to Bambi, and work permitting, he would pay respect to his God as often as he could. Today though, he was here for a different reason. It was thirty-six years to the day that his mother was shot dead and he was in church to feel as close to her as he could. He was only six years old when his mother was murdered and it seemed that everyone assumed he didn't remember the day and the event.

They couldn't be more wrong. He rememberd every detail of the day, and the events that led up to the murder.

He later found out that his mother had been involved in a minor capacity in helping with the shipment of drugs. She had worked as a secretary at the local dockyards and had advanced knowledge of which containers the customs officers were going to spot check.

For the equivalent of a measly fifty pounds a week, she would pass this information on. The fifty pounds a week wouldn't be much to a lot of people, but for her it meant a different life for her son.

It enabled him to go to after-school clubs, to attend school trips and to eat food with a roof over his head. All his mum ever wanted, was for her son to have the best life possible with every opportunity available to him.

One day however, the customs officers seized a vast shipment of heroin via an anoynomous tip-off. The container had not been due for a spot check and was only searched based on the tip-off, so therefore Bambi's mother, had no way of knowing that the container would be searched.

The head of the minor league drug cartel was angry about the loss of drugs, but they also had a lot of other people in similar positions as Bambi's mother and he had to send a message. He was never going to get to the big leagues if he wasn't respected.

The same day that the drugs were seized, a local gang member was paid the equivalent of five hundred pounds to take someone's life.

The next day, as Bambi's mum was walking from work to catch a bus home, a local gang member who had never met her and had no idea who the woman was, pulled the trigger of his Glock 9mm pistol three times. This ended her life.

Bambi still had fresh memories of his mother in his mind. The smell of her shampoo, the feeling of happieness and safety he felt when she gave him a hug, and her incessant patience.

Also, the times after she'd finished a long night shift and would still spend every minute playing with him until school, and again after school, before she began another night shift.

To this day, Bambi had never spoken to another soul about her murder. Eight years ago, twenty-eight years after his mother's murder, and after many years of painstaking research, he managed to hunt down the gang member who shot his mum.

This man was in a maximum security jail, serving a life sentance for two seperate murders. He was seemingly unreachable to Bambi. However, two weeks after he had hunted down this man, the murderer was found hanged in his cell and the verdict, without doubt, was rulled as suicide.

The coroner's report was correct. It was a suicide. Bambi had hunted down the man's family, including his wife and three kids.

Bambi had given him an ultimatum. Either he kills himself within forty-eight hours or his family will die, one by one.

Initially the man had called his bluff, but after the first forty-eight hours, the murderer found out his brother had been tortured and slaughtered. Bambi got back in touch with him that day and assured him that if he hadn't killed himself within the next forty-eight hours, his son would be next, and the torture and murders would get progessively worse.

The next morning the man was found dead in his cell.

It was three years after Bambi found the gang member, that he hunted down the cartel boss who was living under a new name in South Africa.

He tied the man up and slowly and methodically began getting his revenge. Using a wood plane, he set about peeling the man's skin off like he was a potato, starting on his back. The coroner couldn't be sure how long it took the man to die, but he was found with not an inch of skin on him.

Bambi left the cathedral with a sense of sadness but also of peace, feeling he had been closer with his mother. He walked to a coffee shop on Rua Santa Teresa, overlooking the park and sat sipping strong Colombian coffee and eating a fresh fruit salad. He checked his work phone, more out of habit than expectation since he had retired, so was troubled to see five missed calls from his agent.

He called his agent back, though he wasn't going to stress himself over a situation he wasn't yet aware of.

Following the phone call with his agent, he became justifiably stressed, but he wasn't about to let anyone else know that. He'd arranged to call his previous client the next day at 4.00pm Sao Paulo time.

He needed time to prepare for the call. In the extremely

unlikely scenario that new technology was available that he was unaware of and his call could be traced, he needed to ensure he was traced in a diffrent location to his.

It was an eighteen-hour drive to Asuncion in Paraguay that bordered Argentina. Using one of his multiple passports, Bambi made the drive stopping only three times. Twice for a bathroom break and to refuel and once for only a bathroom break.

The next day at 3.45pm in Asuncion and 7.45pm in the UK, an express delivery package was delivered to a post box. It was address to Jerry.

Inside the package was a brand new phone. Fifteen minutes later the new phone rang and Jerry answered quickly.

'Hello?'

'What do you want?' Bambi answered.

'We have a problem. Winter has evaded authorities.'

'Sounds like your problem.'

Jerry took a minute to calm himself before answering, 'They know you were involved.'

Bambi was silent for long enough for it to be threatening.

'Did you tell them?'

'Of course not. We bugged the home computer of the woman leading the investigation for MI5, Sahira Basha. Winter and her have fairly conclusive evidence that you were involved.'

Jerry gave an overview of the evidence and comparison to a job in Germany.

'You still haven't said what you want from me?'

'If Winter and Basha disappear, all of this goes away.'

Bambi considered this.

'No one knows who I am or where I am, I'm still safe. Not interested.'

'Maybe, but do you really want to spend the rest of your life worrying that there are the best and most competent intelligence agencies in the world searching for you? Make no mistake, the British will share this with the US, with Germany, with Israel, with... fill in the blank. Maybe even with the Chinese.'

'Sorry. Still not interested.'

'I will pay you ten million dollars.'

This was a game changer for Bambi. He had been going through his finances and he would be absolutely fine, better than fine, but an extra ten million dollars would make his life exactly how his Mum had always wanted his life to be.

He owed it to her.

'Same deal as last time. Transfer quarter of the money upfront, the rest on completion. I will contact you for help if I need to, otherwise there is no contact. I do this my way.'

With that Bambi hung up, got in a new rental car and began his journey back to Sao Paulo.

22

Ignatius had spent the last couple of days holed up in the house. He was still unsure what his next move would be. All that changed when he had a call from Justin at 5.00am, who was currently on his way over to see him.

After Justin arrived and they were both sitting down with a cup of coffee, Justin began his update.

'Sorry, it took me a while. It seems the algorithims have changed since my day, but I managed to get in Simmonds' and Peters' phones. Long story short Iggy, someone is screwing you over.'

Ignatius didn't comment so Justin continued. 'I found an email address and managed to hack the password. Within the draft folder was a message outlining their plan. They were going to kill you, then plant evidence in your flat that linked you to the assassination.'

'Why was the message still in the folder?' Ignatius asked.

'The password to the email account had just been changed, which suggests that there was a lack of trust between the parties. I also found messages between Simmonds and Peters that shows they were saving emails as an insurance policy for themselves.'

'Do you know who they were communicating with?'

'Afraid not and there is no way of us knowing that with what we've currently got.'

'Surely this proves I'm innocent though?'

'Iggy, we both know it's nowhere near enough. Firstly, the

nature of how the phones were acquired means they would never be allowed as evidence by themselves. Secondly, it will be seen by many that you tried to murder two government officers, who no doubt have a spotless record. And then you took their phones and coincidently on these phones was evidence that says you are inncocent. And finally, we both know this goes high up. If this is all we approach them with, it will be simple and easy for them to make you disappear. We need more, a lot more.'

'So, it's effectively useless?' Ignatius replied.

'Come on, Iggy, leave the dramas for me. It's not useless. It's a piece of the puzzle, a big piece, but if we are going to prove you innocent and keep you alive, we need the whole puzzle. The rest of the puzzle is Bambi. We need him.'

The biggest thing that Ignatius took from all of that, is he couldn't believe Justin had called him a drama queen. They carried on chatting about minor details for a while before Justin headed of to his day job.

Ignatius had washed his clothes a few more times in the past couple of days, and had finally managed to get the stench of burnt flesh from them. He was pissed off with Simmonds and Peters for making him do that. He hated washing.

He now needed to put his face back on and was pleased to find it hadn't been damaged in the car crash and worked just as well. He was annoyed though that he had to hide his own beautiful face.

He went round the corner to his bike and searched his skinny tom tom look-alike and headed out on his journey. The nearest florist was less than ten minutes away and he went in the shop and bought the cheapest pair of flowers he could find. It was a bunch of budding daffodils. He wrote a note which he sealed in an envelope and paid the owner of the shop more than he paid for the flowers to ensure they were delivered today to the penthouse at One Hyde Park.

He then put a new search in his system and headed into London to a shop that described itself as a spy shop. He'd never been in a shop like this before but was pleasantly surprised with the contents. He didn't need especially high-tech equipment and wouldn't find it here, but for what he needed, they had solid and varied gear.

He bought the equipment he needed and realised he still had over twelve hours to kill. He didn't want to risk going back to the house so headed out of London to the place where he needed to be. He had been craving some fried chicken so got himself a feast of chicken, then booked himself into a cheap Bed and Breakfast for the day.

He rested well over the last couple of days, but when you were operational, you never knew when the next sleep was coming, so he planned on taking advantage of this free time and get more rest.

23

Sahira only had a few weak leads on the assassination. Ignatius had taken the evidence showing Bambi's involvement, and she had no idea where he currently was.

She was sitting in Sayer's office, waiting for him, so she could update on the latest developments. She didn't want to tell him about meeting Ignatius outside of a face to face encounter. Sayer had been at a meeting of European Intelligence heads in Munich for the past couple of days, so she hadn't had any opportunity before now, to talk things over with him.

Sayer walked in his office and handed Sahira a peppermint tea he had bought from the onsite cafe. Rather than sit behind his desk he took a seat on a chair next to Sahira and inquired,

'So, where are we?'

Sahira outlined every detail of Winter's contact with her, what had happened with Simmonds and Peters and most importantly, in her opinion, the evidence she had seen of Bambi's involvement.

If Sayer was surprised by all this, he didn't show it. Before he discussed anything further with her, he got on his phone and spent five minutes making some inquiries. When he had finished he said,

'There are no records of a Simmonds or Peters on the government payroll nor any operatives who have been put on medical leave for those injuries.'

'Matt, I'm positive they're part of a government organisation of some description.'

Sayer answered matter-of-factly.

'I've no doubt you're correct. Enough government officers are completely deniable and their existence is hidden even from us, so there wouldn't be any record. I can and will dig deeper though.'

'What's been troubling me though Matt, is that they weren't amateurs by any means, but equally they weren't top level. They were definitely sloppy in parts. Surely this level of staff wouldn't be in a deniable capacity?'

'In theory, it wasn't a top level operation. What was asked of them should have been fairly standard even for a sloppy professional. They were probably recruited specifically for this, which would normally be outside of their remit.'

Sahira gave an internal sigh before she asked what had been on her mind since the incident.

'The fact that this happened and how it happened means that they knew where we'd be, and it shows that someone who is high up in our own goverment is somehow part of this.'

Sayer was still calm and collected even with all this information.

'The evidence does suggest that, but that doesn't really change anything without proof. The same with Bambi's involvement.'

Sahira appreciated the fact that Sayer hadn't said 'alleged involvement', but trusted what she told him outright. Sayer continued,

'So, what are our other leads?'

'Not much, I'm afraid, not much. Winter clearly has external help to get a lot of the information he has. I have searched his known associates, looked to see who would have the expertise to do this and one name stands out: Justin Wilson.'

Sayer searched his brain before answering.

'I don't believe I know him.'

'When he worked at GCHQ he was Justin Sangster, he has since married Ricky Wilson who is ex Six.'

Sayer nodded whilst responding.

'Yes, yes. I know of both of them. Ricky was a top R&D guy and Justin was one of our best cyber lot.'

'They're the ones. They also have a strong allegiance to Winter. He saved both their lives during an operation three years ago, but my clearance doesn't allow me to read into the details of that.'

Sayer gave a dismissive hand gesture.

'I'll make sure you are given access to that by the end of the day.'

'Thanks, Matt. I was planning on paying Ricky and Justin a visit later. They set up a business together a few years ago and should both be at their offices, according to our sources.'

Sayer thought about this for a few seconds before replying.

'Hold that thought for a bit. Let's not spook them unnecessarily, we may actually need them on board. If we go in too soon, they might well shut down on us. Who is our top cyber person now?'

Sahira didn't hesitate before responding.

'Sally Dalton.'

'Ok, read her in. When we approach the Wilson clan, she may be able to speak with them on a level neither you nor I can.'

'Will do. Matt, I know you said we need proof before action, but you haven't really said much on Bambi's part in this.'

'Sahira, I can assure you I'm not taking that lightly, but he is so elusive that we would just be wasting our time trying to follow it up without any evidence. You need to somehow get back in contact with Winter and get that evidence, because the resource we'll need to follow this thread won't be given to us without the proof.'

Sahira and Sayer finished the meeting by arranging when their next meeting would take place and as Sahira was leaving the room Sayer said,

'Sahira, I know you've been doing fourteen-hour days in the office the last couple of days, as well as another two or three hours at home each day. You're making me tired just thinking of it. Go home now and come back tomorrow morning fresh. I'm not asking, that's an order from your Director General.'

Sahira smiled and despite thinking, 'you're one to talk' said, 'Yes, sir.'

It was just after 1.00pm and Sahira had decided she would obey Sayer's order. She checked a schedule on her phone and realised if she was quick she could make a hot yoga class. After the yoga class she was feeling healthy for the first time in the last few days but was also shattered so decided she'd have a lazy afternoon on the sofa, watching mindless TV and sleeping.

It was just after 3.00pm when she'd got back to her home, put on her comfortable clothes and crashed on the couch. She was dozing off, when she had a call from the concierge. They informed that she had a delivery and asked if she wanted them to bring it up. She couldn't think of a delivery she was expecting, so out of curiousity more than anything else, she asked them to bring it up.

A polite young woman delivered a bunch of flowers, which

Sahira initially thought were from her Dad, who was always thoughtful and seemed to know when to send her a card or flowers or something to cheer her up when she needed it.

But when she read the note in the envelope she realised she was wrong. They were not from her Dad. The note read,

The key to our hot date is my tool.

p i s w o i c u u u m r j s k e a i p

B. Vigenere

24

Ignatius managed to get a couple of hours' sleep early on in a chicken coma. He was still stiff from the car crash when he woke up, so stretched out his whole body slowly. He believed he would be needing to use the mechanics of his body a lot in the near future. After spending a large part of the day wasting away the hours and going through his plan in his head, he was now doing his usual pre-meeting reconnaisance.

A few minutes before 10.00pm, Ignatius let out a sigh of relief as he saw Sahira approaching.

When Sahira had first received the note, she had realised immediately that it was from Ignatius. As much as anything else, she didn't know any other human who would start a note with,

The key to our hot date is my tool.

She had got the reference immediately *'hot date'*. I guess you could call setting two people on fire *'hot'*, but what sort of sick son of a bitch would refer to the situation as a date?

The next line would take some working on:

p i s w o i c u u u m r j s k e a i p

The final line, *B. Vigenere.*

She knew she'd heard of Vigenere before so she started there. A quick Google search of B. Vigenere, brought up the answer she was looking for straight away.

Blaise de Vigenère was a French diplomat, cryptographer, translator and alchemist. He lived between 1523 -1596 and was wrongly attributed with the creation of what is now known as the Vigenere cipher. It was actually first described by Giovan Battista Bellaso, but Vigenere had created a stronger autokey cipher version of Bellaso's original.

A Vigenere cipher builds on a Caesar Cipher where each letter of the alphabet is shifted along a number of places. So, for example, a shift of 2, A would become C, B would become D, Y would become A and so on. The Vigenère cipher has several Caesar ciphers in sequence with different shift values.

To encrypt the cipher, a table of alphabets can be used, termed a Vigenère table. It has the alphabet written out twenty-six times in different rows, each alphabet shifted cyclically to the left compared to the previous alphabet, corresponding to the twenty-six possible Caesar ciphers. At different points in the encryption process, the cipher uses a different alphabet from one of the rows.

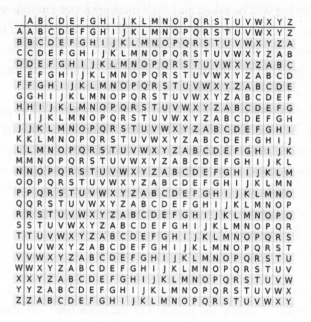

The alphabet used at each point depends on a repeating keyword. So, if the plain text that needs to be encrypted is:

CHINESEASSASSINATION

The person sending the message chooses a keyword and repeats it until it matches the length of the plaintext, for example, the keyword 'MOBILE.'

MOBILEMOBILEMOBILEMO

Each row starts with a key letter. The rest of the row holds the letters A to Z (in shifted order). Although there are twenty-six key rows shown, a code will use only as many keys as there are unique letters in the key string, here just 6 keys: (M, O, B, I, L, E).

For successive letters of the message, successive letters of the key string will be taken and each message letter enciphered by using its corresponding key row. The next letter of the key is chosen, and that row is gone along to find the column heading that matches the message character. The letter at the intersection is the enciphered letter.

For example, the first letter of the plaintext, C, is paired with M, the first letter of the key. Therefore, row M and column C of the Vigenère square are used, namely O. Similarly, for the second letter of the plaintext, the second letter of the key is used. The letter at row O and column H is V. The rest of the plaintext is enciphered using the same pattern.

Plaintext: CHINESEASSASSINATION
Key: MOBILEMOBILEMOBILEMO
Ciphertext: OVJVPWGOTALWEWOIEMAB

To decrypt, you go to the row in the table corresponding to the key. Finding the position of the ciphertext letter in that row and then using the column's label as the plaintext. For example, in row M (from MOBILE), the ciphertext O appears in column C, which is the first letter of the plaintext. Next in row O (from MOBILE), the cipher text V is located in column H, so H is the second plaintext letter.

Sahira got her head quickly around the concept of the cipher, and now she needed to solve it. She had the ciphertext, *p i s w o i c u u u m r j s k e a i p,* so she now needed the key.

The key to our hot date is my tool.

She looked again at the word '*date*' and shook her head thinking, 'what a dickhead'.

She tried to get in Ignatius' head from the minimal amount she knew of him. She jotted down a few words- she wouldn't usually write down in day to day life- as the key and came up with gibberish.

Then a thought occured to her and she used this key on the plaintext,

Ciphertext: PISWOICUUUMRJSKEAIP

Key: DEODORANT

Using the key in a repeating fashion, the cipher text after adding the appropriate word spaces translated to,

MEET ARCH BRIDGE TEN PM.

Sahira had to admit that it was clever of him to communicate in this way. It was secure on several levels.

The cipher text obviously hid the message from a glancing look, even if the cipher used was easy to figure out by signing the name of the cryptographer. The key word was only known to her, Sayer and Ignatius as no one else knew the exact events of what had gone down in the car.

She hadn't mentioned an arch bridge to anyone, as why would she, so the location was unique to her and Ignatius. Finally, the time frame that he had given her to solve it would be minimum. This would be especially true for someone who wouldn't know the key and the significance of arch bridge.

It was only by coincidence that she got the message when she did. On a normal day, she probably wouldn't have got the message until around 8.00pm.

25

Sahira walked up to the empty arched bridge over the lake in Verulamium park and looked out to the lake. She didn't have time to begin to second-guess whether she had made a mistake in her identification of the location, as out of her peripheral vision she saw a man approaching.

She turned to face the man and saw the masked version of Ignatius that was familiar. He walked up, stood next to her, and both of them looked out at the lake.

'So you trust me now?' Sahira asked.

'I trust that you want to find out the truth about all of this and I know that I want to clear my name, so our agendas do align in that respect.'

'Fine. Then what do you want from me?' Sahira asked.

Ignatius outlined what had been found on Simmonds' and Peters' phones. Sahira weighed up the situation and had to agree with Justin. The information they had, most likely wouldn't be enough to clear Ignatius.

Although she never verbalised it, she had no doubt in her mind that if Ignatius went to authorities of any sort now, she would never see or hear from him again, such was the nature of this situation.

She asked Ignatius what his plan was now and he told her what he had planned. Sahira did have some reservations, but due to the fact that she had little else to work on, she agreed to go along with him for now.

They both walked back to Sahira's car, which she had parked at the Waffle house again. Sahira got in the driving seat and looked back to Ignatius who was standing about seven feet away.

'Are you coming or what?' she asked?

'I think I'll take my own transportation this time.'

Sahira gave a 'whatever' shrug and then Ignatius explained where they were to meet.

The traffic was very light at this time of night and Sahira arrived in the Sainsburys car park in Balham at 11.30pm. Ignatius was already there and told her to wait while he did his decreasing circuits of his flat to locate the surveillance team.

Sahira was just starting to wonder what was taking him so long, then, five minutes later Ignatius climbed into the passenger seat of her car, looking a combination of confused and pissed off.

'What's wrong?' Sahira asked.

'What's going on? Why is there no surveillance team there?'

Sahira's head raised up straight and looked hard at Ignatius.

'You must have missed them, they're there somewhere.'

'No, they're not Sahira, just trust me on this. If they were there, I would have seen them.'

Sahira, still feeling sceptical, got out her phone and called her office. After ten minutes of subtle questioning, she hung up and looked at Ignatius.

'The surveillance team was removed today. Apparently, the justification being that if you haven't shown up by now, you're not going to. No one seems to know where the original order came from.'

'We both know that's a load of crap, Ignatius responded. You don't take the surveillance team off this quickly in this sort of case. Something is going down tonight and they don't want anyone to see it. Let's just hope we haven't missed it already.'

Sahira was still not feeling quite as conspiracy orientated as Ignatius, but she had to agree. What he was saying was a definite possibility. Ignatius clearly wasn't in the mood to debate this anyway.

He took the lead and, with his backpack full of the equipment he needed, they went back to the offices across the road from his flat.

Ignatius gave Justin a call again to disable the alarms, then he retraced his steps from a few nights back and got up into the buildings' attics. Once he had pulled himself into the loft, he turned around to give Sahira a hand but found her pulling herself into the loft, just as easily; if not more easily than he had.

They had nothing to report for the first couple of hours but around 2.30am in the morning, Ignatius saw a Honda Africa Twin AS motorbike pull up and park just down the road from his flat. This bike was renowned for being a top on/off road bike and it piqued his interest. The rider of the bike turned the engine off but remained on the bike. A couple of minutes later, two other men walked round the corner and headed towards the first man.

The man on the bike was parked between two street lamps and was fairly well hidden in the shadows, but the other two men had to walk directly under street lamps to reach the first man. They were both wearing jeans, boots and t-shirts with jackets over them. Ignatius had done enough undercover operations in his time using motorbikes, to know the telltale signs.

The movement of the cloth of their jeans showed, to his

196

expert eyes, that they were wearing knee pads and the boots they were wearing were clearly durable bike boots. These men had also arrived on bikes, but had parked out of sight to avoid too much suspicion.

He also knew that they were equipped with shoulder holsters and concealing pistols. Ignatius had his supermarket scanner and used it to get the details from the mobiles of all three men.

As the two men walked past the bike, the other man got off his bike and followed them to the front door of Ignatius' flat. The three of them did a visual scan of the surrounding area, before they walked up the path. They were blinded from view at street level, but from Ignatius and Sahira's elevated view, they could still see the men who were highlighted from the neighbour's porch light.

Before they entered the flat, they drew their weapons. The weapon of the man at the front was blocked from view by the others, but the two behind him had their weapons clearly displayed. He identified them as a Heckler & Koch semi automatic 9mm pistol and a Jericho 941 semi automatic pistol. The Heckler & Koch pistol was often used by French special forces and the Jericho 941 was the pistol of choice within Israeli Special forces.

Ignatius realised these weren't British government officers. They were mercenaries.

One of the men stayed on vigil at the front door whilst the other two went inside. Before Sahira had time to ask Ignatius what he was thinking, he had grabbed what looked like a contact lense case from his bag and had jumped down from the loft saying,

'Wait here.'

Ignatius knew he had limited time, so he double-timed out the back of the terrace house / converted office building and ran around the back of the street, so that he could approach the parked motor bike, out of view from the man on the door of his flat.

He approached the bike, which he noticed had been adapted in a similar way to what he would do for an operation, and took out the contact lens case. He pulled out a gel circular object that Ricky had given him and was about the size of a fingertip. He peeled off a film of plastic and stuck the gelled object on the inside of the metal frame of the bike, just above the engine.

The gel encased a transmitter that would pass any radio frequency scan as it was only made live by vibration and heat combined, and as it needed both of them at the same time, it would only become live when the bike was in motion.

Ignatius was about to run back to the loft when he heard movement and even sensed it before he looked. There was a low level hedge protecting the small front garden of one of the terraced houses on the street. He launched himself over the hedge as soon as he heard movement.

Whilst in the air he sneaked a glance and caught the front of a boot just before he went out of sight behind the hedge. He rolled upon landing, partly to displace the impact but mainly to ensure the noise was at a minimum. Whilst in his roll, he drew his weapon and had it pointed at the hedge.

He did a quick scan of his surroundings and realised his exit strategies were limited, to say the least. His only realistic way of getting out of this in one piece was to pray he hadn't been seen or heard. His training had taken over though and he was in a flat firing position, ready to shoot and move if required.

The three men stopped by the hedge and there was, what seemed like a lifetime of silence. Ignatius wondered if they were positioning themselves for an attack.

The silence was then broken by one of the men speaking.

'What now then?'

Another one of the men answered in English with a hard to place accent, but based on what Ignatious had seen earlier, he guessed Israeli with a hint of American.

'Use your nav systems to go back to the camp. I'm taking alpha route, you two use different routes. Get some R&R and wait further instructions.'

Ignatius heard two sets of footsteps walking off, then after a short period, he heard the Honda fire up and disappear into the night. He exhaled loudly and within a few seconds of them leaving, made his way back to the loft via the route he had originally used to approach the bike. When he got in the loft and settled down, Sahira asked,

'What was that all about? I saw you had a close escape.'

'I've put a tracker on the bike. Thery were using US Military slang, but I'm pretty sure they're not US soldiers. The choice of weapons, their operational protocols, they don't match.'

'I don't understand what you're getting at?'

'Neither do I, but there's something else wrong. I can't put my finger on it, but something's not right.'

Sahira nodded whilst responding,

'Ok, well just sit on it and hopefully it will come. What now?'

'Now we find out what the Three Musketeers were doing in my flat.'

Before Sahira and Ignatius made their way out of the building, Ignatius took out a surveillance camera from his bag and set it up in the loft to keep a vigil on his flat. They left, making sure to leave no trace of their presence. Ignatius was the first to approach the door of his flat and tried his key.

As expected, the authorities had changed the lock, so he took out his lock pick bag and made short work of the door. He turned around, smiling proudly to Sahira. She was standing there with the new key dangling from her left hand. Ignatius turned back around in silence and went in the flat.

They spent the next half an hour searching through the flat without finding any evidence that the men had even been there, let alone that they had planted anything.

Ignatius was looking over his kitchen counter top whilst mindlessly rubbing his hand along it and thinking where he needed to search next. His hand picked up grease and dirt from the counter and he had a look at his palm to see the damage. He noticed a couple of coffee beans on his hand.

After a short period he called Sahira over.

'What is it?' she asked.

Ignatius held up a USB stick.

Once he saw the coffee beans on his hand, he had a light bulb moment. He realised that on the morning of the assassination he had run out of coffee and had to buy some from the supermarket. He hadn't had time to open the new jar of coffee and remembered wiping down the counter before he left for the supermarket.

He took the coffee jar out of the cupboard and saw that it had been opened by someone so he put his fingers through the beans and felt the plastic of the USB stick.

Ignatius was half expecting her to question the find, but she didn't and said,

'It seems someone is desperate for you to go down for this.'

'Yep, lucky me. I need to set up some surveillance in the builder's yard behind the garden'

'OK, I'll come with you.'

'Fine, but we need to be quiet, the neighbours can hear everything from outside.'

Ignatius and Sahira left using a key to the back door and Sahira locked up again as quietly as she could. The garden was nightmare-dark and at the end they could see the illuminated builder's yard inviting them in. As they approached the fence, in unison they sped up and catapaulted themselves over. In mid air, Ignatius looked to the landing site and thought, 'Shit!'

On the ground there was a team of four Chinese men. It seemed that Ignatius had missed one, the other day in his flat. Dressed all in black and clearly just getting ready to climb over the fence, the Chinese were as surprised to see Ignatius and Sahira as they were to see them.

The Chinese team were professionals though and their surprise was short-lived. Not only were they professionals, they were also good and preparing to attack.

In actual fact, they were very good, but they weren't SAS.

In mid air, Ignatius noted the positions of the Chinese and what his attack plan would be.

He couldn't take on all four at once, so he'd have to deal with what was in front of him, before helping Sahira.

As he landed he bent his knees to help with the impact, but he also used it to throw his body up and backwards whilst swinging out his right elbow. The elbow impacted partially with the neck and chin of one of the Chinese men.

He fell to the floor with his body involuntarily gasping for breath as he was severly concussed, flirting with unconsiousness. As Ignatius had thrust upwards and back he used the fence to stop him from falling over.

He had both his hands by his side ready to help stabilise his body. His hands rested against an old pile of bricks that had been stored against the fence and left over from a previous job.

Ignatius picked up a brick in each hand and faced off against the Chinese man directly in front of him. He went to throw the brick in his left hand. The Chinese man ducked whilst stepping to his right, like a Sunday walker ducking under a fence in a field.

The brick didn't hit him, and no, Ignatius didn't miss. He had never thrown it. He was feigning.

The Chinese man threw a right cross punch, a move that Ignatius had known was coming. Ignatius met the hand in mid punch with a punch of his own, but instead of knuckles clashing, the Chinese man's punch made full impact against the brick that Ignatius was holding.

His digitus medius or middle finger was pushed back and now rested halfway up the back of his hand. He screamed in pain, but knew he had to carry on fighting, even though his right hand was now useless.

Ignatius caught the movement of a left fist out of his peripheral vision. He knew it was a feint though.

The man was wearing a tight black t-shirt that accented every part of his chiselled torso, which was where Ignatius was staring. If you watched the legs or arms, by the time that you saw them coming for you, the majority of the power had already been commisioned from the body and it was so much harder to avoid.

The man hadn't engaged any of the muscles within his core to throw the punch, so Ignatius took the calculated guess that it was a diversion. If he was wrong, he knew there wouldn't be enough power to cause serious damage and he would just have to dip his forehead and wear the punch.

The punch was a feign though, and then Ignatius saw the man's lower left side of his torso tighten and knew what was coming. Ignatius threw out his left hand in a cross punch and met the Chinese man's kick, with a brick to his knee. The brick didn't make perfect contact and his knee cap stayed in place, but it stunned the man enough to wince in pain and gave Ignatius his window.

He widened out both his arms and brought the bricks crashing together like a pair of cymbals with a brick on either side of the man's jaw. He collapsed on the floor with his mouth wide open. Dribble and blood was falling from his broken jaw.

Ignatius searched for Sahira who was up against the fence with one of the Chinese men's hands wrapped around her neck.

Before Ignatius had time to rescue her, Sahira bent her knees and thrust her right arm in the air like an olympic front crawl swimmer. As she brought her arm down across her body to finish the stroke, it dislodged the mans hand from her neck, put him of balance and shifted his whole body to the right, exposing the side of his left knee.

Sahira raised her right leg and kicked down on the side of his knee, dislodging it from its joint.

She hadn't finished though and followed up quickly with her left knee into the man's face, which spread his nose across his face. The man crumbled to the floor beaten and immobile.

Ignatius scanned around for the fourth Chinese man and saw him lying unconsious on the floor. He looked at Sahira thinking, 'damn, this broad has some skills' and also thinking he wouldn't call her a 'broad' to her face.

Sahira caught Ignatius eye and said,

'That might have been more noise than we were hoping for.'

'Possibly a fraction more.'

26

They found another exit out of the builders yard that would save them going back through Ignatius' flat and via a circuitous route, headed back to Sainsbury's car park.

They both got in Sahira's BMW Nazca C2 and sat there with the internal lights switched off. Sahira broke the silence.

'Where are you going now?'

Ignatius looked across at her.

'I have no idea. The Chinese have seen me with my disguise, so they'll be able to describe what I look like when they come round. I need to keep a low profile, which won't exactly help me hunt down Bambi.'

'I wouldn't worry about the Chinese. Part of the deal was that we would do the investigation and we would share everything we have with them, so the Chinese aren't about to admit an incident in which they have their own operatives involved.

They will not share this outside themselves and I suspect they'll put a hold on any other investigating, until they see what the fall-out will be from this incident.'

Ignatius gave a half nod before saying,

'That's still too big a risk for my liking. I need to disappear for a bit and figure out what to do next.'

'Ignatius, if you run away now you will just give whoever's doing this time to set you up again. And this time they won't fail and then you'll have no way to clear your name.'

'If you've got a better idea I'd love to hear it, rather than just hear what I'm doing wrong.'

Sahira ignored the dig and said,

'I could set you up in a MI5 safe house.'

'Yeah, I'll pass thanks. Last time I was at the house of some-one attached to MI5, I had two people try to kill me.'

'I remember, I was there too. We have multiple safe houses across London and the UK. I can get you in one, where no one will know you're there apart from me.'

Ignatius knew this was true and was surprised how ready he was to accept Sahira's help.

'Fine, but don't tell anyone, and I mean anyone, otherwise I'm gone for good and your chances of ever getting Bambi also go.'

There was a silence between them before Sahira asked,

'Do you want the address and I can meet you there in ten minutes?'

'It's nearby then?'

'Just around the corner in Clapham.'

'My vehicle is in a safe place here and I can get to it easily from Clapham. Let's go in your car.'

They drove to Clapham in silence, both with multiple differ-ent thoughts racing through their minds. Ignatius also took this time to send Justin the scanner information he had from the three mercenaries.

The streets were empty and Sahira pulled up outside the front of a block of flats which was eight stories high. Sahira let them in via a key swab and they took the lift to the eighth floor. They got out of the lift and the flat was the last one on the left.

Sahira let them in and Ignatius was amazed to see how fully furnished it was and the detail behind the furnishings. There were pictures on the wall, half-full bottles of wine and olive oils and vinegars on the kitchen counter. He half-seriously asked.

'Are you sure we've got the right place?'

Sahira understood the question.

'The place legally belongs to a Katie Watkins. She is thirty-six, single, has parents living in Florida and is a microbiologist who works for a government funded, medical research laboratory. She is officially currently working at a medical research lab in Manchester on a two-year secondment.'

Ignatius looked around the flat and saw a blanket over the sofa with a periodic table printed on it, a doctorate certificate on the wall and other subtle science related pieces.

'And who is Katie Watkins really?' he asked.

'She doesn't exist. Well not any more. She is a poor girl who died thirty-one years ago of pneumonia when she was five years old. We brought her back to life legally for the sake of a cover.'

When Ignatius worked at Six, this wasn't the type of work he would be involved with, but he knew the safe houses were under multiple guises.

He went around and checked out the rest of the flat. It had windows with a street view of the only entrance to the building, and just outside the front door on the left was a large window that opened up onto a fire escape that took you down to the side of the building. He was relieved to know that he had somewhere comfortable to stay for now.

Sahira showed him where things were that he needed to know. She said she'd pick up some food and essentials for him and come back in the morning, or just a few hours' time as it was. As she was leaving, she asked him.

'Why mantress?'

'What?'

'We spoke to some of your old army mates and they said you were known as mantress.'

'Oh, right. I was only known as mantress for a very short time. I had another nickname for most of the time I served.'

'Oh yeah? What was that?' Sahira asked.

'Foot Long.'

Sahira walked out the door without saying anything and shaking her head in despair at him.

Ignatius thought he was funny, but clearly army humour didn't spread far beyond the barracks. This obviously hadn't been his nickname but had always got a smile when he claimed it jokingly to other army members. He might need to adapt his jokes outside of army personel. He still sat back on the sofa with a smile on his face.

27

Sahira had only managed to steal a couple of hours' sleep before she woke again. There was a momentary wave of exhaustion from the last week and all it had entailed. This exhaustion, rather than overwhelm her, inspired her and she got out of bed with determination spiralling through her DNA.

She spent the next ten minutes doing several yoga moves that she made sure engaged every part of her body.

It was already an uncharacteristically warm day for May in the UK and Sahira had as cold a shower as her body would allow. It was so much more energising than she had expected and, despite what was bordering on torterous sleep deprivation, she was ready for whatever the day had in store for her.

She decided to take her Range Rover this morning and was now sitting in London traffic on her way to Clapham, after stopping at a mini supermarket to buy food and toiletries for Ignatius. She didn't know his culinary preferences, but based on what she knew of him, she guessed meat, and the shopping bags had plenty of it in them.

Sahira entered the flat to find a barrell of a Sig Sauer P226 in her face. It was quickly lowered as Ignatius said,

'Oh, it's you.'

'Yeah, good morning to you too. I've brought you some food and other bits.'

'Thanks.'

Ignatius had moved to the couch and was playing with a

Rubik's cube that had been resting on one of its corners in a plastic black holder.

'So what's your plan for the day?' Sahira asked. 'Although I don't think there will be any fallout from the Chinese incident, it might be worth lying low for the day.'

Sahira stopped talking and looked at Ignatius who was playing with the Rubik's cube and clearly not listening to a word she said.

'You ok there, Ignatius?'

'Yeah, fine. What sort of an adult has one of these?', Ignatius waved the cube in Sahira's face. 'It's a kid's toy. Any clown can solve it.'

Sahira kept quiet as she watched Ignatius for the next couple of minutes become increasingly frustrated as he tried unsuccessfully to solve the Rubik's cube. Eventually, she snatched it off him and said,

'Can you please focus on the whole, people trying to kill you thing, set you up for an assassination etc etc.'

'Yeah, yeah. I can't really do anything until I get the results back from Justin with the phone data from those guys. I will keep an eye on the tracker to see if they go anywhere special.'

'Ok, I've got to go to work. Unless anything comes up urgently, I will pop back tomorrow morning and check in. Oh, and remember, don't go anywhere. Clown!'

As she said this, she was walking out the door and threw the solved Rubik's cube at him.

28

It took Sahira painfully long to drive from Clapham to her office in Millbank and she was in desperate need of a herbal tea and some cereal. By the time Sahira had finished her breakfast she didn't have long until her meeting with the British Intelliegence avengers.

She didn't need to prepare any documentation for the meeting, as everything she needed to share was in her head.

There were a collection of hard chairs arranged in a broad circle in Sayer's office. Evidently, this meeting wasn't meant to be conducted in comfort. It wasn't long until the group was assembled in the chairs and Sayer informally began the meeting.

Sahira briefed the group regarding the last few days, including Bambi's involvement, her meetings with Ignatius, the incident with Simmonds and Peters, The Chinese and the mercenaries.

Sayer had known about this from a previous meeting and a phone call this morning, but the others were hearing about it all for the first time. After Sahira had finished, Maguire jumped straight in, looking incredulous.

'Are you kidding me, we have Winter? Why the hell isn't he in custody? Why didn't we arrange to have him detained the second we knew about the first meeting?'

The question wasn't rhetorical. He was defintitely requiring an answer, which came from Wyatt.

'Winter worked for me for a while. I know him well. He's like a rat. No one wants him around, but he sure as hell knows how to survive. He would have known if we'd been surveilling the meet. She made the right call.'

Maguire accepted this information without argument, even though he didn't look at all appeased.

It seemed that Wyatt was the one person who had the ear of Maguire. 'Good to know', Sahira thought.

Forrester involved himself.

'Where's the safe house he's in now?'

'He's asked me not to say', Sahira said

Forrester looked a bit taken aback but let it go.

'He's certainly not shy. Fine. I'll give you a bit of rope here, but only because Matt has vouched for you so much. I still haven't seen any concrete evidence that he's innocent here. If I don't soon, we're bringing him in.'

'Yes, sir', Sahira said. Then she asked, 'What do you want me to do about the Chinese situation?'

Sayer responded. 'Nothing. We'd have done exactly the same if the situation was reversed. We just pretend it never happened.'

The rest of the group nodded their agreement.

Sahira was amazed that the involvement of Bambi hadn't been the top priority here and thought the meeting was over, but Maguire hadn't finished yet.

'Miss Basha, you have been given a lot of freedom here. A lot more than I would have allowed you, or the PM for that matter.'

He looked at Forrester as he said this, but got no reaction to his look. 'What are your next moves?'

'Find Bambi, sir.'

'Why we are wasting our time chasing a ghost, rather than bringing in the prime suspect whose whereabouts we know, is beyond me. Either way, make sure we have real results and soon, or we'll find someone who can get actual results.'

'Yes, sir.'

Now the meeting was defintely over and Sahira excused herself while the rest remained behind. She walked back to her desk, stopping for a quick catch up with a friend of hers from HR who was also a big Chelsea fan.

She reflected that the meeting hadn't exactly gone well, and her main issue moving forward, was that she didn't yet know where she was going to get the results that Maguire was shouting out for. She had just sat down at her desk and logged in to her computer when her phone rang.

'Sahira speaking.'

'Can you come back here, please?'

'Yes, sir.'

Sahira took a minute to catch her breath and then walked back to Sayer's office, fully expecting to have her arse handed to her. When she walked back into Sayer's office, she was surprised to see it was only Forrester and Sayer in the office. She remained standing and said, 'Yes, sir?'

Sayer smiled at her formality and wondered if he should mess with her a bit, but thought he'd save it for another time as she did seem genuinely worried.

'Relax, Sahira. Grab a seat. Tom and I just wanted a discreet chat with you.'

Forrester sat down opposite Sahira. He had taken off his tie and unbuttoned the top two buttons of his shirt, and Sahira could just make out the top of Homer Simpson's head. Sahira hadn't before noticed quite how handsome he was and with the smile he now had on his face, it helped to accentuate this point.

'Sahira, we just wanted to let you know that you're doing a fantastic job. We wouldn't be anywhere near where we are now, without you.'

'Thank you, sir.'

'I can't help but feel though, that we are hindering your investigation. It might be best from now on, if you just report to Matt and myself and I'll deal with the information share elsewhere. We need to find out exactly what happened here, wherever the leads may take us, and I don't want anything getting in your way with that.'

'Yes, sir. Thank you.' Sahira's formal response hid the relief she was feeling internally. She was able to read between the lines enough to understand that he was telling her to carry on with the investigation and not worry about Maguire's attempts to disrupt or whatever the hell it was, he was doing. She also realised that Forrester would never say this to her directly, so she wasn't going to push the point.

They spoke briefly for a few more minutes before Sahira was once again dismissed. As she was walking back to her desk, she received a call from an unknown number.

'Hello?'

'Sahira, when you finish work, I need you to come over.'

'What's going on?'

The words went unanswered though as Ignatius had hung up straight after he finished talking.

Tank was cruising along the A24 on the outskirts of Horsham. He was driving a modified Jaguar XJ that was similar in appearance to the model the British PM was using.

It had the extra seating as he needed it for five passengers. He had liberated the vehicle from an MI5 carpool.

He shortly pulled up outside a farmhouse in Mannings Heath and knocked on the door. John Harrington answered and Tank showed him a fake security service ID.

John and Sarah Harrington didn't know what to look for in an MI5 ID, so they wouldn't know a fake one from a real one to start with. But even if they did, the fake ID that Tank was using was indistinguishable from the real thing, courtesy of Ricky.

Tank told them they needed to pack bare essential belongings and be ready to leave their house within fifteen minutes.

Their natural hesitation was dealt with by Tank in a calm but urgent manner and the Harrington family, with Tank, were on the road within twenty-five minutes. No one ever managed to get it done within fifteen minutes.

Tank drove them to a multi-storey car park on the outskirts of Gatwick Airport and switched the family into a white panel van with comfortable seating installed in the back. From there, he drove around the M25, joined the M1 and began his journey up to Yorkshire, where Tank would be keeping them in a non-discript, terraced house.

Sahira had stayed in the office until 7.30pm as otherwise she would have spent most of the time sitting in London's evening traffic. She drove to the safe house in Clapham and knocked on the door this time. She didn't really fancy being on the end of a gun being held by a former SAS soldier again. When Ignatius opened the door, she held up a bag of Chinese takeaway, and for the first time she was sure she saw a genuine smile on Ignatius face.

They sat down to start eating the Chinese whilst Ignatius began telling her about the two pieces of information he'd received today from Justin, which he had earlier, rather rudely, let Sahira know he needed to discuss with her.

'Ok, Justin intercepted the messages from the phones of the three guys outside my flat. They weren't great. The main guy had a message from Bambi, which Justin knew from the coding used to encrypt the message. He had directed them to kill the Harrington family in Mannings Heath. They apparently are a loose end that needs tying up. He was a gentleman though, and directed the team to make sure it was a quick and painless death, and one that they wouldn't know was coming.'

Using an empathy that Sahira wasn't aware he possessed he said, 'Sahira, I'm sick of this prick.'

'What? Are you serious? We need to get protection for them now. Why the hell didn't you tell me about this as soon as you found out?'

Ignatius held up both hands in a gesture of keeping the peace.

'Don't worry. The family is safe. We have moved them to a safe place. We actually borrowed one of your cars for it, and no one knows where they are.'

'So you kidnapped them and stole a MOD vehicle?'

Ignatius raised his voice, which gradually lowered during his response.

'We didn't kidnap them, we saved their lives. The team is going down tomorrow to kill them. The family won't be there, but I will be, so I can have a little chat with them then.'

'Ignatius, where is the family?'

Ignatius looked at Sahira accusingly.

'They're safe. I don't even know where they are. That way, if I was to be forcibly questioned, I wouldn't be able to give up their location, even if I wanted to. Why are you so desperate to know?'

'We need to make sure that they are completely safe. Forgive me if I'm not ready to put the lives of innocent people in the hands of a fugitive.'

Ignatius ignored the dig.

'There is someone inside the government who is involved in this. There is no way I would tell a government employee where they are, even if I did know. They are safest this way.'

Sahira's anger cooled a bit. He had a very good point.

'Ok, fine, but we need to stop these guys from doing any harm to anyone.'

'On it.'

Sahira wasn't happy about this, she felt that more and more areas of the situation were spiralling out of her control.

'What was the second bit of information that you wanted

to tell me about?' she asked.

'You know the other night when we were surveilling my flat and I planted the tracker on the bike?'

'Yep.'

'Well, there was something that was bothering me and I couldn't put my finger on it. I know now what that was. The sat nav system on the bike is only used on UK black ops and not outside of that.'

'Ok. How do you know that this was one of those devices?' Sahira asked.

'Because I've got exactly the same one on my bike, and there are distinctive parts to the exterior of the device which means it is unmistakeable.'

Sahira took on board this information.

'Ok, what makes this device so special, compared to other sat nav systems?'

'How much detail do you want?' Ignatius asked

'Whatever you know. I want to know.'

'Ok. I'm not the greatest technical person, but I will describe it as best as I possibly can. The device has a super computer on it, that mines data from hundreds of different sites. It accesses all military satellites and all the usual traffic ones, as well as the likes of Google Earth and any private company that has surveillance in the sky. It uses these to analyse every inch of ground in real time, not just roadways or paths, but also parks, farmed fields, wooded areas, or open moorland. In the wooded areas for example it knows the density of the trees and fooliage. In the fields, it knows exactly what is being grown. It then makes use of all the information from local councils, woodland trusts, wildlife trusts, national parks et cetera. Every time a tree is cut down or a footpath resurfaced or a residential property has an extension, these are logged on a database somewhere and the computer acesses it. It will then communicate with the meteorlogical office, and use the information of recent rainfall and other weather that affects the condition of the ground in any given place. Finally, it will access any geological database to know the make-up of the ground in any spot, whether you're on tarmac, soil, or sandstone, and what the condition of that ground will be; taking into account recent weather conditions, any works carried out, and fill in the blanks.

With all this information to hand you put in the make, model, length, width, weight and engine size of the vehicle you're using. In absolute real time, it analyses your route and tells you the best one to follow; even giving you routes that people don't generally know exist.

So if you were driving along a road and needed to get to the next road across but there was no through way, only fields or a wood in between - it would use all the data it has access to and give you an option of a route through the field or woods, assuming there is an option of course. It will take into account the date, day and time and what the expected foot or vehicle traffic would be, or even wildlife or farm animals, on top of all the other information.

Given your speed, the suspension on the vehicle you're driving or riding, and all other relevant details, it will give you a probability of success. So say it gave me an option of a route directly through a field with a churned up surface and bogs and puddles due to rainfall. If I was going at one hundred miles per hour, it would no doubt show my chance of success to be near zero percent. As I decrease speed, the probablity of success will increase, and it calculates and informs me on the screen instantaneously. So to sum it up, it's pretty pimp.'

Sahira looked impressed and astounded at the same time.

'Did you just say, it's pretty pimp?'

'Yeah, so what?'

'You're thirty-nine and you're not a gangster rapper, just please don't say things like that. I'm embarrassed for you. Ignoring that though, it sounds an incredible bit of kit. However, couldn't someone else have made something very similar to the one you've got, and not be issued from the UK government?'

Ignatius was too involved in what was currently going on to care about Sahira's admonishing of him, so just answered dealing with the facts.

'No, I don't think so. Sure for their own countries but a non UK organisation, be it government or otherwise, wouldn't be able to have such full access to so many UK Government sites and satallites. It's just not feasible.'

Sahira covered both her eyes with the tip of her middle fingers and answered mid gesture.

'Yeah, I know. I know, you're right. I really keep hoping that it's just a big mistake or something and there isn't someone within our own government involved. But we both know that isn't the case.'

'Yeah, we do, so on that note, I need you to keep this from your people. They can't be looking for the Harringtons and can't know what I'm up to.'

'Fine, but I can only do that for a very short time. I need you to get these people to open up tomorrow.'

Ignatius nodded but didn't say anything, so Sahira continued,

'Right, I need to get home and get some sleep. I will come by tomorrow night after work. Is there anything you want me to bring you?'

'It's going to be a long day tomorrow. I'd love it if you could bring me a big bucket of fried chicken when you pop over?'

'Sure thing', Sahira said while smiling.

Sahira picked up her bag and headed for the door.

'Are you not even going to wish me luck for tomorrow?' Ignatius shouted. I'm up against three highly trained professionals. There's a good chance, I'll get my arse kicked.'

'I certainly hope so.' Sahira replied as she walked out the door

31

Ignatius was awake, showered and ready to leave by 5.00am. He had spent the previous evening speaking to Ricky and going through operational tactics. He also asked for his help with a few bits of equipment he would need.

Ricky was a bit flustered by the requests and had told Ignatius to give him more notice next time, but he'd make it happen. Tank had also called and pleaded with Ignatius to let him come down and help. Ignatius wasn't sure if it was an act of friendship or if Tank was just missing the old days. Ignatius would have loved the help of Tank. He was a war machine and as far as Ignatius was concerned he was at war, but he declined the request.

He was pretty sure his life was screwed. He had no intention of making the same happen to someone else. But more importantly, he needed Tank to keep an eye on the Harringtons. It would take very good men indeed to get through Tank and onto the Harringtons, who definitely didn't deserve anything untoward to happen.

Through the messages that Justin was monitoring, Ignatius knew that the mercenaries weren't planning on being down in Sussex until this evening. So he had a short time at least to reconnoitre the battle ground. He was down in Mannings Heath by 6.20am and began a meticulous recon of his surroundings.

After a few hours riding around on his bike, his plan was beginning to finalise. What he did realise is that the farm and surrounding areas were a lot busier than he was expecting, because of public footpaths, a nearby school and the nature of the village intimacy. He would need to adapt his plan slightly, now that he had a good knowledge of the battle ground.

He couldn't engage on the farm, due to the risk to others. That was ok, though. He couldn't remember an operation, where given the opportunity, the immediate action plan, didn't take on some level of adaptation.

Ignatius called Ricky and asked for a few more bits of equipment. They were easily accesible to Ricky, and any work required on them was minimal with the resources he had available. Ricky was intrigued but confirmed he'd do as requested and then head down as soon as he'd finished making some tweaks to the equipment.

Ricky spent a couple of hours working on what Ignatius had asked for, and loaded up his van with the new equipment, on top of what he'd already sourced for Ignatius. He added a rectangular piece of steel, which was 2.3metres long, 15cm wide and 2.5cm thick, a chainsaw, some matte black paint and the cat flap from his workshop.

Ricky was down in West Sussex for 11.30am and met Ignatius at a local village pub for a sausages and mash early lunch, and to discuss what was needed from Ricky.

After lunch, Ignatius and Ricky set to work and they were finished with the preperations by 3.00pm. On Ignatius's insistence, Ricky left and headed home to Justin who was adding his support in another way.

At any one time, the MOD has surveillance drones in an automated circular holding pattern ready to be located to any given position, should they be required for assistance due to an act of terrorism or other scenarios that require air surveillance and support.

Justin was fully aware of the protocols of these drones. He knew which ones were likely for immediate reaction, based on current threats, and which threats had the most credibility. Therefore he also knew which drones were less likely to be commandeered and called to action.

Since they were in an automated holding pattern, they weren't being monitored with any level of vigour. Justin had singled out the drone within the relevant proximity that was least likely to be missed, and had taken control of it to use as air support for Ignatius when needed.

Ignatius was in one of the barns on the farm which had the required viewpoints he needed. The mercenaries showed themselves shortly after 5.00pm. One was still on his motorbike while two of them had parked up and were on foot. walking route reconnaisance.

They were still wearing pads below their jeans, but clearly weren't wearing kevlar vests. Ignatius assumed it was due to the fact that they would be conspicuous wearing bulky clothing on a warm day, and they clearly weren't planning on a fire fight.

Using a parabolic microphone, Ignatius was listening in to what conversations he could. He was mainly focusing on the one who had parked his motorbike nearest Ignatius' flat as he was clearly the officer in charge or OIC, using miltary terms when he reported to Justin via a two-way field operations radio.

Ignatius was disappointed to see the close proximity of the route recconaissance that the mercenaries were using, as well as the amount of civilian presence round the farmhouse. He realised he'd need to adapt his plan to draw them in to the actions he wanted them to follow.

He had a look around the barn and saw a wealth of farm engine titbits; some fence posting, a large wooden mallet that was clearly used to hammer in fence posts and some old discarded hubcaps.

Justin was giving him real-time updates on the positions of the three men via the drone he had borrowed. Ignatius had removed his mask as he wanted to be recognised by them, to ensure he got their attention. He then repositioned one of the hubcaps and picked up the large wooden mallet which had a head of close to a foot squared.

When he heard the required position of one of the men, who he refered to as man two, he walked out of the barn and showed himself clearly without his facial mask. The man was clearly shocked to see him and got on his field radio immediately, before drawing his weapon and giving chase. Ignatius had ducked back into the barn before Man Two had time to shoot, but the mercenary was already sprinting after him.

Ignatius was using the reflection of the repositioned hubcap to trace Man Two's route and distance. Using reflection to gauge distance is difficult at best, but Ignatius who had twenty years of experience doing this, was skilled at making accurate judgements. As the man was approaching the narrow barn door, Ignatius swung the mallet feeling just like a man hitting a gong on a gameshow.

His timing was as good as he could have hoped. The large, heavy wooden mallet connected with Man Two's face at full-force, using the forward momentum of the running man and the counter momentum of the mallet's swing.

The impact, which he would later describe as sounding like

a cannon ball hitting a floor of wet concrete, decimated the maxilla, the zygomatic and nasal bones within the face. Shards of these bones entered the brain killing the man instantly, who was now lying motionless on his back, on the floor.

Ignatius obviously couldn't see that these bones had shattered and killed him, but he knew enough about anatomy to know the man was dead. A man's face shouldn't look like bubble wrap that has just been popped.

Ignatius jumped on his bike and fired up the engine. Justin had confirmed to him that Man One and Man Three were now both on their bikes and heading in his direction. He went out the main door of the barn and waited until the two bikes united on the same path as him, albeit from differing routes, and he accelerated off with his bike's 1198 cc engine and 158 bhp.

Ignatius took the route less travelled and rode into a nearby wood on a path often used by mountain bike enthusiasts.

The constant changing gradient and rugged surface of the ground meant that the men who were following him couldn't afford to take one hand off their bikes and shoot at him. On his advanced sat nav screen he could see the location of Man One's bike via the tracker he had placed on it the other day. For detail however, he had to rely on radio comms updates from Justin, and on his wing mirrors for the location of Man Three.

Man Three was chasing Ignatius, pushing his Honda Africa Twin AS motorbike to the limits to catch him, but wasn't making much progress. Then he noticed Ignatius made a mistake. There was a sharp left turn coming up and Ignatius was going too fast and narrow into the turn. He had to break hard to make the corner and nearly came to a stop as he forced his bike around the corner, whilst almost brushing the outside of his right leg against a tree.

Man Three had to make sure he would approach at a wider angle and take the corner at speed, allowing him to make up the distance between them.

Ignatius had decelerated significantly on the last corner, and now ignited the bike's power to get as far away as possible from that spot, but just a matter of seconds later he heard an explosion.

Earlier in the day, Ricky had placed the cat flap on the tree that Ignatius's leg had almost brushed, then he sewed a chip into the outside of the right leg of the trousers that Ignatius was wearing. As Ignatius' leg had come within close proximity of the cat flap, the chip had released the magnetic lock of the cat flap. This time, rather than letting a cat enter a house, Ricky had adjusted the mechanisms, so that the opening of the lock released a laser beam across a path, two metres before the cat flap.

As the front wheel of Man Three's bike broke the beam of the laser, it set off a shaped charge of an explosive that Ignatius had made earlier with equipment Ricky had given him.

A shaped charge causes an explosion to expel in a controlled direction. This particular shaped charge was on the ground by the cat flap tree and exploded at a forty-five degree angle towards the approaching Man Three. The shockwave of the explosion meant that Man Three was effectively riding into a fast approaching brick wall at incredible speed and was unfailingly fatal.

Ignatius, being a man of detail had also added ball bearings and metal offcuts to the explosive material, causing Man Three to become a human collander.

Ignatius could see the path and progress of Man One - the OIC of the group -on his sat nav system and pushed his bike hard to make sure he stayed well ahead. He approached a steep gradient in the path and opened the throttle to ride up it. As he neared the top, he swung the back tyre of his bike around so as to stop and look down the hill into a wooded area of the path.

He saw Man One approaching at speed through the woods beside the path. Suddenly, Man One's bike shot from under him and he was suspended in mid-air, still in a riding motorbike pose. It looked like a scene from a cartoon, when a character is suspended in mid-air after running off the edge of a cliff, staying stationary before they eventually fall.

Both Man One's arms - halfway down the biceps - fell onto the ground and blood spurted from the stubs of the arms left below his shoulders. Then the top third of his body folded back, like a pencil being snapped, and both parts of his body also fell to the ground.

Earlier in the day, Ignatius had ridden this route as part of his recconaissance. His sat nav system had given an option for a more direct route through the wooded area, rather than the circuitous route of the path.

He realised that one of the bikes would likely try and take this route in a effort to cut him off. He had instructed Ricky to sharpen one of the side lengths of the steel rectangle to a razor edge; one a butcher would be proud of.

They had then used the chainsaw to cut slits into two trees either side of the sat nav path and placed the steel sheet into the slits, so it was wedged in place. They had painted the steel matte black to ensure no reflection or glint from light and give its presence away.

Man One had driven into the razor steel at close to forty-five mph and it had cut through skin, bone and organs as easily as a wire would cut through cheese.

Ignatius turned his bike back into the forward position and rode back towards a main road before beginning the journey to his safe house in Calpham.

32

Ignatius made good time and was back in the flat by 7.30pm. The adrenaline of today's events and an early wake up meant he was feeling hungry and lethargic. He had his mask off so was careful not to show his face until he was alone inside his flat. He sunk into the sofa and put on the TV, dozing lightly, catching short periods of sleep, dreaming of the fried chicken that Sahira was bringing him after she finished work.

It was near 11.00pm when he heard the front door erupt open. Instinctively, he rolled behind the sofa and drew his Sig Sauer. He saw it was Sahira and holstered his weapon before she saw. She looked pissed off but so was he.

He couldn't see any bucket of chicken with her.

Ignatius stood up and nodded 'hi' to her when they made eye contact. She didn't reciprocate but unleashed.

'What the hell is wrong with you?'

'Uh, hello to you too. What's your problem?'

'What's my problem? Are you kidding? You caved one man's face in, you blew up another man and you cut a third man in half.'

'You told me to get them to open up.'

Sahira hadn't thought she could be more outraged, but Ignatius, somehow, just managed to make it happen.

'You're a psychopath. This is a mistake. I should have just taken you in when I first met you.'

There was a silent pause while Sahira gave Ignatius an 'explain yourself stare'. He didn't respond so she said,

'Have you got anything to say at all?'

'Did you get my chicken?'

Sahira stormed into the bedroom making no reply. Ignatius could see the fire in her eyes and thought, 'with her skills and the mood she's in, she might even give the rumble in the jungle, Muhammed Ali, a good fight right now'.

Ignatius sat down feeling a bit pissed off. He didn't appreciate her anger, but did still know he needed her help to get through this, and could on some level understand her rage. He gave it another ten minutes to allow some time for the anger to recede. He walked in the bedroom and sat on the bed next to her.

'They were there to murder children. I wasn't willing to let that go unpunished.'

Sahira was clearly still angry but was calm in her response.

'We could have arranged to bring them in and interrogate them.'

'It would have been pointless. I know what they know. They were hired by Bambi, but have no information outside of that, they're just paid help. This doesn't resolve itself until we get Bambi. I needed to send him a message to draw him out of his hole.'

Sahira turned her face to look at him for the first time since he'd sat down and said,

'You went too far. You can't just go around and leave scenes behind from a horror movie. No one knows it was you yet, but they'll figure it out soon. This doesn't help you.'

Ignatius went to console Sahira with an arm around her. She stood up and said,

'Are you kidding me? You're actually hitting on me again. Is this your first day as a human?'

Ignatius looked wounded and replied.

'No, I'm not. I saw three men who were willing to kill a family, including three kids and I stopped it. I appreciate this puts you in a difficult position, but I did what I needed to do to protect that family.'

Sahira felt guilty now and her face showed it.

'I'm sorry Ignatius, I appreciate you were saving a family and I realise you're involved in this unfairly, and through no fault of your own.'

Ignatius looked at her, still a bit wounded. He had genuinely meant what he said and his priority was to protect the Harringtons.

'Don't worry about it. The whole situation is messed up,' he said.

Despite the fact that his intentions were to protect the innocent, he didn't want to push his luck too far.

He had after all, been trying to hit on her.

33

Bambi had just left the Diamond Gym on Pedra Azul Street in Sao Paulo. He had needed to clear his mind, and a ten kms run on the treadmill followed by a pilates class had gone a way to help him gain the mindfulness level of serenity that he was used to.

He had been planning to go to the Burle Marx Park to lay some flowers by a tree for his dear mother. She had never been to the Burle Marx Park but Bambi remembered her at her happiest, while sitting and watching him run in any park. Her laughing with pleassure while he unsuccessfully chased the wildlife around, he felt, would be a fitting tribute to her memory.

The message on his untraceable phone had changed his plans though, and had eradicated his serenity. He sat in his rented Chevrolet Onyx, which was the most popular car in Brazil and therefore the most inconspicuous, and dialled a number he had hoped he would never need to dial again.

Jerry picked up on the first ring and said,

'Your plan didn't work. Your boys are dead and Winter is still very much alive and putting together more and more pieces.'

Bambi responded peacefully though he wasn't calm.

'I wondered why I hadn't heard from them. I assume Winter is responsible?'

'It certainly looks that way, but he's not working alone. He's getting help.'

Bambi took a pause to try and capture his inner zen before responding.

'You told me there wouldn't be a problem after I killed the Chinese Minister, but this is becoming a major problem for me. My price has just gone up by another two million.'

'It's not that simple. This all still goes away if Winter disappears.'

'Two million, or I walk.'

Jerry was beginning to regret using Bambi, but he was too involved now.

'What do I get for an extra two mllion?' he asked

'I come and take care of this myself and it all goes away.'

'Ok fine, but make it happen quickly. The longer this goes on, the harder it's going to be to pin everything on Winter.'

Bambi was getting sick of Jerry telling him things he already knew, but retained his calm and said,

'Tell me about the help he is getting?'

Jerry and Bambi continued talking for the next few minutes and then Bambi drove back to his temporary residence and collected necessary belongings. He made a call to his long standing contact in London to source the equipment he would need, and then headed for the airport. He caught the 4.05pm flight from Sao Paulo and arrived at Heathrow airport in London at 7.00am.

He hired a car under an alias that he had never used before and drove to Aldgate where he met his contact and picked up all the equipment he required. He then drove to the hotel he was intending to stay in for a few days, under the guise of a successful business man.

He pulled up to the Mandarin Oriental, where a valet parked

his car for him. He checked-in and headed to the three-bed-room penthouse, costing a cool twenty-seven hundred pounds per night.

34

B ambi had been staking out the residence for over twenty-four hours now. He had let himself into the property last night and had done a full search. His target's movements weren't set by a clear routine but there were enough re-occurrences for him to pick a window that would work.

He still had two hours until this window of opportunity opened and hated to operate on an empty stomach, so he went into an upscale café and ordered eggs benedict, orange juice and a pot of black coffee. This was an indulgence for him, but since this was a part of his last operation, he had decided to operate with a bit of class and make sure he savoured every moment of these next few days. He knew that in two hours' time he was going to look forward to what he was about to do.

Bambi ate slowly while reading a paper. He made a point of not reading anything about the current situation that was unfolding as a result of his assassination of Xu Hua. The breakfast was one of the best he could ever remember. In the unlikely event he was ever back in the UK again, he would make sure that he came back to this place for breakfast. He sat and slowly finished the rest of his coffee, inhaling the strong aroma. The ingestion of caffeine made him feel awake, alert and ready for the day.

Following on from a week of good climate, the weather had reverted to the UK type, and there was a light drizzle throughout London. Bambi didn't mind this at all. In actual fact, he found the rain refreshing. He stood up and left enough cash to cover breakfast along with a generous tip. On his way out, he noticed a plastic box full with the cafe's business cards. He took one as he had decided that he would make a point of visiting this place again, at least once more. He couldn't remember the last time he had felt this happy and he thought the eggs were a key factor in that.

He slowly made his way back to his surveillance point and only kept a half-hearted eye on his target. He knew what was about to happen and how it would unfold. As always, he had done his due diligence. Finally, the time was right and he had already decided the direct approach was going to be the most effective.

He walked up to the front door and allowed himself a brief smile and then knocked loudly four times. It took an annoyingly long time for the door to be answered, but eventually it was and the occupant looked at him in surprise before asking.

'Who are you?'

Bambi was standing with the chin close to his chest. He raised his head, smiled and said,

'Hello Justin.'

35

Justin knew instinctively he was in a lot of trouble. He wasn't a field operative, so didn't impulsively react to this situation but knew enough to try and buy some time.

'Um, Justin isn't in at the moment I'm afraid. I'm a neighbour looking after the cats for them, whilst they are out.'

Bambi smirked at Justin.

'I can't blame you for trying. I know it's you Justin. I know what you look like. Also, you gave far too much detail in your answer, to questions I didn't ask.'

Justin turned around and ran back into the house. Bambi chased him and was hot on his heels. They ran into the kitchen with Justin just far enough ahead to get to the other side of the kitchen island, so they were opposite one another.

'Running will just make this harder, Justin,' Bambi spoke.

Justin suddenly pulled out a M-26 taser gun that had been strapped to the underside of the overhang from the island. He aimed it at Bambi and pulled the trigger.

The taser didn't fire although Justin kept pulling the trigger more and more desperately, but it never fired. Bambi held up the battery and said to Justin,

'You need this for it to work.'

As Justin's body deflated, Bambi took this opportunity to pounce and ran around the island. He was on top of him before Justin had time to react.

Justin was standing on a chair in his sitting room with a

noose around his neck and the end tied to the ceiling rafters. His whole body was shaking and he had tears streaming down his face whilst he begged for mercy.

Bambi was slowly circling his prey. 'It's nothing personal, but you've become a bit of a nuisance, so you've left me with little options.'

Justin couldn't talk between his sobs, and Bambi slowly started teasingly rocking the chair back and forward with his foot. Eventually he pushed the chair over and watched as the life drained from Justin's body.

Four phones vibrated simultaneously and it interrupted the evenings of all four men.

Director General of MI5, Matt Sayer, was at Soho House private club in London on a wreath-making evening with his wife. It was a bit early in the year, but it would be something they could hang on their front door at Christmas time.

Director General of MI6, Tim Wyatt, was at an interview in Weybridge to try and be accepted as a member of an exclusive golf club. The course wouldn't help his approach play, but he figured he'd rather be shit on a good course.

Home Secretary, Tom Forrester, was at an evening art class and working on what he considered his best piece of work yet, although he was happy to concede that he was far from a top-level artist.

Foreign Secretary, John Maguire, was at home with friends from University playing a lot of bad hands of poker. His friends kept using his favourite film to mock him and shout at him 'show me the money'.

The news they all received on their phones troubled each

of them for different reasons. They all made their excuses and headed to the Home Office at number 2, Marsham Street.

Forrester was the nearest and first to arrive and waited for the others. The rest arrived soon after and the meeting was conducted without any level of formal structure, as it wasn't necessary for this group.

Maguire jumped straight in.

'As sad as this news is for everyone, I don't see the urgency in conducting a meeting based on the death of an ex GCHQ member?'

'Justin Wilson was far more than ex staff,' Forrester responded.

Maguire caught his breath and said,

'Sorry, Tom. I didn't mean to undermine his death. We will obviously offer any support we can to his family, but we don't usually get called to an urgent meeting for the death of every ex intelligence service officer who has passed; especially when it is suicide.'

'I guess you got the call from the police as well,' Forrester said. Maguire nodded whilst Forrester continued. 'We don't believe that it was suicide. We think he was murdered.'

Maguire hid his unease well.

'What's your basis for that, Tom?'

'We think he was helping Winter with his search for Bambi.'

'It wasn't a big secret that he and Winter were close, Tom. We all knew that and knew he was likely helping him, but why do we think that he was murdered? Surely if it was a murder, his boyfriend would also be dead?'

'Husband,' Sayer said

'What?' Maguire asked

'He is married to Ricky Wilson. He is his husband, to answer

your question. We believe that Justin was the one who identified Bambi's involvement in this and he could help Winter in
technical support in a way no one else can, so without Justin,
Winter's task is a lot harder.'

Maguire slammed his fist on the table. 'What task?' he
shouted. 'I didn't realise we'd given him a task and I still haven't
seen any definite proof that Winter isn't behind all this? Do
you know something I don't? We need to bring Winter in now
and put an end to all of this.'

Forrester picked up the reigns.

'John, I don't think we could bring Winter in, even if we
wanted. For now, we have to keep an eye on what's developing
and make sure we control the information.' He turned to Wyatt
and Sayer. 'Tim, Matt, let's see if we can figure out what Justin
Wilson knew and why someone would want him dead. John
and I have to update the PM in the morning at 7.00am, so
we'll all meet here at 6.00am and bring Sahira also.'

Wyatt looked at the group and said,

'Are we done? Matt and I have work to get on with.'

Forrester looked at Maguire, who was too deep in his own
thoughts to comment, so he gave a dismissing nod to Wyatt
and Sayer, who left without further words.

Sahira had been out of bed since 4.00am. She had gone to
the gym, but hadn't fancied a rigurous workout this morning.
She spent twenty minutes stretching, then sat in the sauna for
another twenty minutes, before she headed to the Home Office
for her meeting. She was told it would be a brief meeting and
that suited her. She didn't have much to share.

Both Wyatt and Sayer gave updates on what their respective
team's progress which was impressive for the amount of work

they had managed to fit in since last night, but unimpressive by the results. They hadn't been able to hack into any of the Wilsons' work or private accounts, in the time given. Justin knew how to protect their systems. Even if they had managed to hack in, they didn't know what to look for. Forrester turned to Sahira next and asked,

'Anything to update your end, Sahira?'

'Not really, sir. Winter disappeared after the news of Justin Wilson's death. He left me a message saying that he wanted to meet me today to chat but would only talk face to face.'

Maguire woke up from his seeming slumber and involved himself for the first time.

'You're meeting Winter today?'

'Yes, sir.'

'Where?'

'I don't know yet. He is going to let me know.'

'We need to take this opportunity to bring him in. It's time to stop this and now's our chance.'

Wyatt answered first.

'It won't work. He is too good to fall into an ambush. He would know if we had a team on site. We need to let this play out and see what he has to say.'

Maguire was visibly and unashamedly frustrated.

'Couldn't we then at least put surveillance on him and see where he goes?'

Wyatt was equally blunt.

'No. He would know and we'd risk losing him completely. He wouldn't trust Sahira anymore and would disappear.'

'For God sake this is ridiculous. We need to stop Winter.'

'We will John, but for now, let's see what he has to say and

Sahira can report back to us,' Forrester said. He turned and looked at Sahira. 'Thank you Sahira, that will be all for now. Please report back to Matt as soon as you can.'

'Yes, sir.'

With those words, Sahira started to leave as Sayer said,

'Oh, and Sahira. We thought you could use some help.'

Sahira's eyes widened in horror as she thought she knew where he was going with this.

'Matt, honestly, I'm better off alone. If I take Larholt with me, it might spook Winter and scare him away.'

Both Sayer and Wyatt chuckled.

'I was just going to say, transfer all your other work to Pete in JTAC, so that you can put your entire focus on Winter. As much as I'd love to send Larholt along with you, I can't. He somehow managed to get a car stolen, one that he'd checked out. He has paperwork to do.'

Sahira nodded and left the room hiding a knowing smile.

36

The previous afternoon. Ricky had contacted Ignatius as a broken man. He had walked in to his house, along with a neighbour, who he'd invited in for a cup of tea when he saw her after parking his car.

He had just returned from his usual two-and-a-half hour meeting with engineers at his and Justin's company. They used the meeting to update on progress for designs they were working on, as well as to discuss future ideas.

He was laughing with his neighbour when he walked into the front room. All that changed when he saw his husband hanging from a thick piece of rope, from a beam in the room.

He cut him down and cradled him in his arms whilst he wept. Later, he would cry until his eyes were dry and then continued to heave in mental and physical pain. He had never known hurt like it and despite his incredible intelligence, he had no idea what to do. He wasn't thinking about practical actions. He was thinking how he could possibly live from now on without the love of his life.

Ricky couldn't remember if it was he or his neighbour who had called the police, and he had no idea how long it had passed since he had first seen his husband hanging, until the police arrived; but it wasn't long.

The police weren't sure whether a crime had been committed or not at this point, but took Ricky to the police station to take a statement. Ricky had been at a meeting with multiple witnesses. His car was caught on Automatic Number-plate Recognition cameras and his neighbour had seen him pull up and had accompanied him into the house.

From when he had left his house to when he had returned, it had been slightly over three and a half hours.

Rigor mortis occurs from a chemical change in the muscles after death. It is first noticeable in the smallest muscles, like the eyelids, fingers, jaws and neck. It is happening in the larger muscles also, but it takes longer for it to affect the movement. The rigor in the small muscles will start being noticeable within an hour after death. There were not yet signs of rigor mortis even in the small muscles.

These facts all meant that Ricky couldn't have committed any crime, had there been one. He was allowed to go home shortly after arriving at the police station, once he had given his statement.

When Ricky had arrived home, he had a period of clarity and there was no doubt in his mind that Justin was killed because they were assisting Ignatius. He thought that Bambi was behind the killing. He also knew that they had chosen to help Ignatius before he had even arrived at their house, and he was more determined than ever to help Ignatius find Bambi and make him pay for the death of his husband.

Ignatius had met Ricky at an address that Ricky had through another work contact. He had spent the night mainly just sitting with him in silence and giving him a hug when Ricky needed one. Ignatius didn't care for many people but he cared for Ricky and Justin. And he was going to get revenge for Justin's death and if necessary, he would do so without mercy, pity or empathy.

Ignatius contacted Sahira that day and told her that he needed to see her the next day. The next morning when Ignatius was heading out, Ricky had come up to him and offered him a hug. He then gave him a package and said that he hoped it would help Ignatius, and he was on-hand for anything needed.

37

Bambi was woken by a call shortly before 7.00am. It was Jerry. He had answered, ignoring any pleasantries.

'What have you got for me?'

'Winter is meeting with an MI5 officer today. I don't know where or when, but she'll lead you to him.'

'What do you want me to do with regards to her?'

'For now, leave her be. We'll need to deal with her at some point later, but this is too public a forum. The key thing is to make sure Winter disappeares.'

In his head, Bambi was thinking, 'I won't be here later', but he let it go.

'Ok fine. Anything else?'

'Winter will know if he's been followed or set up. Be careful he doesn't spot you and it's likely he'll be in disguise to beat the facial recognition cameras.'

'He'd know if a team were there, or if he was going to be detained. I have no intention of detaining him or being with a team.'

'Let me know when it's done.'

'Fine.'

Bambi hung up and got himself out of bed. He went and took a shower and then ordered some breakfast.

He got in his rented car and drove to the address in Aldgate to meet his contact again. He was aware that Ignatius may be wearing body armour, so from his contact in the back of a mechanics garage, he bought XM1158 7.62mm Advanced Armor Piercing (ADVAP) rounds.

ADVAP penetrates armor by using a heavy tungsten core penetrator. The combination of weight and velocity—and a dart-like tip—would penetrate the weave of Kevlar and enabled the round to defeat other armours, including steel.

The issue with these bullets is that they require M240 machine guns and larger battle rifles to deliver their rounds, so he would need to conceal this weapon, but he had already come up with a plan for that.

He couldn't risk testing these rounds in case the noise alerted people and drew unnecessary attention, but he had never been let down by his contact before and trusted the equipment that was provided.

Bambi had everything he required now, so he took out his Glock 17 with a silencer attached and shot his contact twice in the head with the 9mm ammunition already in his pistol.

His contact had been good to him over the years, but if he was to retire in peace, he couldn't leave any loose ends. Bambi drove back to near Westminster and circled around the area in a holding pattern, waiting until he received a call.

Ignatius had phoned and told Sahira to go to Westminster tube, take the jubilee line to Green Park station and then walk north up Stratton street and wait on a window seat inside Café Nero.

Bambi had taken to foot and had watched Sahira walk into the Café Nero, and was currently waiting for Ignatius to turn up. He hoped it wouldn't be long as he was getting hot.

Ignatius walked cautiously up Stratton Street. The drizzle of the previous day had gone and it was a bright, hot day, which pleased Ignatius as it meant he could wear sunglasses without it looking suspicious. As an additional benefit they would also hide his eyes which were searching the perimeters.

Walking up the street, he passed two business women and a business man who were all wearing suits and carrying a bag from a local supermarket. There was also a postman wheeling his post trolley, a road cleaner with his cleaner barrow and brush, and a UPS delivery man with a large package.

Nearing the café he glanced right and saw Sahira sitting in the window across the road, reading The Sun newspaper, low enough to show her face. The Sun newspaper was the signal showing Ignatius it was safe to approach. As he crossed the road, Sahira walked out the café and started walking by his side as if they were two strangers who just happened to fall into step.

Many soldiers have told stories of how they have been patrolling while in a war zone, and suddenly have a heightened sense that something is about to happen. Sometimes it can be subliminal, such as lack of women or young children in the street. Sometimes for an even more abstract reason, like a trodden plant in a field, and, sometimes, it might be for no reason at all. However, soldiers have learnt to trust these instincts, especially Special Forces soldiers who are more often in volatile environments. It was worrying for Ignatius, but he was now having one of these feelings.

Ignatius was rattling his brain to try and think, to find a reason why he was having this feeling. He was struggling to make sense of his perceptions.

Then it hit him: the postman. He was wearing thick trousers and a shirt and jacket on a hot day, but Ignatius knew that postmen had options to wear summer appropriate clothing. More than that though, he had wheeled his trolley past three or four tall buildings, that each had shop units at street level, with additional flats rising up above and forming each individual unit.

What were the odds that none of these flats would have any mail, be it a bank statement, a bill, or some form of junk mail?

Ignatius swung around searching for the postman.

Bambi had realised that the man Sahira was walking alongside was Ignatius Winter. He crossed the road and walked behind the pair slowly catching up but always moving away from his escape route.

He got near enough, pulled out his M240 machine gun from the post trolley and took aim.

Suddenly he saw Ignatius was agitated and frantically looking around. The movement of Ignatius' head meant that he couldn't risk missing a head shot, so Bambi aimed at centre mass.

He had the gun on semi-automatic and pulled the trigger twice.

Winter was knocked back and, on his way down to the ground, he dragged Sahira with him to cover her from the bullets.

Despite what Hollywood might tell you, people very rarely die immediately from being shot, unless it is a head shot. They usually have a few seconds, at least, before the body completely shuts down. As Winter was falling, he saw him pull his gun and begin to aim straight for him. Bambi had no intention of being shot, so turned around and began running for Green Park underground station, making sure to put obstacles between him and Ignatius. These obstacles were predominantly people.

He never did hear a shot from Ignatius.

Bambi had left his trolley and dropped his machine gun, but pulled the pistol he had concealed within his jacket, in case anyone had thoughts of being a hero. He had covered his hands in a layer of super glue, which ensures leaving no prints or DNA, so didn't care about the evidentiary value of the machine gun or trolley being left behind.

He had not used a silencer on the machine gun for a couple of reasons. The main one being, a silencer reduces the velocity of a bullet, so it might hinder its chances of piercing a Kevlar vest, but also the sound of gunshots would cause panic and that panic should assist his escape.

Bambi was sprinting down Stratton Street, listening to screams in the background. He suspected Winter would be close to death by now. No one survived two high velocity body shots.

He ran into Green Park tube station and swiped his Oyster card to get through the barrier and bounded down to the Piccadilly line, brushing other commuters aside, in order to head west towards Hyde Park Corner.

He got on the platform as a tube train pulled up and the doors were opening. Rather than getting on the tube, he ran to the end of the platform and hurdled the metal barrier then down the tracks heading towards Hyde Park corner.

When he knew about this job, he had made a few assumptions based upon how he would have arranged the meet, if he was Ignatius. He had planned his escape routes based upon the likely scenarios he had run through in his mind, and if the operation had fallen outside of these routes, he would have aborted for a later day.

As he ran down the track, he could sense the vibration on the line and he flattened himself against the side of the tunnel on the walkway. The tube shot past him and he started chasing after it.

The next stop from Green Park was Hyde Park Corner, but halfway between the stations, Bambi jumped up onto a platform.

Located between Hyde Park Corner and Green Park stations, Down Street had a short life as a working station between 1907 and 1932. It became critical to winning the Second World War when covertly transformed into the Railway Executive Committee's bomb-proof headquarters. Winston Churchill would use it during the worst of the bombing raids throughout the war.

Bambi was now running along the disused platform of this abandoned station, steeped in history. He took a moment to pause and strip off his postman's outfit, under which he was wearing workman's overalls.

He took a tin of lighter fluid out of his pocket and sprayed the clothes he had just taken off, before setting fire to them on the platform floor.

He ran upstairs towards street level and found a locked door onto the street. He picked the lock easily and slipped out the door into the middle of some ongoing street works. He picked up a spare tool laying close by and joined the other workers on the street while wearing the matching overalls.

The area was already swamped with police, searching for a psychopathic postman so Bambi continued working until there was an opportunity to sneak between the police patrols.

He made his way to a department store, bought some clothes

and used the changing room to change outfit and then headed back to his penthouse at the hotel.

He rested his head on the bed, satisfied that Winter was dead and he was now retired.

He would wait in the UK until his money for this job had cleared, just in case he needed to employ some persuasion for his payment, then he'd decide his next destination.

38

Bigelow Aerospace is an American space technology company, based in Northern Las Vegas, Nevada, that manufactures and develops expandable space station modules. Ricky had always been fascinated with the organisation and it was the first and only organisation that had ever rejected him, when he had applied for a role with them fifteen years earlier.

He had however kept a close admiring eye on their work. The cutting-edge nature of the work they carried out often led to rumours about the company.

These rumours were fuelled after the owner of Bigelow Aerospace, Robert Bigelow, bought Skinwalker Ranch, southeast of Ballard, Utah, for two hundred thousand dollars.

The ranch has long been associated with paranormal activities and is often dubbed the UFO ranch. In 2016, Bigelow sold Skinwalker Ranch for $4.5 million to 'Adamantium Holdings', a shell corporation of unknown origin. After this purchase, all roads leading to the ranch have been blocked, the perimeter secured and guarded by cameras and barbed wire, with signs everywhere designed to inhibit people from approaching the ranch.

Ricky didn't believe in the UFO theories associated with the Ranch and therefore by association, with Bigelow Aerospace.

He believed that unknown technology was being worked on, although he couldn't prove it.

One bit of technology he could prove though, was the use

of Vectran shield fabric, that the company had used to develop an expandable module of the International Space Station.

Vectran shield fabric had twice the flexibility and more importantly, twice the strength of Kevlar. The morning that Ignatius had left to meet Sahira, Ricky had handed him a package that contained a vest made of Vectran.

A XM1158 7.62mm Advanced Armor Piercing round might be able to penetrate Kevlar, but it was no match for Vectran.

Once Ignatius had realised that something was wrong and he had searched for the man who was impersonating a postman, he had almost instantly come face to face with a M240 machine gun pointed straight at him, about to give him the good news.

Instinctively, he had covered Sahira and he took two bullets to centre mass as he positioned his body in front of hers. The impact had rattled his bones and he was going to know about it. He was very lucky not to have cracked ribs, but they hadn't pierced the body armour Ricky had given him.

As he was falling, he drew his Sig Sauer and was getting ready himself to return fire. He wanted to hit back but the man who he believed to be Bambi, was already running away. The fire cracker sound of the shots had caused panic amongst the public. People were frantically running in all directions, preventing him from shooting for fear of hitting an innocent.

Once Ignatius saw that immediate danger had passed, he allowed himself a brief moment to lie on his back and groan. Sahira had jumped to her feet and was standing over Ignatius, with her hands tracing over his body in an unqualified attempt at a medical review of his body.

She didn't actually touch him though as she didn't want to

cause any more damage to him. She whispered, 'Where are you hit? How bad is it?'

'It didn't go through my vest. I'll be ok.'

Sahira looked surprised but she let it be.

'Wow, you're lucky. That must have hurt.'

'It tickled a little. Come on, we need to get out of here.'

Ignatius, gingerly got to his feet and noticed a slowly calming crowd was descending on his position. He didn't need attention of any kind and was about to act, when Sahira took control. While Ignatius was trying to catch the wind that had been knocked out of him, Sahira brandished a badge and shouted, 'British Intelligence, please keep away and move yourselves to a position of safety.'

The stunned crowd was trying to figure out what was required of them and what their next movements should be. Sahira and Ignatius took off, with Ignatius moving like a drunken baby.

He managed to get around the corner with his ribcage 'screaming at him' and climbed on his bike, which had the helmet dangling from a handlebar and thankfully hadn't been stolen. Ignatius couldn't risk chaining it to the bike in case a quick escape was required, so he took the calculated risk of leaving it hanging on the bike's handlebars and hoped the passers-by were honest.

He started the engine and Sahira was standing next to him looking worried. She asked him if he was going to be ok to ride it.

'I'll be fine, meet me at the safe house', he said, then took off at speed.

Within seconds, he had passed the first police car with its sirens screaming almost as loudly as his ribs. Soon he was passing multiple police vehicles, including armed response.

One eagle-eyed police officer gave him a hard stare, but it was left at that. It wasn't clear whether it was because the police officer realised that by the time he turned around, Ignatius would be long gone or because he dismissed his instincts. But either way, gradually, Ignatius put distance between himself and ground zero.

He parked his bike in the side alley, by the fire escape of the safe house, and slowly made his way to the front door, grimacing, but doing his best not to draw attention to his pain.

The lift ride up to the top floor was painful and stopped at seemingly each floor on route to allow residents access to their flats. The minimal jerk of the lift stopping, felt like him falling onto concrete every time. 'Do none of these jokers work?'

When he finally got into the flat, he very gingerly took off his clothes and did a self-inspection. Nothing was broken, but he was going to be sore for a few days. He took some frozen meat out of the freezer and wrapped it in a tea towel, gently resting it against his progressively bruising sternum. He promised himself was going to hurt Bambi for this.

It took at least half an hour, with Ignatius lying motionless, before Sahira walked into the flat and saw him lying in just his boxer shorts and a scrunched up tea towel across his midriff. She had a moment of gratefulness and affection as she walked over to him with a bag in her hand.

'Hey, Ignatius, thank you so much for saving my life. I genuinely appreciate what you did back there. Is there anything I can do for you?'

'I wouldn't say no to a bed bath.'

Sahira's affection for him dissipated as quickly as it had

formed. She ignored his request and motioned the bag in front of him.

'I picked you up some painkillers and fried chicken.'

'Thanks.'

Ignatius opened the bag and dry swallowed three strong painkillers, even though the packet advice suggested only taking one at a time.

He took one bite out of a piece of chicken and realised the pain he got from chewing wasn't worth the reward of the fried chicken taste. He put the chicken back in the bucket and lay down on the couch. Sahira sat next to him quietly for the next fifteen minutes as he slowly became more and more drowsy and fell into a restless sleep; part drug induced and part exhaustion. He was between semiconsciousness and sleep for the next three hours, before he finally gained some level of lucidity. He woke up to see Sahira typing away on her phone. Once she noticed that Ignatius was awake, she put her phone down and focused on him.

'How are you feeling?'

Ignatius was still a bit groggy and his voice rather husky.

'Feel a bit better. It's going to be sore for a few days, but no major damage has been done.'

'I'm happy to hear that, Ignatius. I would be dead if it wasn't for you, I can't...'

Ignatius cut her off.

'I don't think they were after you. If anything, I put you in more danger by getting in front of you, but we have bigger things to worry about.'

'Ignatius, we don't need to do this now. Get some rest and we can figure it out later.'

'We do need to do it now. We were ambushed and someone is feeding Bambi information. How many people knew of our meeting?'

Sahira looked troubled as she responded,

'I only told four people and they are the elite four of our Intelligence community. They though, almost certainly told others for political and operational reasons, so I'm afraid I can't say exactly how widely this was shared. Do you want me to ask them?'

'No. Definitely not,' Ignatius said.

'We seem to have a lot working against us. So, what on earth do we do?' Sahira asked.

'We make it work to our advantage.'

39

Sahira spent the night at the safe house with Ignatius. She wanted to keep an eye on him, in case other damage that neither of them foretold, manifested itself. Ignatius was comfortable on the sofa and didn't want to move, so she took the bedroom and was surprised how well she slept.

She woke early and was ready to go to the gym, before she met her Dad - who was in London on business - for breakfast. As she was about to leave the flat, she changed her mind and went to the kitchen. She did an inventory check and was not surprised to see that most of the shopping she'd done for Ignatius was still available.

She cooked a breakfast consisting of sausages, bacon, eggs, beans and toast for Ignatius, with a generous pot of tea and some orange juice on the side. She took the breakfast over to the coffee table and put it down, then gently woke Ignatius.

He seemed genuinely surprised and even partially confused by the breakfast. He clearly wasn't used to this sort of gesture. For the first time, Sahira thought she saw a hint of humility in him whilst he ate.

A vast portion of his upper body was different shades of purple, starting with aggressively dark, where the rounds had impacted the vest and gently lightening as it expanded away from the centre.. The pain had eased a little and he was moving more freely, albeit with noticeable restrictions. He was able to eat his entire breakfast quickly, and Sahira took it as a very positive sign his appetite was still intact.

There was almost an exclusive silence whilst Ignatius ate and Sahira didn't know how she felt about the fact that the silence was a comfortable one.

When Ignatius had finished his entire plate, he very gently let himself sit back against the sofa cushion with his cup of tea in his hand. He looked at Sahira without a hint of sarcasm.

'Thanks a lot, Sahira. That was lovely and good of you.'

Sahira smiled whilst giving a 'you're welcome' nod. This was the first time she'd ever seen Ignatius lower his guard even a small amount. She wondered how long it had been since the last time he'd done that.

Ignatius's focus remained intact though and he spoke with operational efficiency as they discussed a workable plan. It wasn't difficult for Sahira to persuade him they should wait a day or two before implementing any plan. Ignatius was stubborn as hell and fat-kid-on-a-cookie keen to get going, but he was also smart, and knew he needed at least forty-eight hours to allow a bit more physical recovery time.

Sahira had picked up the Rubik's cube and was twisting it randomly with clearly no intention of solving it.

'What's going on? What's wrong?', Ignatius asked.

'Ignatius, it seems that you're taking a big risk with this plan. Is there no other way?'

'I don't know. If there is, I'm all ears, but I can't see it.'

Sahira was in no way comforted by this, but she didn't have another suggestion, so changed the subject.

'I'm going to meet my Dad for breakfast, then I'll pick you up something for the bruising, do you need anything else?'

'Nah, I'm all right. I got a few things I can do today. I'll see you later.'

Sahira had already done Fajr prayer so she left for her breakfast. When her Dad was in town, she always told him he should stay with her. He had bought the place after all and she had plenty of room, but he insisted he didn't want to intrude on her space and always stayed in the same room at the Ritz hotel, which is where they were meeting for breakfast.

Sahira had an avocado benedict and her father a poached smoked haddock. He was in a jubilant mood and was animated in describing what the family had been up to. It was a welcome distraction for Sahira and she bathed in his mood as much as she could. She loved hearing about her family's life back in Saudi Arabia.

After breakfast, she gave her father a big hug and walked down the street to the pharmacy before a quick stop back at the safe house. Then she was going to work.

Sahira opened the front door to the house and saw Ignatius quickly put the Rubik's cube down on the table. She pretended she hadn't noticed. After giving him the arnica cream and some vitamin C tablets for the bruising, Sahira headed for work.

Ignatius had slept while Sahira was at breakfast and slept for another couple of hours after she left the second time. When he woke up, he took a warm shower to help with the blood circulation. He gently patted himself dry and rubbed in some arnica cream. He gave Tank a call to check in.

Tank and the Harringtons hadn't encountered any problems, but they were starting to ask some testing questions and Tank was worried that they were questioning the legitimacy of the whole situation. While Ignatius knew he'd need help for the next part, he also knew that he needed Tank to stay with the

Harringtons, so he made a call he never thought he'd ever make.

Ignatius spent the rest of the day resting and rubbing arnica cream into his bruises. Mid-afternoon, he was feeling bored so picked up the Rubik's cube again. In an impressively impatient amount of time, he was all ready to dismiss it, but then remembered something and walked into the bathroom.

He walked back into the sitting room and sat down with the Rubik's cube and the tweezers he had just borrowed. Slowly, he removed each individual coloured sticker of the cube, then replaced them so each side of the square matched colour. By 7.00pm, Ignatius was bored out of his mind. He used to be able to control his impatience and still could, but each year it got harder.

Sahira got to the safe house at 8.30pm and walked in to see Ignatius throwing the Rubik's cube in the air and catching it. She looked at him and said,

'Hey, good for you, you solved it.'

'Oh, yeah, did it ages ago, just after you left this morning.'

Sahira picked up the cube and rolled her eyes as she saw the individual coloured stickers on the cube not quite aligned, and then saw the tweezers on the table. Something told her that Ignatius wasn't a man who tweezed. Ignatius was pretending he hadn't seen Sahira notice what he'd done, so tactically moved the conversation on.

'So, are we set for tomorrow?'

Sahira considerately looked Ignatius up and down.

'Are you sure you're fine to go ahead? We can wait another day or so, until you heal a bit more.'

'I'm fine. We can't afford to wait any longer. Let's go for it.'

Sahira wanted to push back some more but she didn't. She

also thought they needed to move sooner rather than later, and she knew this stubborn manchild wouldn't change his mind, especially if he was asked to do so.

40

Sahira woke in her own bed offensively early. She was starting to wonder if she would ever get a good night's sleep again? Her mind was working overtime and didn't seem bothered by the sleep deprivation, but it took her fifteen minutes to convince her body to get out of bed. She dragged herself down to the gym and swam, what was for her, a leisurely fifty lengths.

She then let the hot shower waterfall down her face and body for twenty minutes before she took her time applying creams and oils and drying her hair. She dressed and walked up to the café within the gym and ordered a double espresso, which she sipped slowly whilst reading a paper. The gym had a prayer room and Sahira used it for Fajr prayer this morning. After the prayer, she went back to the café for a superfood smoothie consisting of spinach, chia seeds, apple, lemon and English cucumber.

The smoothie helped her feel fresh again. It was another beautiful London morning, so after going upstairs to brush her teeth and straighten her outfit, she made her way to the office on foot.

Sahira had already updated Sayer on the events of the past few days but had requested an emergency meeting with The Big Four today for important intel sharing. They were not available first thing this morning, so Sahira spent her time doing some paperwork before pushing the boundaries of her access levels, to gather information for Ignatius.

After three infuriating hours, she hadn't been able to get Ignatius exactly what he wanted, but had narrowed down the search parameters. She didn't think it would be enough, but it was all she could get for now. They might need to adapt the plan.

She got a call at 10.45am to say that the meeting would happen at 1.00pm, but then ten minutes later she got another call to say that she should go to Sayer's office now to brief them. It seemed they were keen to hear what she had to say, or at least one of them was.

Sahira made her way to Sayer's office with a bottle of water in hand and nothing else. She briefly said 'hi' to Sayer's new assistant Ian Parslow, whom she had known well when he was an assistant to her usual boss. Parslow was a rotund and cheery man who was a great source of fashion advice and celebrity gossip for Sahira. It was her guilty pleasure that she shared with very few people.

After a brief chat, a light on Parslow's phone lit up and without answering, he looked at Sahira and said,

'They're ready.'

Sahira thanked Parslow and made him promise they would meet for a glass of Sauvignon Blanc soon, and he could scratch her celebrity gossip itch.

Sahira walked in the room and saw four men she was used to seeing well dressed, looking even more immaculate than usual. Forrester must have picked up on this and without being asked he said,

'Morning, Sahira. We've just had a meeting with Chen Lim, head of Ministry of State Security for China.'

Maguire picked up the thread from Forrester.

'They are not happy with our progress and want to know

why we still haven't found Winter. I hope you have good news for us?'

Sahira didn't commit to an answer to his question just yet and waited for the room to settle.

'You wanted this meeting, Sahira. The floor is yours,' Sayer said.

'You're all aware that, when I had an arranged meeting with Winter the other day, we were ambushed and he was shot twice.' Sahira began. 'There have been rumours about his fate, since his body was never found. I called this meeting, amongst other reasons, to let you know he is alive and well.'

Sahira discretely scanned the room to see if there were any specific reactions to this news, but not one of them signalled their thoughts, with four faces remaining passive so she continued, 'He contacted me early this morning. Not only to let me know he's alive and well, but also to confirm he has proof of who's behind all of this.'

Maguire spoke up, whilst the rest of the room sat quietly with a vast combined brain power working hard in the silence.

'What proof does he have? How did he get it?'

'I don't know, sir. I asked the same questions, but he just told me he needed another day to verify the intel, and would be willing to present it to all of you at some point, the day after tomorrow.'

'So, you haven't seen this proof?' Maguire asked.

'No, sir. I haven't and I don't know what this proof shows.'

'So, there might not be any proof? He could just be playing us?'

'Yes, sir. It's a possibility, but I don't see to what end? He hasn't mislead us about anything so far.'

'You mean, other than telling us he was not part of this?' Maguire snapped.

Sahira felt the question was rhetorical so didn't answer, but Forrester jumped in before she would have looked insubordinate.

'Ok, Sahira. Let's assume what Winter is telling us the truth? Where and how does he plan on sharing this intel with us?'

'I'm afraid I don't know that either, sir. He says, he is having help verifying certain parts of the intel, which he will show me tomorrow, before he is willing to present to a larger audience. I have assured him complete safety, once he returns from wherever he is now, in one of our safe houses in Clapham until he provides us with the details.'

This bit of information produced an almost indistinguishable glance between Wyatt and Sayer. One that no one would have picked up on, unless they were a highly trained Intelligence officer, like Sahira.

Sayer took charge of the room.

'Ok, Sahira. Let's get some security on the safe house and ensure there is no repeat of the other day. Tell Winter he can have whatever he needs in the meantime to assist him to show us this intel. Make no mistake though, if he is playing us, we're either taking him into custody or taking him out. That's his call.'

'Yes, sir, I will let him know. But I don't think we should add security to the safe house. He has major trust issues amongst other things.'

'Ok, fine, but we need him to show us this, Sahira. We are drawing a line in the sand here. He's not going to be given other opportunities, especially if he messes us about.'

'Yes, sir.'

41

Bambi was officially pissed off now, and when he was pissed off he was nasty. His money hadn't been paid for the last job. He didn't know exactly who had hired him, despite his best efforts to find out from the beginning, so he could use the knowledge as a bargaining chip for these exact situations.

He had taken precautions though. He had recorded every conversation that had taken place between Jerry and himself. He had tried to contact Jerry a couple of times with no success.

He had sent a message saying that they had until midday today to pay the money owed to him. Otherwise, he would release what information he had, and he swore to find out who the person was and then kill them. It was just after 11.30am when he received a call from his client.

'Where is my money?' he simply asked.

'I will pay you, when you get the job done. Winter is still alive and well,' Jerry replied.

'That's not possible. I shot him twice in centre mass with high velocity armour piercing rounds. No human can survive that and even if by miracle they did, they certainly wouldn't be well.'

'I don't know what to tell you, but I do know that not only is he alive, but he also has proof of both of our involvement.'

'What proof? How is that possible?' Bambi asked.

'I don't know yet. He is verifying the intel he has now and is showing it for all to see the day after tomorrow.'

Bambi wished he'd never taken this job. The money wasn't worth this crap, but he was too involved now to back out.

'We can't let that happen,' he said.

'I know. I also know where he'll be tomorrow.'

'Ok, I'm listening.'

Jerry told Bambi about the safe house and gave him the address.

'The MI5 officer, Sahira Basha, may know a lot more than she is letting on, or certainly might soon. She has now become too much of a liability,' he said.

'I will take care of her also, ' Bambi said and then hung up as he had work to do.

Bambi couldn't understand how Winter had survived? Was this guy Iron Man? He would make sure that didn't happen again though. He accepted that he hadn't given Winter the credit he deserved. He would have to force him into making a mistake if he could.

42

Ignatius had left the safe house and was staying in a small Bed and Breakfast in Hertfordshire that was happy to take cash and not ask too many questions about his reasons for an overnight stay.

He was waiting on a friend of sorts to turn up and also for a call from Sahira. He had rested as much as possible and had worked the arnica cream into his bruising as well as taking his painkillers, but he still was in a fair amount of discomfort and wasn't moving as freely as he would have liked.

Eventually his phone rang and he answered half way through the first ring.

'Hey.'

'Hello, Mr Winter.'

'Who is this?'

'If I were you, I would cut my losses and disappear. I'm sure you know how to do that.'

Ignatius paused. He had a cacophony of emotions shouting through his head, but remained calm.

'Bambi. How's it going? I hear you told people you'd killed me. That must have been embarrassing?'

Bambi counted slowly and quietly to three in his head to calm his anger, then began his speech.

'Justin cried as I wrapped the rope round his neck. He was begging for his life as I slowly rocked the chair under him. I decided not to let him drop and have his neck break for a quick death, but just to remove the chair gradually and let his body weight suffocate him to death. He had tears rolling down his eyes even as the air left his body. The fear in his eyes was pathetic. Almost as pathetic as when he lost control of his bowels and shit himself.'

Ignatius was clenching his jaw so hard that it would have only taken a minimal amount of extra pressure to turn his teeth to chalk.

Bambi continued, 'How many more of your friends are you going to be responsible for me murdering, Mr Winter? Do you want me to tell you how I'm going to kill your next friend? Any questions, any details at all that you want to know?' Bambi asked and then paused for effect.

'I have one question,' Ignatius said.

Bambi smiled as he asked,

'What's that Mr, Winter?'

'How's your mum?'

Bambi yelled expletives down the phone and shouted out details of what he was going to do to Ignatius, but it didn't matter. Ignatius had already hung up.

43

Ignatius was angry and was having some graphic violent thoughts, but he reverted to training and managed to take control of his emotions. His training and experience had taught him, that ninety-nine percent of the time, if he was acting under a high emotional charge, his decisions were not his best ones.

He knew that the point of the phone call from Bambi was to try and get him angry, to act irrationally and therefore make him an easier target. It took some effort due to the nature of his emotions at this point, but he managed to overcome them eventually.

A couple of hours later there was a knock on his room's door. He checked who was at the door before opening it, and found himself staring at Squadron Sergeant Major Andy Atkin-Berry. The history between the two of them was complicated and they had both led interesting and raw lives. When they saw each other they both gave a formal nod and a firm handshake. They were British at the end of the day.

After Andy had been dragged to London for five minutes' worth of talking nothing about Ignatius, he was intrigued enough to do some research into the situation. Once he heard news of the death of Justin, he felt compelled to involve himself in the situation.

Justin had led technical support on some of his operations and many other operations for the Special Forces. There was no doubt in Andy's mind that Justin had saved multiple lives with his expertise and support. Yesterday he had managed to get hold of Ignatius to offer any support and that's why he was here now.

After spending a few hours finalising details for their plan for tonight, Andy got in his Land Rover Series 2 and went to run some errands for the upcoming operation.

It was 11.30pm and Ignatius and Andy were on the roof of a building in St Dunstans Road in Barons Court, London.

St Dunstans road was made up of two sides of terraced housing. They were at the end of the road nearest to the station. Both were dressed in black and were well equipped for what they needed to do.

British Intelligence run multiple satellite offices across the country in the UK. Some of these are fully functioning Intelligence offices, some are staging offices for operations and others are used for a variety of different reasons. They are disguised in an array of different buildings, be it residential properties, farm outbuildings or industrial units.

The street they were on now was entirely residential, except for one building that was used by British Intelligence as a fully functioning hospital, albeit on a much smaller scale.

These hospitals were used to treat patients that British Intelligence might not want in the system. The patients might be people in, or about to join, witness protection, operational officers who were wounded in the field, or even enemies of the country they wanted to keep alive for Intel gathering purposes. Often these people were assumed dead by the outside world.

The point of these hospitals is that if you had no need to

know of their existence, they were a very closely guarded secret, even from people who worked within the Intelligence services.

Earlier in the day, Sahira had tried to use her DV clearance to gain access to the exact location of a specific hospital which was holding patients of interest to them. Unfortunately however, even with her status and clearance she wasn't able to find the address so she had to get creative.

The Intelligence Service offices, both head and satellite need to use a variety of external suppliers to provide a multitude of different products. Everything from stationary, coffee beans, office equipment, weaponry, technical equipment and much more.

The suppliers of this equipment are thoroughly vetted, but the diverse nature of all the requirements, and therefore the use of differing suppliers, mean that a continuous close vetting of all the suppliers is impossible. For that reason, along with reasons of secrecy, all the equipment rather than being sent to the individual offices directly, are sent to a large warehouse.

There, every item is scanned for traces of a radioactive or biological signature, an electronic signature, and many other things to ensure that no explosives, diseases or unwanted surveillance equipment is hidden amongst the materials and could compromise the offices awaiting their goods.

Once the materials have had a thorough scan, they are then delivered to the required places via delivery people on the government payroll, who are continuously monitored and vetted.

Although Sahira hadn't been able to access the exact address of the hospital, she knew what equipment the hospital would require to treat her patients of interest. Therefore she had managed to access the procurement system and get the dates and times of the delivery to the warehouse, for the medical supplies.

She had then accessed the Vehicle Location trackers on the delivery vehicles for those days and followed the routes the vehicles had taken. Using a process of elimination from deliveries over the last few days, the only address that the hospital could be was on St Dunstan's road.

The fact the street was residential meant that there weren't any delivery bays for the individual properties. Sahira had managed to gauge the delivery vans had always parked at one end of the street, and always on the same side of the street. But they were not always in the same spot as they had to park wherever they could find a space, depending on what was available. That meant the closest Sahira could get to the address was within five properties.

Ignatius and Andy didn't have time to do any surveillance to find out the correct address between five houses and certainly couldn't breach each property. So they had to use another method to find out which property housed the hospital.

It was 11.38pm now and they needed to be ready for 11.40pm, so they got the equipment out of one of the rucksacks and set it up. At 11.40pm, the street went completely dark and using an electronic current infrared ray barrier detector that Ricky had super charged with his own unique skill set, they scanned the five properties.

Earlier in the day, Andy had used his Security Services ID he had as a member of 22 SAS, and five hundred pounds in cash as a sweetener, and approached an engineer who worked for the National Grid and would be working this evening.

He told the engineer it was a matter of national security that the power on this particular grid pattern, covering St Dunstan's road, went out for thirty seconds at 11.40pm. Thirty seconds was long enough for them to achieve their task, but short enough time to ensure the residents of the street didn't have time to call the electric companies to register a complaint. It would just be a nuisance for a minimal period.

As a hospital, there would be backup generators that would kick in immediately in case of a power cut, to ensure equipment such as life support machines wouldn't skip a beat both figuratively and literally.

A residential property wouldn't have this sort of generator. The generator would support the machines and low-level emergency lighting. Andy and Ignatius couldn't rely on the visibility of lighting through shutters and heavy-duty curtains, such as a top secret hospital would undoubtedly have in place.

The current detector picked out the only property that was spitting out an electronic signature during the blackout, with the level matching that required by heavy duty equipment.

They had found the hospital.

The hospital, being located in a building designed as a residential property had a small garden at the back, which backed onto Margravine Cemetery, separated by a six-foot brick wall.

The two men made their way down from the roof, across the road and walked around the corner to enter the graveyard. They climbed over the wall from the graveyard, into the back garden of the hospital.

They were both fully dressed in black, including black balaclavas they had pulled down to cover their faces, just before they breached the wall. In the shadows at the back of the garden, they crouched and watched the property for any signs of staff being alerted to their presence.

The property was three floors high and the first floor had a small balcony. They both knew that the front door, and very likely the back door, would have heavy duty locks and security systems, that would take time to circumvent, but they doubted that a first-floor door onto a balcony would have the same level of security.

They simultaneously jumped up and grabbed the edge of the balcony and pulled the weight of their bodies and equipment up onto it. This comparatively simple action caused Ignatius a great deal of pain, but he side-lined it for now.

Ignatius let Andy do the honours with the door, as he suspected Andy's skills were employed more often and more recently. It took Andy less than thirty seconds to beat the lock and his eyes showed disappointment it hadn't been a bigger challenge.

The two elite trained soldiers freed the shotguns attached to their backpacks and set about silently clearing the hospital rooms. The property didn't have a lift, and the two men assumed the patients of interest would be on the ground floor, saving the necessity to move up and down stairs.

Ignatius went down the right hand side of the stairs in a crouch, while Andy descended upright on the left hand side. As they did so, a man in jeans and a shirt walked past the bottom of the staircase.

By the way he was wearing his shirt, both Ignatius and Andy knew he was carrying. The man obviously caught a movement out of the corner of his eye and shot his head round to look up the stairs, where he saw two masked figures.

Before he had time to draw his weapon, he was hit by two rounds Ignatius and Andy had fired simultaneously.

The non-lethal bean bag rounds hit him in the sternum and he was bounced back against the wall. Almost immediately, both masked men were on top of him and whilst one handcuffed him to a radiator, the other one stuffed a cloth in his mouth then duck taped around his face covering his mouth, so the victim couldn't make a sound. One of the men then took his key card. The bean bag rounds would hurt like hell and he would be in quite a bit of discomfort until he was found and released, but he would have no lasting damage and would get over it. It was all part of the job.

Ignatius and Andy searched a room on the right of the front door as you walked in, which was empty, so they looked in the room on the left, which had two patients in beds. Both were either asleep or passed out but since they couldn't be sure, Ignatius approached one of the beds and Andy the other.

They put their hands over the patients' mouths and injected them in the neck with a syringe they carried in their respective backpacks. Both patients' eyes opened wide and the screams were muffled as the injections stung.

The fact they hadn't already awoken to the noise in the corridor, suggested to Ignatius they had been in a heavily medically assisted sleep. Within seconds, both patients were out cold. With some effort Ignatius and Andy carried each one over their respective shoulders, out the front door, using the key card from the handcuffed security guard.

Andy skipped down the front steps, whilst Ignatius almost crawled down under the weight and pain. Both patients were dumped into the back of a panel van which was already waiting in the street. Ignatius and Andy climbed into the front two-seater passenger seats and the van took off down the road, toward their digs for the night.

As the van pulled onto the A4 heading out of London, Ignatius and Andy looked at each other and both gave a nod that said everything.

44

Ricky let himself back into the house carrying three poly-styrene takeaway boxes. He handed one to Andy, who was stretching the sleep out of his bones and one to Ignatius who had just come out a shower and was moving sluggishly.

Last night's activities had clearly taken a toll on his already battered body. Ignatius said thanks to Ricky and gave him a pat on the shoulder, one that also meant 'how you doing?'. Ricky gave Ignatius a forced but genuine smile. He had been, understandably, very quiet since Justin's death. Since Ignatius wasn't a leading expert on counselling, he had kept schtum and just made sure he was available for Ricky if he reached out.

They opened their polystyrene boxes and saw a full english breakfast of sausages, bacon, beans, mushrooms, black pudding, fried eggs and toast. None of them could think of a meal they'd prefer more than this right now. Andy walked over with three mugs of piping tea and they sat down and ate greedily in silence for a couple of minutes. When they paused for breath, Ricky asked,

'How are the patients?'

'They'll be fine for what we need,' Ignatius replied. He then looked at Andy and said, 'Andy, I really appreciate your help, but you shouldn't be here. You can't get caught up in this.'

Andy kept eating and looking at his box of break-fast responded,

'Operationally, without my help, can you pull this off?'

'No.'

'Well, shut up then. Anyway, I'm not here to help you. I'm here for Ricky and mainly I'm here for Justin.'

Ignatius nodded.

They finished the rest of the breakfast in silence then Andy began clearing up the minimal mess they had produced. Ricky said he wanted to go through all the details for tonight once more. The other two wouldn't have it any other way and sat down as Ricky once again went over the plan in minute detail.

After they finished, Ricky said he had work to do and left them, whilst Ignatius and Andy spent the day in their own subtle and unique pre-operation rituals.

Sahira treated the start of today as she would any other day, with a trip to the gym, a superfood smoothie and a morning prayer. She was in the office just before 8.00am and went about catching up on some paperwork and administrative activities.

There was no point searching for Bambi. She had a pretty good idea where he was going to be later on anyway. She was going to meet her father for a quick lunch, before he flew off this afternoon to the US for business. Those plans had to change though, when Ian Parslow called her and said Sayer wanted to see her.

As Sahira approached his office, Parslow smiled and waved her straight through. She entered the office where Sayer was typing away at his computer. He smiled and apologised, saying he would be with her as soon as he finished the email he was typing, and to take a seat.

Sayer finished his email, then got up from his desk and walked round to sit in one of his comfortable armchairs facing

Sahira. His demeanour was easy as he smiled at her.

'How are you doing, Sahira?'

As simple as the question was, it did catch Sahira temporarily off guard. One of Sayer's best attributes, in Sahira's opinion, was the way he looked after his staff. She'd seen it too many times; people treat their staff like shit and in return they acted and worked like shits. In Sayer's case, he treated his staff well and they responded by working well.

Despite this though, Sahira thought the matters at hand might take priority over her wellbeing.

'I'm fine thanks, Matt. Do I not look well?'

'You look like shit, Sahira.' Sayer's serious face turned into a grin and they both started laughing. Sayer tried again, 'You look fine Sahira, I didn't mean it that way. I just want to make sure that you're not going to do anything stupid and get yourself into a difficult situation, shall we say.'

'I don't know why you'd think that, Matt?'

'You gave up the location of the safe house quite freely yesterday. It was a surprising change of heart from before when you were adamant that only you should know?'

'I just felt that it was the right time to bring everyone fully in the loop.'

Sayer pondered this.

'Ok, fair enough. Well, my job is to make sure I'm here to support you and enable you to do your job, so make sure you take advantage of that.'

'Thanks, Matt, I will do.'

Sahira made her excuses and left his office feeling conflicted.

Bambi was finishing his final preparations to leave the hotel and the UK either today or early tomorrow, depending on how it all played out. He just had one small task to do first. Kill Ignatius Winter and Sahira Basha.

After that, he would fly to Bangkok, then get a connecting flight to Koh Samui, where he would spend a couple of weeks relaxing in anonymity before he decided on his full retirement plan. He put his belongings in a case and wiped down the penthouse to rid as much of his presence from there as possible. He checked out, paying his bill with a credit card that would never be used again.

He couldn't use his previous contact to source weapons any more as he had already killed him, but that wasn't a major issue as he always had a back-up plan. He had pre-paid and arranged to pick up the materials he would need for tonight.

He made his way over to a storage facility near Clapham, picked up what he needed, before heading over to the safe house in Clapham.

He did a foot route reconnaissance of the area. And quickly found his spot across the road and slightly to the right of the safe house.

He made a call and was quickly sent the architects' plans of the building directly to his phone. It was an old Victorian building which had been converted into flats many years ago. He waited until a resident left the entrance to the building, catching the door before it shut and locked. He strode up the staircase to the top floor, and then picked a lock to a seemingly inconspicuous door with a sign on it saying 'MAINTENANCE'.

In this room was a single-story staircase that led to a door onto the roof. He picked the lock to the door and walked out onto a vast roof, with a mass of aerials, a water container and a hut that housed workings relevant to the flats.

Bambi initially secured the door with some industrial steel wedges. These wouldn't stop any serious effort to get through the door to the roof, but it would give him enough time to make his escape if required. He then removed a kernmantle rope from his bag and hung it down the back westernmost corner of the building. Using a drainage hole in the lip of the roof, he had a perfect view of the entrance to the safe house and also of the flat itself.

This is where he set up the sniper's nest.

He had viewed the safe house all day and hadn't seen any sign of Basha or Winter. He was beginning to question if the intel he had been given was solid. He would wait out the night and morning, but if there was no sign of either of them by 8.00am, he would leave the country regardless. That wouldn't be ideal for him as he would miss out on a big pay day and would also have to look over his shoulder for the rest of his life. He was pissed off with Basha and Winter for putting him in this position.

Bambi didn't need to wait until the morning. Shortly before 10.00pm, he saw a couple approaching. He thought they were the potential suspects, but he couldn't be sure in the dark.

He only had one chance at this, and needed to make sure he hit the right targets, as armed police would be on site in a matter of minutes. The pair briefly stopped by a bus stop and became part of a crowd. Maybe it wasn't them.

The couple started walking again towards the safe house and his interest was piqued. He would know for certain shortly, when they walked under the glow of a street lamp and were completely illuminated.

He had his sights trained on the couple and as they walked under the streetlamp, he saw their faces and was able to confirm it was indeed Basha and Winter. Winter was still in his disguise, but it was definitely him. He noticed that Winter was moving with a certain awkwardness. It was good to know he wasn't completely indestructible and the bullets had at least some impact on him.

It was a shame he wouldn't be able to chat with him in his own unique way first, and find out how he had managed to survive the shooting, but Bambi readily made his peace with only being able to kill him.

Bambi put Winter in his sights first and was just about to take the shot, when a bus drove directly in his sight line. By the time the bus had passed, Basha and Winter were just entering the building housing the safe house. It wasn't a major problem, he had anticipated it was unlikely he'd be able to take the shots whilst they were on the streets.

He adjusted the sights on his weapon and turned on his RANGE-R through-the-wall sensor (TTWS) technology he had attached to his weapon.

This technology works in a similar way to radar and usually operates within the frequency ranges of 1-10 GHz, but Bambi was using a higher frequency. A higher frequency had less penetrative power through walls and windows, but higher frequencies increase the accuracy of object size and distance measurements.

TTWS has to combine several technologies and advanced data processing methods in one device. The reason he was comfortable using the higher frequency is that the walls of the building were not going to be able to block the radar and he intended on making the shot through glass anyway, to avoid any bullet trajectory distortion.

After Basha and Winter entered the building, they paused in the lobby, which Bambi assumed was because they were waiting for the lift along with one other person who was already there. While they were waiting, three other residents entered the building and made their way over to the lift. Eventually the lift arrived and the four residents and two temporary residents, who happened to be his targets, entered the steel cubicle.

The main restriction with TTWS is that the radio waves cannot penetrate metal. Thus, detecting a person in the closed body of the lift which is made with steel sheeting, wasn't possible.

The lift stopped at the first floor and Bambi saw that two of the occupants exited the lift and made their way to separate flats. It next stopped on the fourth floor where one occupant departed and went into a flat. The lift then made its way up to the top floor and Basha and Winter exited along with one other resident.

Even the distorted thermal imaging figures that Bambi saw through his sights, showed Winter's difficulty of movement. They headed towards the far end of the corridor and Bambi wondered for a moment if they had someone else with them; someone else he might need to kill. That decision would depend what mood he was in. As it happened though, the third person was the resident who lived in the flat opposite the safe house, which was a lucky break for them.

Basha and Winter entered the safe house and almost seemed lost with what to do next, but slowly made their way to the kitchen. Despite the fact that the figures on his screen looked similar to how figures should look through a thermal imaging sight, the TTWS sight couldn't detect differences in temperature, so Bambi wasn't able to see if they were cooking or boiling the kettle. But the movements suggested that they were making a drink and casually chatting.

Clearly, they had no idea what was about to happen to them. He kept a close eye on their every movement. He couldn't risk making the shot until they were in the front room and there was only glass between them and a bullet.

It was a painful seven minutes' wait while they chatted in the kitchen and drank their coffees, or whatever it was they were drinking. Eventually, the pair made their way to the front room. The curtains were drawn but that didn't matter with TTWS technology. Bambi lined Winter up in his sights first. He was facing away from Bambi's position and slowly turned around, and for a moment it almost seemed as if they were looking directly at each other.

The round hit Winter centrally in the forehead and he dropped instantly to the floor. Bambi mumbled to himself 'Survive that one, Iron Man.'

Before Winter even hit the ground, Bambi had begun lining up Basha in his sights. He was a little bit surprised to see her cartoon-like figure on his screen looking clearly panicked. She was rooted to one spot and he could see her head wagging around. He expected more from a senior MI5 officer. He pulled the trigger and once again, it was a direct head shot.

For the first time in the last few days Bambi gave a genuine smile and felt a momentary wave of serenity.

Ignatius Winter and Sahira Basha were both dead.

Bambi, started stripping down his QBU-88 sniper rifle

which chambered 5.8×42mm cartridge with a longer stream-lined bullet with steel core.

He had specifically used this rifle as it is a Chinese bull-pup designated marksman rifle developed for the People's Liberation Army.

He wasn't going to be so blatant as to leave the rifle or shell casings, but the shot bullets found in the safe house would suggest the rifle and therefore suggest that the shot had originated from a Chinese marksman. Jerry had assured him that such data would be quite sufficient to stop the investigation.

Everyone would assume the Chinese were behind the killings, but without definitive proof, the British government couldn't act on it, and there would also be a level of understanding as to why the Chinese did this. It would be spun as an assassin and a rogue Intelligence officer were killed. It was seemingly a way to finally put an end to it all.

Once he had stripped down the rifle sufficiently to ensure it would fit in his rucksack, he picked up the two shell casings and put them in his bag also. He attached the bag tightly to his back, and made his way to the back westernmost corner of the building where he rappelled down the side of the building.

He unclipped his rigging from the rope and left it as it didn't matter. He took a second to compose himself, before turning round with a huge feeling of relief, ready to begin his new life; apart from one fact: when he turned around, he was staring into the barrels of two guns. Behind those guns stood Ignatius Winter and Andy Atkin-Berry.

Bambi looked into the sky and stretched the back of his head onto the top of his spine and exhaled slowly and loudly. Eventually he looked back at the two barrels and said,

'Will you at least tell me how?'

'No,' Ignatius replied.

Bambi then started convulsing uncontrollably, and shortly after that everything went dark.

45

Ricky pulled the car up beside Ignatius and Andy and pressed a button on the console to open the boot. Within the large boot of the 4x4, Ricky had placed a cage that many dog owners use to transport their large pets. Ignatius and Andy, with little consideration for his wellbeing, stuffed the unconscious and heavily restrained Bambi into the cage, and then Andy got in the front next to Ricky leaving Ignatius to sit in the back.

Ignatius had his Sig Sauer with silencer attached resting on his lap. The plan was to get Bambi to the next location, but if for some reason, the anaesthetic wore of early and he woke on the ride and started making a nuisance of himself, then Ignatius would shoot three or four rounds through the back seats to quiet him down.

Ricky looked into his wing mirror and caught Ignatius' eye. He said, 'I wasn't sure you'd be able to pull this one off, Ignatius. Well done.'

'We pulled it off, Rick. You, me and Sahira.'

Andy looked across at Rick and then looked in the mirror at Ignatius, indignation plainly showing on his face.

'Yeah, no problem guys. You're welcome. Pricks!'

Both Ricky and Ignatius laughed a lot.

The plan that had been put in place was ambitious, but they felt it was also their best choice of very limited options.

It had all started with Sahira, not so subtly, giving up the location of the safe house. By letting Sayer, Wyatt, Forrester and Maguire know the location, she had known that inevitably this information would filter down to others in the relevant organisations.

She had filled in the paperwork for use of a safe house and 'accidently' forgot to save it on the Intelligence Service database, requiring the correct level of security clearance to access; meaning the information was accessible to all within British Intelligence. Anyone looking for the place where Ignatius was being holed up, wouldn't need to look that hard now to find the location of this particular safe house.

Ignatius and Sahira had waited until it was dark to approach the block of flats to ensure they couldn't be identified and shot on the way there.

As they were nearing the flat, they paused at a bus stop nearby so they could time the bus's approach.

When they saw the bus coming, they continued walking towards the flat, making sure they passed under the street light, so that they could be positively identified. The bus drove by them within seconds.

They entered the doors into the relative safety of the lobby. To view them within the building, Ignatius had known that Bambi would need to use TTWS technology. They halted in the lobby to wait for the next part of the plan. There was already a resident waiting for the lift, so they dutifully waited alongside her.

The previous night, Ignatius and Andy had broken into the secret hospital and the patients they had liberated were with Andy as they all entered the block's lobby.

Both Sahira and Ignatius turned around when they heard the door open and they saw Andy entering behind Simmonds and

Peters. Both of them were wearing a mask that covered their heads and faces with just holes for the eyes, nose and mouth. They were wearing aloe vera masks to treat the burns on their faces and head.

The resident who was waiting for the lift with Ignatius and Sahira, almost had a heart attack and didn't know whether to run or pretend she hadn't noticed them.

Ignatius took a different approach and when they came close enough, he smiled and in a very below average Anthony Hopkins imitation, he said,

'Hello, Clarice.'

Simmonds and Peters didn't look amused and even Sahira gave Ignatius a 'what the hell' expression. Clearly, she wasn't a *Silence of the Lambs* fan.

The lift eventually arrived and all six got on. Ignatius would have preferred there was no resident with them, but nothing could be done about that now, and it would have looked too suspicious if they hadn't got in the lift with her.

Ignatius pressed the button for the first floor and when the lift stopped, he and Andy got out of the lift and went into separate apartments which they knew to be empty. One flat was still waiting for new tenants and the other flat's tenants were away on a holiday.

They waited five minutes until they knew the lift would have reached the top floor and Bambi's focus would be seven floors higher up. Then, both men used a folding grappling hook and rope and lowered themselves out of the window down to street level. Ignatius at the side of the building and Andy from the back of the building.

Using non-line-of-sight (NLOS) radio communications kits,

Ignatius talked normally without needing to press any buttons to transmit, letting Ricky know they were both at street level and mobile on foot.

The lift's next stop was the fourth floor and the resident who had travelled in the lift with them, couldn't get away quickly enough and hurried to her apartment. Her front door was already open before the lift doors had time to close. The lift eventually reached the top floor when Simmonds, Peters and Sahira exited.

During the day, Ignatius and Andy had sat down with Simmonds and Peters and told them they needed to be moved to a safe house, for their own protection. The two soldiers told the pair they were going to be questioned about the roles they played in the kidnapping and attempted murder of Ignatius and Sahira.

If they told the truth about their involvement, who else was involved, and who gave the orders, the National Crime agency would put them on the Protected Person Scheme, also known as Witness Protection. They would be given full immunity and relocated abroad to start a new life. Ignatius had warned them that if they didn't do exactly as they were told, he would kill them.

They believed him.

Both Simmonds and Peters had protested they had no idea who was behind the order and couldn't help them. Ignatius knew this was true, but that was ok, as he had no intention of helping two people who were readily going to murder him and Sahira in cold blood.

The size difference between Simmonds and Ignatius, and Peters and Sahira was an area of concern in the planning, but

Ignatius had hoped that the relative difference in size between the two couples would be enough to fool Bambi.

As the three of them were walking along the corridor towards the safe house, Simmonds was still walking with discomfort due to his face being blow torched and the car crash.

At the end of the corridor, Simmonds and Peters went in the safe house and Sahira went to the flat opposite, where the residents were expecting her.

She had spoken to them earlier, and using her credentials had asked to speak with them tonight about a fabricated matter of national security. When Sahira entered the flat, she told the couple she would be with them shortly, but quickly needed to return a call to her office.

Using a separate NLOS radio from Ignatius and Andy, she communicated with Simmonds and Peters and told them to wait in the kitchen, whilst the team did an outside perimeter search to ensure it was safe.

When she heard from Ignatius, that he and Andy were in position, she radioed Simmonds and Peters to inform them all was clear and they would be in touch in the morning to arrange a time for the testimony. She had previously let them know that the flat was being watched by her people, and they must not leave it under any circumstances.

Simmonds and Peters were troubled by everything, but felt they were backed in a corner and had no choice but to comply.

After a couple of minutes, they made their way into the front room to get some rest as both were in a lot of pain. They entered the front room and cautiously looked around. Simmonds could see a red light above the curtains, attached to a camera, and his eyes were drawn to it. He knew they were being watched and his feeling of hopelessness multiplied.

Peters wasn't looking at Simmonds when she heard the explosion of a gunshot. She swung around to see Simmonds lying dead on his back, with a hole through his head.

A mixture of exhaustion and the effects of the drugs she had been taking for her wounds, meant she couldn't process what was happening immediately. Before she had time to drag her compromised thoughts into some reaction, a bullet entered her head, broke through her skull and pulverised her brain.

Even before Ignatius and the others had first entered the building, Ricky was on the roof waiting. He was under a thermal myler blanket to hide himself from any Thermal or TTWS technology.

On the lip on the roof he had set up a Raytheon Boomerang Warrior - X.

Once the first shot rang out, the Warrior - X began its work. The incoming shot announcement was heard from a built-in speaker with a display telling Ricky the range, azimuth and elevation of the shooter from both shots, which were identical.

He got on his radio to Ignatius and Andy as they walked a circular holding pattern, based on most likely locations of the nest, and gave them the exact location. Both of them double-timed it over to the building, knowing there was limited time before the shooter made his escape, and they needed to identify the escape route.

As they were taking a circuitous route of the building, Andy spotted a rope and immediately got on his radio.

'Ignatius, I'm at the back western corner and there is a kern-mantle rope hanging down from the roof.'

Both Ignatius and Andy had used a kernmantle rope

thousands of time in training and operations, in order to abseil down the sides of buildings, structures, mountains and many other objects. They knew Bambi's escape plan.

They hid themselves from immediate view and watched as he lowered himself to the ground. When he hit the ground, he disconnected his rigging and turned around.

He took it well in his stride, and even had the nerve to ask them how they managed to trap him.

Ignatius gave him short shrift and then shot him with a M-26 taser gun that was often used by the American military, and had been provided courtesy of one of Ricky's American clients. The taser crippled him and Ignatius then injected him with anaesthetic.

Once Ricky had given the location, he had made his way down to the waiting car and had driven to a side street by the building where Bambi had taken the shots. Ignatius and Andy were waiting for him and they piled Bambi into the cage in the back of the car, like a rabid dog.

The mood in the car was contradictory, swinging from moments of levity to periods of sombre reflection, as they made their way to a warehouse by Greenwich docks.

46

Bambi woke to find himself lying on a raised platform, his arms cuffed behind his back and a rope around his neck with a hangman's knot. By the weight of his pockets, he could tell that they had been emptied and all his possessions had been taken from him. They'd even taken his shoes, the dicks!

He would need to negotiate his way out of this current dilemma. He wasn't exactly in a position to fight his way out, and he didn't fancy taking on his opposition using that route anyway.

They had seen him wake up, but gave him time to lose the immediate after-effects of the anaesthetic before they decided to go into the room within the desolate warehouse on the banks of the river Thames.

Ricky pulled on one end of the rope which encircled Bambi's neck. It was attached to a pully system and as Ricky slowly pulled, it forced Bambi to stand up on the platform underneath him. Then, when it was completely taut, Ricky tied off the end of the rope to a railing.

Bambi's heart was racing, but he was trying to remain calm as he stood in front of them as they were watching him. He knew a lot about each of them, as Jerry had shared profiles on everyone who they believed to be involved with helping Ignatius, as well as everyone who had played any part in the investigation. He focused on Andy first.

'Mr Atkin-Berry, you are a serving member of the most elite

army unit in the world. You can't be involved in my illegal killing. You know that you need to take me in and let the judicial process deal with this.'

Andy smirked, but with no humour attached to it.

'You might not fully understand what the SAS do.'

Bambi changed his tactics with Andy.

'If I know who you are, so do others. Don't you at least want to know how I know who you are?'

'Nah, not really.'

With this response, Andy turned his back on Bambi who had cracks starting to appear in his calm persona. Bambi changed his approach and addressed Ignatius.

'If you kill me, you won't know who is behind all of this and you'll still be blamed for the killing of the Chinese Minister.'

Ignatius stared at Bambi in silence for a few seconds.

'This is the only deal you'll get. You tell us now, who was behind this and you live. You don't and you die.'

'I don't know who was behind it, but I can find out. I've kept recordings and intel from dealings with the man who hired me.'

Ignatius didn't reply but just lifted a USB stick that they had taken from Bambi's belongings and waved it in front of his face. He then also turned his back on Bambi and walked over to Ricky and Andy.

As Ignatius joined them, he put an arm on Ricky.

'Listen, mate, I understand your hatred of him and although we can't begin to understand your pain, are you sure you want to do this? Taking a man's life changes you. However much of a dick he is, don't let his death be a burden to you. Let me do it for you.'

'Thanks, but it's something I need to do myself and more

than that, something I want to do,' Ricky said. 'Also, I don't want you two implied in his death. Leave the room and I'll meet you by the car in a bit.'

Ignatius and Andy looked at each other and walked towards the door. Both went either side of the door, turned around and sat down, so their backs were against the wall by the door, in the same room. Neither said a word.

Ricky walked over to Bambi, looked him in the eye and pressed the button of the remote he was holding. The manual mobile lift table that Bambi stood on, started to slowly lower.

Over a period of minutes, Bambi's heals lifted and soon he was on tiptoes, then shortly after that there was a gap between his toes and the table. His neck and face started swelling and turning red as his airways were cut off.

Bambi died shortly afterwards, in a small room, in a warehouse by Greenwich docks.

47

Ricky walked over to Bambi, moved the mobile lift table and replaced the table with a chair on its side. He didn't even look at Bambi. As far as he was concerned, Bambi was past history and didn't deserve any more of his thoughts or time.

He wheeled the table into a far corner of the warehouse and wiped it clean, then walked to the car where Ignatius and Andy were waiting. Ricky looked at them and said, 'Let's go.'

'This is where I leave you guys,' Andy replied.

'We're in the middle of nowhere, how are you going to get, well, wherever you need to go?' Ricky asked.

'I'm a resourceful guy.'

Ricky nodded and said, 'Andy, I can't thank you enough. What you've done is above and beyond.'

'Anytime, mate. I'm really sorry about Justin and here for you whenever you need.' He then looked at Ignatius,

'Ignatius...'

'Yeah,'

'Go fuck yourself.'

After a couple of seconds, both Andy and Ignatius smiled and shook hands.

'Will do.'

Ricky and Ignatius got in the car and drove off leaving Andy standing outside the warehouse. They headed to North West London and parked up in a multi-storey car park in Harrow.

Shortly after they parked, Sahira walked up and got in the

back seat.

'Is it done?' she asked.

Ignatius nodded his confirmation and gave her the address of the warehouse, so she could send a team to pick him up. She handed Ignatius a key card.

'What's this?' he asked

'I've booked you a room for a week at The Grove Hotel in Watford. Let's face it you can't stay at the safe house. You should be fine there. I spoke to Sayer and although you are still officially a person of interest, there's not going to be any effort put in to finding you for now. Still it's probably best if you stay in disguise.'

Ricky raised his eyebrows at Ignatius. The Grove was one of the top hotels in the country. It seemed Ignatius would be staying in comfort.

'Thanks, Sahira. Here's what we got from Bambi.'

Ignatius handed over the USB stick to Sahira along with every other thing they took from him. Sahira would give it to the relevant people to extract all data and evidence that they needed. That was the hope anyway. 'So, what's the plan now?' he asked.

'We'll get the evidence to clear you and then, well, it's up to you. You can disappear or we can bring you in and clear it all up, but I can't promise there won't be any repercussions. Some pretty extreme stuff has happened.'

Ignatius nodded his agreement.

'Once it's been proved I wasn't behind this, I'll hand myself in and face whatever comes my way. I can't spend the rest of my life on the run. It's not worth it. Can you do me a favour, Sahira?'

'Sure. What do you need?'

'My mum and dad, and brother and sisters... All they know is that my face has been all over every bit of media as an international assassin. Can you contact them and let them know a version of what happened? I haven't been able to as I couldn't risk putting them in danger.'

'Of course. Don't worry, I'll talk to them.'

'Thanks. Do you want their details?'

Sahira gave him a 'really' look.

'Sorry. Of course, you don't. You've got them already. Thanks though. Maybe leave out the cutting people in half bit.'

'Yeah, I was thinking along those lines too.'

As quickly as Sahira had entered the car, she was getting out and told Ignatius she'd be in touch soon.

Ricky put the car in gear and pulled out of the parking spot.

'I guess I'm dropping you at The Grove then?'

Ignatius spent the next three days in luxury. He knew he probably had some tough times ahead, so was in no rush to move to the next phase. He spent a lot of time in the black tiled pool, which gave an impression the water was black. He had also done some light stretching in the gym, but was careful not to do anything too heavy as his ribs were still very sore. He ate well and was surprised to realise he hadn't drunk any alcohol and hadn't wanted to just yet.

On the fourth day he received a call in his room, telling him there was a package for him at reception. He made his way down there where the woman working behind the reception desk handed him the parcel, which was a bunch of budding daffodils with a note attached. The note read:

Even a clown can solve this.
Wybbrvltxesljkuduoagflupozaibzd
S. Xx
    Ignatius laughed and headed back to his room to solve the
code, already knowing the key word.

48

Sahira was sitting at the bar with a glass of wine and kept checking her watch, then it occurred to her. She thought, 'oh no, this can't be happening, this is the worst possible scenario. Surely, it's not true?'

She realised she was both anxious and excited to see Ignatius. Was she was falling for him?

Her internal dialogue, running on overtime, was saying, 'Come on Sahira. You're better than this. He's an asshole, he's misogynistic, he tells crap jokes, he's very likely a psychopath and he cheats at the Rubik's cube. Who does that?'

At the same time, another part of her, the bit she was trying with all her energy not to listen to, was saying, 'he's handsome, he's clever, he's brave, he is loyal to friends and they are loyal to him. Maybe he's not that bad after all? No, stop thinking like that. I cannot fall for him. He's everything I don't want in a man.' Before she had time to process other thoughts she heard,

'I didn't know you drank?'

She turned around and smiled.

'I don't often, but thought I'd have one tonight, fancy joining me?'

Ignatius hadn't considered having a drink, but suddenly thought. Why not?

'Sure, I'll join you for a drink.'

He sat down on a stool next to her and ordered a beer from the blonde barmaid. As they waited for the beer to arrive, Sahira told him about her conversation with his parents and siblings and that they all sent their love.

Ignatius kept quiet, but was grateful. Afterwards, Ignatius pulled a wrapped gift out of his bag and gave it to her. Sahira ignored the fact it looked like a five-year-old had wrapped it, and opened the present. Inside was a QWERTY Rubik's cube. A Rubik's cube with the symbols of a computer keyboard on it, and rather than each side being made up of three by three squares, it was made up of four by four squares and to solve it, you needed to align the squares in the order of the keyboard. It was a puzzle lover's dream.

Sahira smiled as she opened it and said,

'Thanks, I love it.'

She gave him a kiss on the cheek and then feeling awkward suggested,

'Shall we talk shop now?'

'We probably should.'

'The good news to start with. I gave Sally Dalton the USB stick and despite the heavy encryption, she got through it quickly. She's good! There were recordings between Bambi and the person who hired him, which were time stamped. They show details of the whole operation, including setting you up. There were details that couldn't have been known unless they were the assassin. What I'm saying is, you're in the clear for the assassination. There was also a card from a restaurant around the corner from the Wilsons, which Bambi had in his posses-sion. We went to the restaurant with a picture of Bambi, and a waitress identified him as being there on the morning that Justin was killed.'

'That's not really news. We knew it was Bambi who did it,

even if we didn't have proof. What is the official line?'

'The official line is still that Justin's death was a suicide.'

'Pricks.'

'That's just the beginning of the bad news, I'm afraid. Whoever hired Bambi, covered his tracks and is untraceable. All we know is that he calls himself 'Jerry'. We're doing all we can to try and find out who he is, but it's not looking good.'

'Ok. So, I'm still a loose end and they can't leave me alone?'

'I don't think so. It might actually be in his interest to ensure that nothing does happen to you now. All that would happen is make people ask more questions. There's nothing to suggest that you have any idea who they are, or have the resources to find out.'

'Ok, just one question. Did he order the killing of Justin?'

Sahira thought about how to word her answer.

'Yes. But if we can't find out who he is, how are you going to? If he gets wind of the fact you're looking, it would put you back at risk. Serious risk.'

'He was responsible for the death of Justin. I'm going to be responsible for the death of him.'

Sahira wanted to try and dissuade him more, but knew she would be wasting her time, so changed the subject.

'The bad news doesn't end there I'm afraid.'

'Go on.'

'There are people fighting your corner, but there are others who think you have some points to answer, and want you to answer for them. Ignatius, I know you don't want to run, but it might be your best option. I can give you money and help you disappear.'

Ignatius was a little shocked and Sahira could see this. It

was an incredibly generous offer, more than he would expect.

'Uh, thanks. Sorry if I seem ungrateful. I'm not, I really am grateful, but I'm not used to people helping me out so much.' Sahira blushed at this, which wasn't unnoticed by Ignatius. 'But I will face whatever is coming my way.'

'Ok. I thought you'd say that. We'll fight your corner as much as we can then.'

'Thanks. Just one more question. Do we know who Bambi is?'

'No, not yet. They're working on it. I don't know why it's taking so long, but I'll let you know when I do. If I do.'

Ignatius and Sahira, then forgot about everything that had happened since May 11th and talked together about each other's past, about football and about many other things. They were the last two customers sitting in the pub and couldn't believe it had gone so quickly. Just as they were about to leave, Sahira got a call. She showed her phone to Ignatius and said,

'Sorry, I've got to take this. It's a friend from Uni.'

Sahira answered, and the caller said,

'Last time I called you, I let you know that the foundations had been put in place.'

'Ok.'

'Well, I've just sent you a photo of where we are now.'

Sahira looked at her phone and smiled. The caller continued, 'We've now laid the first bricks and every day it is rising, and the building is starting to really take shape.'

'I can't talk right now Jen, but seriously, that is amazing news.'

Her friend Jenny from University, who was now the CEO of the Basha charity, told her no problem and she'd call again as soon as she could. It might be a while because there were limited facilities to call from this place. She was in a remote part of the Congo and was overseeing the building of an orphanage that the Basha charity had commissioned, in the name of Allah.

Sahira walked back over to Ignatius with a big smile on her face and impulsively said,

'I was thinking, we could maybe have a night cap at the hotel bar, if I'm invited of course?'

Ignatius was trying to be cool, but his response was higher than he expected.

'Of course. Sure, let's do that.'

Sahira smiled and they started walking towards the taxi rank. On the way, Sahira put her hand into his.

49

Sahira called in early the next morning and asked for a day off which was happily granted by Sayer. He had, after all, interrupted her last holiday break. Sahira and Ignatius spent the day in the hotel's robes. They went to the spa, ordered room service and stayed the rest of the day in bed. It was around 5.00pm when Sahira got a call from her office. It was Sally Dalton.

'We have a likely suspect for Bambi. Thought you'd want to know.'

Sahira shot up in bed.

'Sally, you're amazing. Tell me.'

'We believe he is called Robert Dawe and is an ex member of CANSOFCOM, a Canadian Special Operations force. He either never had any prints, dental records or DNA on record, or more likely, had them deleted at some point in time. He was registered as dead in 2005 after the vehicle he was in hit an IED in Iraq. This man has also had extensive plastic surgery, so any old photograph are not of use.'

'Ok. Why do you think it was him if he is presumed dead and there are no prints or DNA or anything else to confirm it is him?' Sahira asked.

'He had two wounds. One was a bullet wound and one was shrapnel from a frag grenade. He still had some shrapnel in his body. We were able to age the wounds from the scar tissue as occurring between 2002 and 2004, and the surgery was clearly done by a medic in the field. He must have been behind enemy lines and wasn't able to get to a medical facility. I was able to access the military databases of each country that had forces in the area at this time and the only match for field surgery on both these kinds of wounds, within this time period, was performed on Robert Dawe. That, and the fact his records have been deleted, I think, tells us with high level of certainty that he is Bambi.'

'Do we think the Canadians had any knowledge of this?'

'No, there's nothing to suggest that and no motive for them to be involved. They also have cooperated fully when we told them what we found out.'

Sahira was trying to process all this information and then asked,

'Does this help us find out who hired him?'

'No. There are no obvious links yet. I just thought you'd like to know who he was.'

'Thanks, Sally. I appreciate the call. I'll pop by and say 'hi' tomorrow.'

Sahira hung up the call and told Ignatius what they had found out. She asked if he'd ever heard of him or had any dealings with him?

'I did some work with CANSOFCOM, but the name doesn't mean anything to me and I didn't recognise him when I saw him. We just need to figure out how this all fits together.'

Sahira agreed, but then said,

'Well, we're not going to figure this all out today. Fancy a shower?'

Ignatius smiled and followed her into the five-star bathroom.

50

Jerry was sitting in his office after hanging up the phone. Despite many difficulties along the way, things might have just worked out how he wanted. The death of the Chinese Minister of National Defence, Xu Hua, had unfolded as he had planned and Britain was safe from a very real and dangerous threat. It also seemed there were no traces of his involvement in any of this.

The main loose end seemed to be Ignatius Winter, but he could make sure that Ignatius disappeared for a long time and then it wouldn't matter. He had to admit that Winter had been a good opponent. He would feel better if he was dead, but nothing on this scale ever went exactly to plan, so he'd make his peace with it.

He checked his watch and realised he had a meeting he needed to attend, so he straightened his tie and smoothed out his suit after standing up from his chair. He walked towards the door to his office and smiled as he looked at his favourite picture on the wall.

It was an original from the famous cartoon, Tom and Jerry.

He left the office and straightened the plaque on his door which read,

Home Secretary

Tom Forrester.

THE END